10+

(2)
Swift

Praise for

R J Anderson's

Also available by R J Anderson

Swift

Knife
Rebel
Arrow

For older readers:

Ultraviolet
Quicksilver

R J ANDERSON

ORCHARD

ORCHARD BOOKS
338 Euston Road, London NW1 3BH
Orchard Books Australia
Level 17/207 Kent Street, Sydney, NSW 2000

First published in the UK in 2014 by Orchard Books

ISBN 978 1 40832 648 0

A CIP catalogue record for this book is available from the British Library.

3 5 7 9 8 6 4 2

Printed and bound by CPI Group (UK) Ltd, Croydon, CR0 4YY.

Orchard Books is a division of Hachette Children's Books,
an Hachette UK company.

www.hachette.co.uk

For Simon,
who helped me get it right.

part one

For a bird, there are only two sorts of bird:
their own sort, and those that are dangerous.
No others exist. The rest are just harmless objects,
like stones, or trees, or men when they are dead.

– J. A. Baker, *The Peregrine*

one

'Knockers! The knockers are coming!'

The shout rang through the fogou, echoing off the rocky walls of the tunnel and into the chambers beyond. The boy had been drowsing, curled on the earthen floor beside his clan-brothers; now he was shocked awake as his father seized his elbow and wrenched him to his feet.

'Take this and hide it,' he commanded, and the boy staggered beneath the unexpected burden of a sack almost as heavy as he was. As he floundered for a better grip, a coin tumbled out of the bag's mouth and rolled across the floor. Instinctively the boy stooped to retrieve it.

'Leave it,' his father snapped, spinning him round and giving him a shove. 'Get out of here! Quick!'

The boy knew better than to hesitate. He clutched the sack to his thin chest and stumbled for the exit. Around him rose shouts and curses, the rasp of knives and the clatter of spears as the men of the clan raced to arm themselves. And from the hillside above, distant but growing louder, came the jeering war-cries of the enemy.

Mother, *the boy thought in sick dismay.* She told them where to find us. Father was right.

But he had no time for regrets now, even if it was his own foolish pity that had brought this disaster upon them. His father had entrusted him with the treasure, and it was his duty to keep it safe. The boy gripped the sack tighter, and ran.

As he burst out of the fogou, scrambling up the steep, overgrown bank that hid the underground passage from view, the first light of dawn was greying the horizon. In the tunnel it had been damp but sheltered; here the cold wind slashed through his ragged tunic and raked at his bare legs. He glanced wildly in all directions, wondering where in this scrub-dotted wilderness he could hide.

The carn! It stood on the ridge to the north-west, a lopsided heap of stones. If he crouched low and moved quickly, he might reach its shelter before daylight robbed him of what little concealment he had. But did he dare to make a run across the open valley? Or would that be his last mistake?

He had only a few heartbeats to decide. A ragged line of knockers were tramping down the hillside – fifteen of them, stocky and muscular, with steely breastplates glinting beneath their cloaks. Some were armed with thunder-axes, the magical hammers they used for deep mining; others wore long knives at their hips, or carried staffs stout enough to crack a man's skull with one blow. But he saw no bows or slings among them – nothing that could hurt him at this distance. Tightening his grip on the sack, the boy bolted for the carn.

Don't look back, *he told himself, panting as his feet slapped the crumbling earth and the sack bumped against his spine.* You can't help Father and the others now.

He knew what they'd be planning, because it was the only strategy that made sense. They hadn't a chance of defeating so many knockers in the open: not with only four seasoned fighters, a one-legged cook, an old healer, and a handful of striplings who'd scarcely earned their names. Besides, they wouldn't want to leave the women undefended. So they'd lure the knockers into the fogou, where the dark and narrow passages would give them the advantage. They'd use their luck-magic to make their enemies trip and blunder; they'd whistle up a wind through the tunnel and blow dust in their eyes. Then they'd drop low and slash the knockers' hamstrings, or duck behind them and slit their throats. It was a filthy way to fight, but the boy's people were outcasts anyway, so they had no honour to lose…and as his father always said, better a live dog than a dead lion.

He'd almost reached the carn now, stones skittering beneath his feet as he fought his way up to the summit. The tower looked crude but it was masterfully built, ancient already when his grandsire was born and one of the many secret places where his people had found refuge in the long years of their persecution. To strangers it would appear a solid heap, but the boy knew how to make the carn give up its secrets. He scrambled to the base of the pile, crouched and pressed his small white hand against a certain stone.

With a grating rasp the carn opened, rocks shifting and rearranging to frame a low doorway. The boy crawled into the darkness, pulling the sack after him, and nearly fell headlong down the stairs. Catching himself, he conjured a glow-spell and crept downward, the magical light bobbing like a will-o'-the-wisp before him.

At the foot of the staircase a chamber opened, rough and bare. It was even darker than the fogou, and musty-smelling too: a forbidding place, with nothing comfortable about it. But in the middle of the floor, on a rough dais of stone, stood a crock piled to the rim with treasure. Coins and goblets and plates of gold and silver, rings and brooches and jewelled pendants, with weapons and armour piled haphazardly to either side. Ancient riches forgotten by the long-dead men and women who had owned them, they belonged to his people now, as much as they belonged to anyone.

The boy hesitated, awed by the presence of so much wealth. With reverent care he approached the dais, upended his sack and let its contents spill onto the hoard. Then he backed out of the chamber. This place was not for him, not yet.

Hurrying back up the stairs, he extinguished his glow-spell and was turning to shut the carn when the air split with a thunderous crack and the ground beneath him shuddered. The boy staggered, lost his footing and fell. As he picked himself up, wincing at fresh cuts and bruises, shouts of triumph rose from the valley below.

The knockers had discovered the fogou. But instead of plunging inside to do battle, they'd split into two parties and surrounded both ends of the tunnel. And between them a cleft in the earth gaped like a mortal wound, while the knocker who'd made it was hefting his thunder-axe and bracing his stout legs for another swing...

They were cracking the fogou apart from the outside. Shattering the great stone slabs that formed the tunnel's ceiling, and bringing them down on the men and women trapped within. The boy's fists *clenched, helpless rage storming up inside him. If only he were bigger, stronger, more skilled at luck-magic or wind-working...*

But along with cunning he had also learned caution, and he knew better than to charge into a fight he could not win. Though his stomach knotted and his eyes burned, he stayed motionless as the thunder-axe smashed down for the second time, and with a roar and a rumble the whole roof of the fogou collapsed.

The boy spun away, shoving his bloody knuckles against his mouth to keep from crying out. He did not want to see what the knockers did next, how they searched the rubble for his people's bodies and finished off any living ones they found. The Grey Man and Helm, Dirk and Ram and their wives, Spit the cook and Needle the healer, Dart and Parry and the other boys – all of them were dead, or soon would be.

And it was his fault.

Ivy bolted upright, gasping into the darkness. Her cheeks felt wet, and her insides roiled with the horror of what she'd just seen. For a few wild seconds she couldn't tell where she was, or even *who* she was: part of her was still back on that rugged hillside with the boy, sharing his agony and shame. But then her night-vision focused, revealing the rocky walls around her and the firelight glowing at the mouth of the cave, and she collapsed onto her bed of ferns in relief.

It was a dream, she told herself. *Only a dream.*

Yet the assurance rang hollow, no matter how many times she repeated it. It hadn't felt like an ordinary nightmare: it had been too vivid for that, too powerfully real...

'Ivy! What's wrong?'

In an instant Martin was beside her, helping her sit up and move closer to their small fire. The lithe strength of his arm around her shoulders should have comforted her, but Ivy's nerves were raw and she couldn't bear it. She squirmed away.

'I'm fine,' she panted. 'Just—'

But words failed her. She needed time to breathe, to think, before she could explain.

Martin sat back on his heels and watched her. The firelight gilded one high cheekbone and made his pale hair shine silver, and for a moment he looked as haughty and remote as a faery prince of legend. Then he turned to toss another stick onto the flames and the spriggan in him leaped out – glittering eyes, sharp features and teeth bared in a mirthless smile. '*Fine*, you say. And I thought piskeys couldn't lie.'

Ordinarily Ivy would have been indignant, but she hadn't the will to argue with him, not now. 'I'm not hurt, or sick, or in danger,' she said. 'I had a bad dream, that's all.'

Martin raised his brows at her, and all at once Ivy was conscious of her own tear-streaked face and tangled hair. She shifted back against the rocky wall, hugging her elbows for warmth. 'I thought you'd gone hunting,' she said. 'I didn't expect you back until morning.'

'It's almost that now,' said Martin. He poked the fire until it collapsed into a glowing heap, and a few sparks flitted up to snuff themselves on the ceiling. 'But you can lie down again if you like. It's not as though we're in a hurry.'

He sounded indifferent, but his back was stiff, and Ivy wondered if she'd hurt him. 'Martin…'

He waved her aside. 'You don't need to explain. I understand.'

Ivy was bewildered – how could he, unless he was reading her mind? But then another possibility dawned on her. It would certainly explain why he'd flown off in bird-shape every night they'd been travelling together, and left her to sleep by their campfire alone…

'Oh,' she said softly. 'Do you have bad dreams too?'

'Me?' He flicked her an odd look. 'I don't dream at all. I never have, as long as I can remember.'

'Then what are you talking about?'

Martin sighed and sat down, folding his legs beneath him. 'I know you wanted to travel together,' he said, 'and in the beginning, it seemed like a good idea. But we've been tramping over the countryside for days and we haven't found a single spriggan, or even a clue to tell us where they might have gone. And you haven't learned anything that would help you convince your queen – or rather, your Joan – that you're not a traitor.'

I banish you from the Delve, now and forever. Betony's cold words echoed in Ivy's mind. *Go where you want and call yourself what you will, but you are no longer a piskey.*

Ivy shook off the memory. She might be half-faery, but she would always be a piskey at heart, no matter what her aunt said.

'Only because I'm not sure what I'm looking for,' she replied. 'It could be…I don't know, a better place for our people to live. Another mine that's just as secure as the one we're in now, but isn't contaminated with poison. Or maybe all we need is proof that the spriggans and faeries aren't a threat to us any more, and it's safe to live on the surface again. I'll know when I find it – but I'm not ready to give up yet.'

'You don't *want* to give up,' countered Martin. 'Because you're loyal, and stubborn, and you don't know when to quit. But you're not made for this life, Ivy. And it's making you miserable.'

'This life.' She spoke flatly, fighting to control her anger. 'What do you mean by that? You think I'm too weak or frightened to keep up with you?'

'Ivy…'

'I was the one who found you chained up at the bottom of the Delve, remember? I climbed down the Great Shaft night after night to bring you food and water and listen to you babble Shakespeare, when for all I knew you might be planning to eat me alive. I was the one who convinced you to teach me bird-shape, and then I risked my life to set you free—'

Martin cut her off with an impatient gesture. 'You're not listening. I don't doubt your bravery. Or your strength.'

'Then what are you talking about?'

'This.' He drew his thumb down her wet cheek. Ivy's heart jumped, and she flinched away.

'You're a piskey,' Martin said. 'And I'm a spriggan. I'd never even heard that word until you accused me of being one, but I've learned enough now to understand.' He let his hand drop and sat back. 'You're afraid of me, no matter how you try to deny it. And you should be.'

'I'm not.' She tried to sound confident, but her voice came out high and squeaky, like a little girl's. Like the child she'd been on the night the spriggans took her mother…

Except they hadn't taken Marigold, not really. Her mother had been captured by the evil faery Empress instead, and spent the next five years struggling to escape and get a message to her family. Until Martin came to tell her that Marigold was alive, Ivy had believed that spriggans were ravening monsters responsible for all the evil in the world – but now she knew that magical folk weren't so easily divided into tribes of good and bad as that.

'I'm not afraid,' she said, louder this time. 'I know you would never hurt me. You saved my life.'

Twice, in fact. And though the healings Martin had performed on Ivy had drawn the two of them together and changed them both in ways she was still struggling to understand, she was almost certain he hadn't meant that to happen. It wasn't in Martin's nature to bind himself willingly to anyone.

'But you are afraid of spriggans,' he said. 'The other spriggans, I mean. You're willing to help me search for them, but you don't really want to *find* them. Not after all the terrible things they did to your people.' He picked up a twig and twirled it between his fingers, transforming it to a knife and back again. 'No wonder you're having nightmares.'

Was he trying to frighten her away? If so, he'd be disappointed. Ivy climbed restlessly to her feet, pacing to the mouth of the cave. 'It's not what your people did to mine,' she said, rubbing her arms as the breeze cut through her light jumper. 'It's more…what my people did to them.'

'What do you mean?'

The suspicion had been growing in Ivy for days now, as she and Martin hunted through seaside caves, old ruins and rock formations without finding the slightest trace of the spriggans' existence. The piskeys of the Delve might live quietly these days, but little more than a century ago Ivy's knocker forebears had roamed the countryside in small armies, killing or enslaving any magical folk who dared to resist them. Ivy's own mother and grandmother had been captured in a raid on a faery wyld… and Ivy wasn't the only piskey with faery blood in her, not by a long shaft.

What if the same thing had happened to the spriggans? The women dragged underground to join the piskeys, the men murdered or forced into exile, until none of them remained? She'd tried to push the thought aside – after all, even if it was true, it had happened a long time ago and there was nothing she could do about it. But her dream had dragged all those dark fears and guilty feelings to the surface.

'There were spriggans in my dream,' she said reluctantly, 'but they weren't hurting anyone. The knockers, the piskey miners… they were attacking them.' She went on to describe everything she'd seen, from the time the boy's father had shaken him awake to the moment the fogou collapsed.

'So when you cried out,' said Martin when she had finished, 'it wasn't for yourself. It was for him. That boy.'

Even now, the memory brought a lump to Ivy's throat. 'It felt so real. Like a vision of something that had really happened…'

'Maybe it was.' Martin moved to join her. 'I've heard of faeries who can see hidden things, or even look into the future – we call it the Sight. Don't piskeys have anything like that?'

We, he'd said. So he still thought of himself as a faery, part-spriggan or not. 'No,' said Ivy. 'At least, not any piskey that I've ever met. And I've never had visions before, have you?'

'Never.' Martin folded his arms and frowned down at them, his brow creased with thought. Then he said, 'What makes you so sure the boy and the others in this tunnel-thing – the fogou – were spriggans? They might have been wandering faeries, or some other tribe of piskey.'

'Piskeys who can bring bad luck and control the winds?' asked Ivy. 'I don't think so. And the boy seemed to think changing shape was normal for his people as well. My brother Mica made it *very* clear to me that piskeys don't change shape.'

'You do.'

True, but she'd always been the exception to the rule. Born frail and wingless in a Delve full of sturdy, moth-winged piskey-women, Ivy had spent her whole life fighting to prove her worth, often in unorthodox and even dangerous ways. Turning herself into a swift – a tiny, quick-darting bird – had satisfied her lifelong hunger for flight and given her more freedom than she'd ever dreamed of. But it had also driven a wedge between Ivy and her older brother, who'd been horrified when he realised what she could do.

'Haven't you heard?' she said. 'I'm not a real piskey. Aunt Betony said as much when she banished me from the Delve.' And Mica had stood there and let it happen, without so much as a word in her defence. 'Anyway, I've never heard of piskeys attacking their own people...'

She trailed off, gazing out the mouth of the crevice to the valley beyond. It was still mostly dark, but she could make out a tall, red-lit metal spire – a radio tower, perhaps? – in the near distance. To the west stood the chimney and bob wall of an old pumping-engine house, one among hundreds of abandoned mine buildings that littered the Cornish landscape. And if she listened closely, she could hear the rumble of early-morning traffic along the road a few miles away.

But in the dream, there'd been no signs of human industry or technology at all. The spriggan clan's weapons were crude, their clothing rough and old-fashioned. Even the knockers had been oddly dressed – who wore cloaks or boots like that any more?

'But if it was real,' she said, 'it happened a long time ago. Maybe even hundreds of years. And I don't know why I'd be seeing something like that.'

'Well,' said Martin, 'perhaps it was only a dream, then. Something your mind churned up from bits of stories and legends you heard when you were in the Delve.'

Ivy nodded, but her eyes were on the horizon, where a rosy glow was seeping through the clouds. This place was a long way from the old tin mine where she'd grown up, or the flat she'd briefly shared with her mother and sister in the human city of

Truro. She'd never seen this wild, rugged valley before she and Martin flew over it last night, and her unfailing instinct for direction, both as a bird and as a piskey, told her she'd never been in this part of Cornwall before.

So why was it starting to feel familiar?

She was still puzzling over the question when dawn broke at last, lighting up the nearby ridge. There stood the metal tower she'd seen earlier, but a sling's throw from its base rose a smaller landmark she hadn't noticed before. A lopsided pile of stones, taller than Ivy at human size and perhaps three times as wide.

Astonished, Ivy stared at the carn, then whirled to look at the crevice where she'd been sleeping. She'd noticed how oddly square its entrance seemed, but she'd assumed it was part of an old mining tramway, or the lintel and doorposts of some long-ruined cattle shed…

'What is it?' asked Martin.

Ivy turned to him, wide-eyed with wonder. 'This is the place,' she said. 'We're standing in what's left of the fogou, and that's the carn up on the hill. The valley I dreamed about – it's real.'

two

There was no use trying to search the crevice – its back wall was one great slab of stone, impossible to move, and the rest of the ruined fogou was so thickly overgrown with scrub that they would have had to dig to uncover it. They did find the other end of the tunnel after brushing away some of the overhanging ferns and foliage, but it was blocked. The knockers had done their work too well.

'The carn, then?' asked Martin, gesturing at the top of the ridge. In unison they changed shape – Martin to the tiny black and white bird from which he'd taken his name, Ivy to a darting swift – and flew up the hillside to land beside the rocky pile. Martin turned back to human size, his personal preference; Ivy felt more comfortable at piskey height herself, but she followed his example. Together they crouched beside the tower, studying the weather-beaten stones that formed its base.

'It was a small one,' she murmured, running her fingers over the rocks. 'More square than the others, and flatter…here.'

She laid her palm against the stone, expecting the carn to open for her as it had for the spriggan-boy. But no matter how she pushed or pressed it, the tower remained as solid as before. Ivy tried all the other foundation stones in turn, then slapped the carn in frustration and sat back.

'I don't understand,' she said. 'I was so sure it was real.'

'It still might be,' said Martin, straightening up and brushing dirt and bracken from his knees. 'But likely the opening spell's worn off over the years. Especially if the carn's been abandoned as long as you seem to think.' He gave the upper part of the carn a shove, but the stones refused to move. 'Pity. I could think of a few good uses for that treasure. A hot bath and some clean clothes, to start with.'

He didn't glance at her as he spoke, but Ivy's cheeks heated all the same. She'd been washing as often as she could, but after a week of tramping around the wilder parts of north Cornwall her jeans had grown stiff and the sleeves of her jumper were filthy. Martin's slim trousers and jacket, on the other hand, still looked as fresh as when they'd set out seven days ago. She was tempted to ask how he managed it, but with her luck it would turn out to be some particularly male faery – or spriggan – kind of cleaning spell that a piskey-girl like herself couldn't do...

'Oh,' she burst out, resisting the urge to smack herself. 'Of course! How could I have been so stupid?' And before Martin could react she seized his wrist, pulled his arm down, and flattened his fingers against the lowest stone.

With a grinding, sepulchural rasp the carn opened, revealing a low doorway and a staircase leading down into darkness. Martin snatched his hand back and swore, his grey eyes wide.

'Well,' said Ivy, satisfied, 'that proves you really are a spriggan. It wouldn't open for anyone who wasn't.' She motioned to the doorway. 'Shall we?'

The space inside the carn was barely large enough for the two of them, even once they'd shrunk to half-size. And though the stones appeared rough from the outside, they were so closely fitted together that not even a hint of sunlight filtered through. Without her keen night-vision, Ivy would have been blind – but when it came to dark places, she had more than a few piskey tricks to rely on. She willed her skin to glow, sending out a pink-tinged radiance that lit up the interior of the carn from top to bottom.

'Incredible,' Martin murmured, so close that his breath warmed Ivy's ear. A shiver raced down her spine, and she hurriedly stepped onto the staircase to put some distance between them. Not that he'd frightened her, not exactly…but right now, she didn't need any distractions.

As she picked her way down into the blackness, Ivy counted six, seven, eight stairs – all of them a little too high for the average piskey, and too low for most humans. One more and she'd reached the bottom, stooping under a rough lintel to enter the dank-smelling chamber beyond.

And there it stood – a great earthen jar, filled to overflowing with tarnished metal and age-dulled gemstones. Armour and weapons lay jumbled around its base, shields and breastplates grimed to blankness, a few swords still intact within their rotting scabbards. It was just as she'd seen in her dream.

Wondering, Ivy edged closer, drawn to a sheathed blade that must have belonged to a child, or a small woman. It looked just the right size for her, but did she dare to touch it? What if there was some kind of protective spell on the trove, and the floor crumbled out from beneath them or the treasure disappeared? She turned, looking for Martin…

And there he stood with hands braced on each side of the doorway, eyes shut and teeth gritted as though he were in pain. Ivy cursed herself for forgetting how much he hated being underground. 'Are you all right?' she asked. 'Do you want to go back outside?'

'No,' said Martin curtly, pushing himself away from the door and striding past her. 'I am all agog to see this treasure.'

Before Ivy could warn him, he walked to the crock and plunged his hands inside it. But it seemed the hoard wasn't enchanted after all, because nothing happened. Daring, she stooped and picked up the sword, pulling it free of its scabbard.

The blade was rust-spotted but unbroken, its edge only slightly notched. She hefted it and made a couple of experimental passes, testing its balance. She had no skill with weapons, but she liked the weight of the sword in her hand: it made her feel strong, purposeful, even heroic. And she hadn't felt that way since she'd fought Gillian Menadue, the vengeful faery who'd captured Ivy's little sister and planned to kill every piskey in the Delve…

Yet there'd been nothing noble about that desperate struggle at the edge of the Great Shaft, and Ivy would never forget the sight of Gillian slumped unconscious over the railing, or the shriek of its hinges as it broke and sent her tumbling to her death. And though Ivy had saved her people that day, there'd been little joy in a victory that had torn her family apart and forced her to flee her lifelong home. She let the sword drop and turned away.

'If I had to put a number on it,' said Martin, rubbing his thumb over a grime-encrusted coin to reveal the glinting metal beneath, 'I'd say this trove's been here at least four hundred years, and most of the treasure would have been old even then. See this?' He handed the coin to Ivy. 'That's Roman.'

They were sitting together on the ridge outside the carn, with the pieces Martin had taken from the hoard – several handfuls' worth of necklaces, bracelets, rings and brooches, plus a small leather purse full of mixed coinage – spread out between them. Martin seemed to think it would be worth quite a bit of human money, though from the way he kept caressing the treasure Ivy wondered if he could bring himself to sell it.

'If you say so,' she replied, passing the coin back. 'But that just makes my dreaming about it even stranger. Why would I see a vision of something that happened centuries before I was born?'

'Cornwall's a strange land,' said Martin. 'Didn't your mother say something once about old powers in the earth of Kernow, and how the spells the piskeys and other magical folk used to fight each other still linger in the ground?'

It was true. That was how Gillian Menadue had discovered

the dark magic known as the Claybane, and turned it against the piskeys of the Delve. Ivy herself had only endured a few minutes of that living death before Gillian's daughter Molly rescued her, but she would never forget the horror of being trapped in a clay shell, unable to move or speak.

'Well, then,' continued Martin, 'maybe this valley remembers what happened here, because the boy felt it so strongly. Maybe that's what you were sensing last night.'

'But why me and not you?' asked Ivy. 'You're the spriggan. By rights, you ought to be a lot more attuned to your own people's memories than I am.'

'Maybe,' said Martin, 'but I told you before, I don't dream. I never have, as long as I can remember.' He paused, his fingers tracing the shape of a pendant he'd picked up from the heap. 'Maybe that's why you had to dream it for me.'

Ivy was instantly wary. 'What do you mean?'

'I think our minds are connected somehow. Ever since I healed you, we've been...' He made a vague gesture. 'Sensitive to one another. Remember when I was trapped in the Claybane, shouting for help, and you were the only one who could hear me? And when we finally managed to communicate...'

Ivy's lips parted. 'It was in a dream.'

But he hadn't just spoken to her in words that night. She'd also glimpsed Martin's memories – not just the recent images he'd been trying to show her, but older visions of his youth and childhood as well. Nothing coherent, just flashes of cityscapes and grimy streets and the faces of people he'd once known. But she'd felt, at that moment, that she was seeing the world through his eyes. Just like she had with the spriggan-boy.

'Maybe dream-sharing is something spriggans do,' she said. 'Maybe it wasn't an accident – maybe the boy left that memory here for other spriggans to find, to tell them what had happened.' And then, as Martin suggested, she'd picked it up from his mind somehow while she slept.

But it was an uncomfortable thought, being the keeper of a spriggan's dreams. Especially in this strange, wild country full of ruins and old battlefields, where there was no telling what dark memories she might uncover next.

'Hm,' said Martin. 'I'm not sure the boy would have wanted other spriggans knowing about his family hoard. But you might be on to something.' He held a ring up to his eye and turned it to catch the light, then dropped it back into his pocket. 'Anyway, it'll take time to get the full value out of this. But I can sell a few pieces right away, and make enough money to spare us eating insects all day, or sleeping in any more caves. As long as you don't mind going back to your mother's—'

'You're going to leave me behind?' Ivy was startled, then annoyed. 'Why? I can fly just as fast as you can.' A good deal faster, in fact. 'Anyway, there's no way I'm going back to Truro now. It was hard enough getting away from my mother and sister in the first place.'

Not that Marigold had forbidden Ivy to go, not exactly. It wasn't in her nature to give orders, and she knew too well how capable Ivy had become in her absence. But she'd looked troubled and a little hurt when Ivy told her that the flat was simply too small for three. And when she explained that she was going to look for a way to clear her name and prove that Betony had been wrong, her little sister Cicely had begged to come with her. Ivy had been forced to sneak away when Cicely was sleeping, and she still felt guilty about that.

'Yes, I suppose it would be a little awkward,' said Martin. 'Especially since you haven't told them you're travelling with me.' He raised his brows quizzically. 'Have you?'

'No,' Ivy admitted, with some reluctance. 'But that's beside the point. Why can't we stay together? Surely there must be someone in Cornwall willing to buy your treasure.'

'*Our* treasure,' corrected Martin. 'You deserve at least a half-share, especially since I'd never have known it existed without you. And maybe you're right about a dealer, but I don't know this part of the country that well. I can find buyers more easily in London.'

'London! But you can't go back there – you told me so yourself. You're still wanted for murdering the Empress and the other faeries—'

'Are looking for me, yes,' Martin said. 'But I can't imagine they're making more than a show of it these days. Nobody mourns the Empress: a few sanctimonious bores aside, most faeries would probably agree I did them a favour.'

He spoke airily, but Ivy wasn't convinced. If he believed he could be safe in London he wouldn't have fled to Cornwall, much less stayed here for so long.

'Even if that's true, you're still safer not travelling alone,' she said. 'And I'm sure I can fly as far as London, even if I've never been there before.'

'Oh, I won't be flying.' He scooped up a handful of treasure from the rocks and poured it into his pocket. 'There's no way I can carry all this in bird-shape. I'll have to travel by magic instead.'

Of course. She'd forgotten that faeries – or half-faeries, in Martin's case – could will themselves from one place to another with merely a thought. Once piskeys had been able to do the same, if droll-tellers' tales were anything to go by. But that magic had been lost over the years since her people went underground, and Ivy had yet to learn it.

'You could teach me,' she began, but Martin shook his head.

'You can't Leap to a place unless you've set foot there at least once already. And for a journey like this, I'll need to stop a few times along the way. Trust me, I can do this a lot more easily on my own.'

'I see,' said Ivy stiffly. 'Well then, you'd better do that. I wouldn't want to slow you down.'

'You're upset.' A line formed between his brows. 'What's the matter?'

Ivy looked past the carn to the neighbouring hillside, and the ruined mine building upon it. There was an old engine house just like that one back at the Delve, where the piskeys used to feast and dance on Lighting nights. She bit her lip, homesickness welling up inside her. She'd taken the company of her fellow piskeys for granted, but now she wondered if she'd ever be part of a community like that again.

'Ivy.' Martin slipped his fingers under her chin, turning her face towards his. 'I won't be gone long. I'll be back tonight if all goes well, or at the latest tomorrow morning.'

'If all goes well.' Ivy shook off the touch. 'But what if it doesn't? I could be waiting for days, never knowing what's happened to you. Just like the last time.'

Though it wasn't really fair of her to say so: it hadn't been Martin's fault she'd misunderstood his intentions when he flew off that night, or that he'd fallen into one of Gillian's Claybane traps and couldn't get back to her. She knew better now than to think he would leave without saying goodbye. But after losing her mother to the human world and her father to the mine, Ivy was all too used to being abandoned.

'Never mind,' she said, before Martin could speak. 'I can do some exploring on my own, and eat and sleep in swift-shape. I'll be fine.'

'Why not go to Molly's?'

'It's too soon for that.' Gillian's daughter was still grieving for her mother's death, and her father would be at the cottage with her. It would be awkward.

'Well,' said Martin, 'it's your decision. But it's getting late in the year for swifts, so be careful. And take this.' He picked something up from the rock beside him, spelled it clean with a touch, and held it out to her.

It was a diamond-cut gemstone on a golden chain, as big and

green as one of Ivy's eyes. 'What—' she choked, then cleared her throat and tried again. 'What do you want me to do with it?'

'Wear it, of course,' said Martin. 'As a token of my good faith.' The corner of his mouth quirked up. 'After all, if there's one thing I've learned about spriggans, it's that they don't give treasure away lightly.'

If Ivy's cheeks had been hot before, they were sizzling now. She could only hope that her sun-browned skin would hide it. 'But don't you think it's a bit – I mean, I'm not old enough – and we haven't known each other that long—'

Martin broke into the first genuine smile she'd ever seen from him: not the usual slow curl of the lips or wicked flash of teeth, but a boy's grin of pure, unbridled delight. 'I'm sorry, did I just propose to you by accident? Is that what piskey-boys do when they want to marry, give their sweetheart a necklace?'

Ivy wished the hillside would open like the mouth of a hungry giant, and devour her whole. 'You mean…faeries don't?'

'Not at all,' said Martin, and Ivy wanted to slap him for looking so amused. Couldn't he at least have the decency to share her embarrassment? 'I only meant to put your mind at ease. All right, what about this?' He dropped the necklace and picked up a copper bracelet.

'You don't need to give me anything,' Ivy protested, but Martin had already clasped it around her wrist.

'Fits perfectly,' he said. 'And now…' He laid his fingertips on the bracelet, and the copper grew warm. 'Just like the old game. If it's hot, I'm close; if it's cool, I'm far away.'

'And if it's cold?'

'Then I'm dead – or else I've flown to Iceland. But I doubt you'll have to worry about that.'

Ivy touched the slim twist of metal. It might not be a pledge of love, but coming from Martin, the gift was anything but insignificant. As a fugitive he could ill afford to promise anything to anyone, let alone make it easy for them to track him down… yet he'd done this, just to reassure her.

'So,' Martin continued, dropping the last few bits of treasure into his pocket and climbing to his feet. 'When the bracelet turns warm again, I'll meet you here at the carn. All right?'

Ivy managed a smile. 'All right,' she said.

three

As soon as Martin was gone the bracelet on Ivy's wrist turned cool, and the hillside seemed lonelier than ever. She glanced at the carn one last time to make sure it was shut and the rest of the treasure was safe. Then she took a running jump off the ridge and transformed to swift-shape.

By the electric feel of the air and the ominous bulk of the clouds lumbering in from the sea, a thunderstorm was coming. The last time that happened Ivy had ridden it out, chasing Martin from one wild air current to the next until her pulse beat hard as the rain on her close-feathered wings and her head reeled with excitement. But a thrill like that was better shared, and Ivy had no heart for games right now. She dived past the ruined fogou to make sure she hadn't left anything behind, then shot into the grey morning sky.

The valley dropped away below her, receding to a mere ripple in the landscape. She rose higher, a tiny black dart against the clouds, faster than any but the swiftest falcon and borne on untiring wings. Her sharp eyes scanned the landscape, marking the deliberate piles of carns and quoits, the lumpen outcroppings of the tors, the lines of drystone hedges – and most of all, the chimneys of the whim-engine and pumping-engine houses that marked the sites of former mines.

Over the past few days Ivy had inspected a few of those shafts first-hand, climbing as far down into the darkness as she could. But none of them had the cozy, welcoming feel of the mine she'd grown up in, and most of them were flooded so deep it would have taken months of hard labour to pump them dry again. It was hard to imagine any piskey, even the toughest knocker, choosing to live in a place like that.

Yet her people couldn't stay in the Delve forever, no matter how much work they'd put into making it their home. With hundreds of disused tin mines to choose from, was it mere bad luck that they'd settled on the one that turned out to be poisoned? Or were all the old workings contaminated in some form or another? Ivy wished she knew – better yet, that she could prove it. But even if she could identify the poison and track it to its source, it would take a miracle for her aunt to listen to her now.

The first drops of rain fell, trickling off her back and wing-feathers. The swift part of Ivy urged her to rise above the clouds and keep flying, but she suppressed the instinct and veered southward, heading for the Delve. Yes, her aunt Betony still held the title of Joan the Wad, queen of the piskeys, and Ivy knew better than to defy her fire-wielding power. But she hadn't seen her old home since the day she was exiled, and surely it could do no harm to fly over it? Especially since Betony had no idea that Ivy could become a swift…

Or at least Ivy hoped not. Her brother Mica might have turned his back on her in disgust when he'd found out she could change shape, but she couldn't bring herself to believe he'd betray her. Surely his determination to hold on to what was left of the family honour would keep him quiet, if nothing else.

Still, it wouldn't do to make herself obvious, or Mica might be tempted to reconsider. She'd make a discreet survey of the Delve from the air, and continue on her way.

But when she caught sight of the engine house that had once belonged to the mine called Wheal Felicity, with its broken-down roof and stone walls overgrown with creeping vines, Ivy's resolve crumbled. She'd grown up in this place, and being sent away from it had left an aching void inside her that not even her mother's love or Martin's companionship could fill. She couldn't bear to leave without seeing at least one of the friends and neighbours she'd left behind, even if it was just old Hew stepping out of the Earthenbore to smoke his pipe.

But that meant she'd have to wait until the storm blew over – not even the most determined hunters would go out in weather like this. As she swooped past the engine house, Ivy spotted the remnants of a jackdaws' nest tucked into the crumbling brickwork, sheltered from the wind and rain. Her short swift's talons were poorly made for such a perch, but she darted into the alcove and landed with only a little difficulty. Then she settled down in the damp straw and began to doze with one eye open, in the strange half-sleep of birds.

She was dimly aware of thunder rumbling in the distance and the clouds roiling overhead, of a hissing downpour pelting the stonework all around her and then gradually fading away. But it wasn't the end of the storm that startled Ivy awake. It was the sound of two people talking.

'I'm tired, lass. And it's so damp today. Can't it wait until tomorrow?'

'It's all right, Mum, I'll help you. Just climb up here, and I'll take your arms, and we'll fly to the top together.'

Ivy hopped upright in excitement. It was Jenny, her lifelong neighbour and best friend in the Delve. If she could only find a way to talk to the other girl alone…

Jenny's mother broke into wheezing coughs, and ended with a groan. 'I can't do it, Jenny. Don't waste your strength on me. Just let me go back and lie down a bit.'

'Mum, please. Just try. Mum!'

There was no answer. The older woman had gone.

Ivy had to move, or she'd miss her chance. She scrabbled off the ledge and swooped to the ground, landing in her own piskey shape and size by the caged top of the shaft. Then she cupped her hands around her mouth and called softly, 'Jenny!'

There was a long pause. Then the reply came, wary and tremulous: 'Ivy? Is that you?'

'Shhh,' whispered Ivy. 'Yes, it's me, but it's a secret. Can we talk?'

Light sparked in the darkness, growing from a pinpoint to a dot and then into a small, luminous figure as Jenny fluttered up the shaft towards her. Her moth-wings made no sound, but Ivy could hear her panting, and by the time she reached the top she looked exhausted. Ivy put her hand through the bars, and the other girl gripped it.

'I can't go any further,' Jenny gasped. She looked paler and thinner than Ivy remembered – or was that a trick of the light? 'You know I can't. But I'm glad to see you.' With Ivy's help she clambered onto the inside lip of the shaft and sat down, with the metal bars between them. 'When the Joan said you'd gone off to live with your mother I was happy for you, but I wished we'd had the chance to say goodbye.'

Ivy hesitated, weighing how to answer. The laws of the Delve decreed that women and children had to stay underground, and Jenny was too mindful of her duty and her reputation to disobey. Yet she'd come this close to the surface, and she'd been urging her mother to do likewise, so she must have at least some doubts...

Besides, Jenny had always been one of Ivy's closest friends. If she couldn't trust Jenny, she might as well give up on the Delve altogether.

'I didn't leave by choice,' Ivy told her quietly. 'Betony banished me and told me I could never come back.'

Jenny's lips parted in dismay. 'How could she? If you hadn't broken the Claybane curse, we'd all have been trapped for the rest of our lives—'

'But if I hadn't gone up to the surface,' said Ivy, 'the Delve would never have been attacked in the first place. Or at least that's what my aunt believes.'

'That doesn't make any sense,' said Jenny indignantly. 'Keeve disappeared long before you did, and so did your sister. If you'd stayed here, that faery would have gone on catching piskeys one by one until the Delve was empty, and we'd never have known what happened to us!'

Ivy's heart warmed. She'd despaired that anyone would understand, but Jenny had always been clever. 'Maybe,' she said. 'But I still broke the law when I left to search for Cicely. And I broke it again when I brought Molly into the Delve – Betony can't forgive me for that.'

'Molly? You mean the human girl? The one who helped free us from the Claybane?'

Ivy nodded. Gillian's daughter had been the only one who could release the trapped piskeys, once her mother was dead.

'But she was only a girl, not much older than Cicely! She wasn't spying out our defences or trying to steal our treasure, she was doing us a kindness. It's not fair to blame you for that!' Jenny drew breath to go on, but her throat rattled and she doubled up coughing instead.

Jenny's mother had always had a weak chest, but this was the first time Ivy had seen her friend like this. 'You're not well,' she said in alarm. 'How long has this been going on?'

'It's only – the poison-spell – that faery dropped – down the Great Shaft,' rasped Jenny. 'I inhaled some when we were helping

Mum and the others escape, and—' She coughed again, and sat back with a bleary smile. 'But it's nothing serious. The Joan's been casting spells to clear the air, and she says we'll soon feel better again.'

Of course that was what Betony would say. The possibility that there had been poison in the mine before Gillian came was unthinkable, because that would mean she'd been wrong to banish Ivy – and five years before that, Ivy's mother – for telling her so. 'I hope you're right,' said Ivy, 'but I'm not sure that smoke-spell Gillian cast was poisonous.'

Jenny blinked at her. 'But it must have been. The way it smelled! And what about your father?'

Flint had given his life to destroy Gillian's smoke-spell, and the memory of the last time Ivy had seen him, standing in the hazy darkness with his thunder-axe in hand, still haunted her. 'I know,' she said. 'But if Gillian could have poisoned us all so easily, she wouldn't have needed to use the Claybane. I think the smoke was only meant to frighten us, so we'd all run for the surface – and into her traps.'

'Oh, Ivy.' Jenny looked stricken. 'But that means—'

Ivy cut in quickly, not sure she could bear it if Jenny finished the sentence. 'I know this may be hard to believe, but the Delve has been poisoned for a long time. Look at me, Jenny.' She crouched closer to the bars. 'Remember how sickly and pale I used to be when I lived underground. Do I look like that any more?'

'No,' Jenny whispered, and tears came into her eyes. 'But I do.

Most of us do, especially the old ones. Mum's chest is getting worse every day. Even my little brother Quartz coughs sometimes, and he can't run half as fast as he used to. But if the Joan's spells won't help us, what will?'

'The same thing that helped me and my mother,' said Ivy. 'She was dying when she ran away from the Delve – so sick she was coughing blood. But after a few days of fresh air and sunlight, she started to get better. And now…I wish you could see her. She's beautiful.'

'She always was,' said Jenny wistfully. She leaned back, her gaze flicking over Ivy, then sat up again.

'I haven't grown any wings, if that's what you're wondering,' Ivy said, and Jenny blushed.

'I'm sorry. I just thought, if being out of the Delve had made you so much healthier, then maybe…' She broke off with a little laugh. 'Never mind, I'm being silly. You don't need them.'

No, she didn't, not now that she could become a swift. But she couldn't say that to Jenny: she hadn't even told her own mother and sister about her shape-changing.

'The point is,' she began, but Jenny gave a start and held a warning finger to her lips. Ivy froze as a croaking voice rose from the bottom of the shaft:

'Eh, Jenny, what are you doing?'

'It's Nettle,' hissed Jenny, her eyes round with panic. 'I have to go.'

Old Nettle was the Joan's attendant, so Jenny had good reason to be frightened. 'I'll come back tomorrow,' Ivy whispered.

Jenny let go of the bars and floated downward, her skirts belling out around her. 'I'm coming, Nettle,' she called, and vanished into the darkness.

Ivy stayed by the Great Shaft after Jenny had gone, hoping to catch some snippet of her conversation with Nettle. Would the old woman scold her for going so close to the surface? Would she threaten to report Jenny to her mistress? When Ivy lived in the Delve she had often climbed to the top of the shaft herself, but she'd always been careful not to get caught. She feared what might happen to Jenny if Betony found out.

Though by the looks of her, Jenny was suffering already. Even apart from the cough, it was shocking how wan and sickly-looking her friend had become. Had the poison in the Delve grown worse since her banishment? Or had Jenny only ever seemed healthy to her by contrast, because Ivy had been ill for so many years herself?

Whatever the answer might be, something had to be done about it. The idea of her proud, stubborn aunt still refusing to let the piskey-women and children go to the surface, all the while enjoying complete freedom herself, made Ivy furious. Someone had to make Betony see reason – and if she'd written Ivy off as a troublemaker, the impertinent, headstrong daughter of a sister-in-law she'd always despised, then maybe she'd listen to someone like Jenny who'd never crossed her even once…

Except that no matter how hard she tried, she couldn't imagine Jenny standing up to Betony. Not that the older girl was a coward, but she was humble, and always respectful of her elders. Besides, it wouldn't be fair to ask her friend to take such a risk when she had her mother and young brother to think of.

But who else would speak up for the suffering women and children of the Delve?

Ivy put her ear to the cage and listened, but all she heard was the slow drip of water falling down the shaft. At last, resigned, she changed back into a swift and flew away.

Ivy swooped and glided through the air, shrieking as she went in the instinctive, ceaseless cry of the swift. Wind-borne spiders tumbled past her, and she snapped them up – a meal that would have revolted her in her own form, but as a bird she didn't think twice about it. When she'd taken the edge off her hunger, she skimmed over a pond for a drink of water, then shot through the clouds to bask in the brilliance of the midday sun.

She never tired of flying like this, darting effortlessly through the air; it was a pleasure she could never take for granted. Especially after all the years she'd spent creeping weak and wingless through the Delve, never seeing the world above her except in the darkness of a Lighting night. Back then she'd envied Jenny for having wings, but now she ached with pity for her friend, and all the other piskey-women she'd once thought so much healthier and better off than herself. She wished they could know the feeling that thrilled inside her now, shining through even her darkest worries: the wild, delirious joy of freedom.

Ivy rode the wind down the coast to the very tip of Cornwall, where there were some ruins she and Martin hadn't visited yet, and stayed there until the clouds drifted apart, shredding into ragged strips of grey. By the time she'd winged her way back to the Delve, the sky was all but clear: the sun had dropped behind the engine house, and the horizon blazed purple and coral. Perhaps now she'd meet another friend she could talk to.

She knew all the secret exits from the mine, the winding paths the piskey hunters took through the gorse and underbrush on their way to the fields beyond. Ivy's sharp eyes swept the hillside, and before long, she was rewarded with the sight of two of the older hunters climbing out onto the surface. First came Feldspar, then Gem caught up with him, and before long they were good-naturedly teasing each other, with plenty of elbow-jabs and barks of hoarse laughter.

She'd always liked the two men, and it was good to know that the time they'd spent trapped in the Claybane hadn't dampened their sense of humour. But did they have to enjoy themselves quite so obviously? Ivy felt a flash of resentment on Jenny's behalf – until she listened more closely, and realised that some of the men's chortles were coughs.

Dread tightened Ivy's chest. If even the piskeys who went outside every day were feeling the effects, the air in the Delve must be even worse than she had feared. What if she'd been wrong about Gillian's smoke-spell being harmless? Gillian had been friends with Ivy's mother once, or pretended to be, so she knew about the poison lurking deep in the mine. Perhaps, in her last act of vengeful malice, Gillian had used her magic to worsen its deadly effects?

Ivy was brooding over the thought when the next pair of hunters emerged, their drab miner's trousers and waistcoats blending almost invisibly with the bracken. It was Pick and his young son Elvar, a skinny thirteen-year-old who'd just started training for the hunt. As quiet as the others had been noisy, they moved off towards the nearby wood, and soon were lost among the trees.

Several minutes passed, and Ivy was beginning to think she'd seen the last hunting party of the evening, when the gorse stirred and a familiar brown cap and pair of broad shoulders emerged from the shadows. A fit, powerfully built young man, as tall for a piskey as Ivy herself was short. He pulled off the cap to scratch his head, and the sunlight glowed in his hair like molten copper.

Mattock. Ivy hadn't known how much she'd missed that square, honest face of his, until now.

She'd had such good luck this morning in finding Jenny, that Ivy half-expected that luck to hold. Matt had always taken her seriously when nobody else did: if she told him what was happening in the Delve, he might help. But before she could land and take her own shape, Matt turned back and called, 'Hey! Mica! Are you coming or not?'

Ivy's hopes deflated. She should have known – Mattock and her brother were practically inseparable. They foraged together every morning and hunted together most evenings; they took turns milking the neighbouring farmer's cows after he'd gone to bed; and when the piskeys of the Delve needed goods that only the human world could provide, it was Mica and Matt who walked to the nearby city of Redruth and did the buying. She'd never catch Mattock alone, let alone convince him not to tell Mica that he'd seen her.

She wheeled to go, but then Matt spoke again, his voice cracking in astonishment: 'Ivy?'

Ivy's wingbeats stuttered. Surely he didn't mean – he couldn't have guessed – Mica would never have told him.

Yet there he stood with cap in hand, looking straight up at her. Somehow, Mattock *knew*.

four

Once Mattock had called out to her, Ivy didn't dare stay an instant longer. Mica had warned her, even before he knew her secret, that the hunters of the Delve regarded taking the forms of birds and animals as a kind of blasphemy. If he'd told Matt about her shape-changing, he might have told the other hunters as well...

Ivy turned tail and flashed away at top speed, plunging into the shadows of the wood. She zigzagged between the trees, their sparse leaves and twisted branches blurring around her, and shot out across the river valley on the other side. Only when the Delve was well behind her could she bring herself to slow down, and even then her heart beat wildly with the nearness of her escape.

Yet now that the first shock had passed, Ivy couldn't understand how it had happened. The first time Mica had spotted Ivy in swift form, he hadn't recognised her as his sister at all. In fact he'd slung a stone at her and nearly killed her, believing she was Martin.

So what had made Matt think that the lone swift circling above the Delve was Ivy?

Whatever the answer, one thing was clear: her swift-form was no longer a safe disguise. If she came back to see Jenny tomorrow as promised, she'd have to make herself invisible and climb up to the engine house on foot.

Gradually her pulse settled and Ivy relaxed, stroking on through the darkening sky with just the occasional flick of a wingtip to steady her course. In bird-form she could not feel the copper bracelet on her wrist – like her clothing, it was tucked away in some magical between-space, waiting until she took her own shape again. But she resolved to check it as soon as she reached the carn. She needed to talk to someone, and if anyone could help her make sense of what had just happened, it would be Martin.

As she glided through the twilight, distracted by the glowing lights of human vehicles chasing each other along the roadway below, she wondered how her companion was faring. He'd seemed enthralled by the treasure they'd taken from the carn, his eyes glittering with pleasure as the riches spilled between his hands. Yet at the same time, he'd been strangely determined to sell it as soon as possible. It was as though the spriggan and faery aspects of him were at war: the part that longed to hoard, and the part that needed to bargain...

Ivy only hoped he wasn't regretting that decision now. Perhaps he'd been right that the other faeries had no reason to begrudge him assassinating their Empress – but they had little reason to trust him, either. From what little Ivy knew of his history, Martin had met the Empress when he was a boy little older than Elvar or Jenny's brother Quartz, and he'd gone willingly into her service. She'd groomed him from a ragged urchin into a sleek young courtier, willing to scheme and betray and kill at her command; she'd even taught him to lie, as few magical folk could. Ivy wasn't sure when Martin had finally turned against his mistress, but she suspected even he would agree that his repentance had come later than it should…

A dark shape flashed through the upper hemisphere of her vision, and something struck her outstretched wing. Knocked off course, she tumbled into a spiral, beak open in a shrill of alarm. She had barely an instant to recover before her assailant plunged at her again.

A hobby! Martin had warned her about these small, fast-stooping falcons, one of the few predators that could catch a swift. She tried to dive away, but too late: the falcon was on top of her, talons clamping around her body. Ivy screamed again, as much with fury as terror, and struggled to escape. But the bird's grip only tightened, and pain stabbed through Ivy as its claws pierced her skin and the cruel, hooked beak came down for the killing blow—

A second, stunning collision buffeted Ivy sideways, the hobby tumbling with her. For an instant its death-grasp loosened, and Ivy twisted and beat her wings in a last attempt to free herself. But then she spotted the newcomer who had crashed into them, and her courage withered.

She'd hoped it might be Martin in his other bird-shape, come to rescue her. But it was an even bigger falcon, raking at the smaller bird with its own powerful talons. The hobby shrieked and dove away, but the other falcon overtook it, swerving around for another strike. Ivy's captor veered aside just in time.

At first Ivy had thought the two birds were fighting over her, but now she understood: the bigger falcon was attacking the hobby itself. And in the whirling confusion of their aerial battle, Ivy finally realised what she had to do. She stopped her frantic flapping, marshalled her fear-scattered wits, and willed herself into piskey shape.

As her weight increased tenfold, the hobby could no longer hold her. Its claws ripped across Ivy's ribcage and then she was falling free, the ground rushing up towards her at dizzying speed. She knew she had to change back into a swift before she crashed, but the wind was deafening and her brain was whirling so fast she couldn't *think*—

She transformed at the last instant, pulling herself out of the dive a mere stump's height from impact. The pain in her side took her breath away, but she forced her trembling wings wide and skimmed over the scrubby ground until momentum could carry her no further. Then she changed to her own shape again and collapsed into the heather, spent.

The falcons were still screaming at each other in the distance, but Ivy had no strength even to lift her head, let alone care who won the battle now. She'd strained every muscle in her arms, her spine ached all the way down to her tailbone, and the hobby's talons had raked deep, stinging scratches along both her sides.

How could she have been so foolish? A lone swift flying through the September dusk, when most of her kind had flown away weeks ago – of course the hobby had been drawn to her. And no wonder Mattock, a hunter trained to know the habits of birds and animals, had guessed that she was an impostor.

She'd been so proud of her ability to take bird-shape, so confident in her powers of flight. She'd thought she could outrun any danger, outfly any predator that crossed her path…but now Ivy understood, with cruel clarity, how arrogant those thoughts had been.

She wasn't strong. She wasn't special. Even in bird-shape, she was small and fragile and vulnerable as ever. And now, no matter what time of year she flew or how many others of her kind flocked around her, Ivy would never feel safe as a swift again.

It was a long time before Ivy could muster the energy to move, and the agony of sitting up forced an involuntary groan from her lips. But she couldn't lie out in the open all night. The sky was almost black now, the air growing cooler, and without the insulation of her close-packed feathers, Ivy was starting to shiver.

This wasn't the valley she'd been flying for, with its circle of low hills and the carn watching over it. The hobby's attack had driven her off course, but her directional sense told her she'd landed a good two minutes' flight south and a half a minute west of her target. Which was no distance at all for a healthy swift in daylight, but an impossible journey for Ivy. Her injuries weren't fatal, but they'd left her too stiff and shaky to fly even if she could find the courage to do so.

Her only option was to grow to human size and limp to her rendezvous with Martin on foot. But she was already weak, and in her current state she'd be lucky to make it more than a mile...

Lucky. She had been, hadn't she, despite everything? If she hadn't dropped onto a downdraught at exactly the right instant, the hobby would have struck her with both feet, paralysing her. But it had just missed her that first time, giving Ivy a chance to fight back. And then that other falcon had swooped down on the hobby and distracted it until she could escape...so that was two strokes of extraordinary good fortune. If the bigger bird had shown up even half a minute later, she'd be dead.

Blood was seeping through Ivy's jumper, and her teeth had begun to chatter. She wrapped her arms around her sides and stumbled forward, one laboured step at a time.

Come on, she told herself. *At least try for the top of that hill; you'll get a better view from there. You can make it that far.*

But the ground was boggy from the morning's rain, and the ridge was further than it looked. Soon Ivy's shoes were soaked through, her socks squelching inside them, and it took all her strength to keep pulling her feet out of the mud and slog on. She slipped and fell twice before she reached firmer ground, and by the time she'd struggled up the rocky slope to the summit, she was spent. She swayed there, gazing dully at the scattered lights of the farms and cottages below – all humans, all strangers, all too far away – then limped towards a nearby outcropping in search of shelter.

Her night-vision was fogged with weariness, and her left side felt as though it had been flayed and then rubbed with salt. The wind up here was harsher than it had been below, but she couldn't go any further. Ivy collapsed against the rocks, heedless of the damp ground, and pressed her fingers against the copper bracelet. Was it growing warmer? Ivy hoped so, but between the alternating chills and sweats that gripped her body, it was hard to be sure.

I'm sorry, Martin, she thought foggily. *I tried…* And with that Ivy's chin dropped onto her chest, and she fell into exhausted sleep.

When he'd first heard the muffled sobs in the middle of the night, the boy had thought he must be dreaming. And even once he wakened enough to know the sound was real, he couldn't imagine where it was coming from. Certainly none of the older boys and men sleeping around him, wrapped in their cloaks, had done anything but mumble and snore for as long as he'd shared their company. And since joining the band he'd discovered that crying gained him nothing but a cuff on the ear, so he'd learned to keep his tears hidden.

Which meant it must be one of the women weeping. But why? Spriggan-wives weren't badly treated, as far as he could tell; they were treasured, protected, sheltered from all harm, and whatever comforts the clan could provide were always given first to them. There were too few females among their people, and they bore children too rarely, for anyone to take their presence for granted.

Yet he couldn't be sure that the women were happy, either. It was hard to know how any of them felt or what they were thinking, because their faces, like the rest of their bodies, were invisible. So if he got up and went out into the passage, he'd either see a shadow or nothing at all...and the boy wasn't sure he liked the idea of talking to a ghost. Not even a living one.

But it was hard to lie there, listening to her weep. Perhaps he had better get up after all, if only to hush her before she woke the others. The boy turned over, unwrapping himself from his cloak. Then he tiptoed around his sleeping clan-brothers, and slipped into the main passage of the fogou. Feeling his way along the drystone wall, moss slippery beneath his fingers, he crept up the tunnel towards the exit.

He'd feared he might trip over the woman before he saw her. But there she sat with her knees drawn up and her head bowed over them, shockingly visible. Her moon-coloured hair veiled her face and spilled down her back to the floor, and what he could see of her skin was covered in jewellery – a ring or two on each finger, bracelets stacked from wrist to elbow, and solid armbands that came halfway to the shoulder. A leather purse hung at her side, heavy with coins by the shape of it, and her belt was crusted with gems and gold.

The boy stood paralysed, his mouth dry. No man of the tribe, not even a boy-child like himself, should ever look at another man's wife or know the size of his hoard, and he had just seen both. His only chance was to back away quickly, and return to his bed before anyone could suspect—

The woman looked up sharply, like a roe deer scenting danger. He caught a glimpse of the emerald circlet on her brow before she flickered out of sight. 'Who's there?' she demanded. 'Show yourself!'

Unforgivable as seeing her had been, to disobey would be worse. That was the voice of the chief's own wife, first among all women. Shakily the boy stepped out of the shadows, walked quickly to where she had been sitting, and knelt by what he hoped were her feet. 'Forgive me, Lady,' he stammered.

The treasure she wore chimed and rattled as she rose. He braced himself for the curse, the spittle, the backhanded blow – but instead an invisible hand, soft despite the weight of the rings, cupped his face and turned it to the light.

'My son,' she whispered, as though he were a wonder.

The Grey Man's wife, his mother? How could that be? True, he'd been taken from his birth-mother as soon as he was weaned and given to another clan for fostering, and by the time the Grey Man and his band came to claim him he'd had no idea who his parents were. But he'd felt sure he was no one important. How could he be when the chief had never spoken to him, or spared him more than an indifferent glance? All he'd been allowed to do these past few weeks was tag along behind the older boys, carrying whatever burdens they gave him and eating whatever scraps they threw his way. He didn't even have a proper name.

But if this strange, lovely woman wanted to claim him as her own, *it wasn't his place to tell her she was wrong. He gazed at the air where he thought her face must be, waiting for her to go on.*

She was silent so long that he might have thought she had gone away, if not for the slight pressure of her fingers against his skin. At last she raised him up, tenderly, and took his hand in her invisible one.

'Come with me,' she whispered. 'There are things I need to tell you.'

five

Alone on the moorland, Ivy stirred restlessly against the stones. The pain in her side was worse than ever, her skin burning with feverish warmth. But the night was still dark, and her exhaustion was stronger than any discomfort. She slumped lower, and soon even the icy rake of the wind across her face could not keep her from falling back into the dream-world she'd left behind.

'Can you work a spell of silence, little one?' the chief's wife whispered as she led him towards the fogou's southern exit, a low portal framed by ferns and long grasses. 'So no one will hear us, even if they wake?'

The boy nodded, shy and proud. He held up one hand, feeling the spell take shape and settle across the tunnel behind them. Then he turned to where he thought she must be and said, 'It's done.'

Her lips brushed his temple. 'My clever boy.' She made him sit down, then with a faint jingling she seated herself across from him and said, 'Look at me.'

The boy squinted, trying to focus on nothing. The air shimmered, the shadows brightened and took shape...

And all at once he could see her, even more beautiful than he'd imagined. Eyes tip-tilted like his own, but large and dark as a doe's. Delicate features in a heart-shaped face, with the points of her ears just visible through the silken fall of her hair. Chains and pendants draped her neck and spread out across her collarbones, like a breastplate of gold and silver with jewels winking out of it. And spread behind her, quivering, were a pair of glassy wings like a dragonfly's – wings unlike any he'd ever seen or heard of before, even in the old stories his foster-auntie used to tell him at night.

'What are you?' he breathed.

She gave a small, sad smile. 'Some call us the Pobel Vean, the Small People of Kernow,' she told him. 'Others call us faeries.'

The boy gazed at her, too awed to speak. She stroked his hair as she went on, 'When I was younger I ran away from home, looking for adventure. I was wild and wilful and sure of my power, and I thought I could be happier on my own.' Her hand stilled, then fell away. 'I was a fool. Before long I was captured by a human who...who was not kind to me, and if your father hadn't found me, I would have died.'

She'd thought the Grey Man hideous at first, and with good reason: he had been wearing the grotesque shape the spriggans used to frighten humans away from their treasure, with a stumpy body and a bulbous head. But when he changed back into his ordinary form, she saw that he was not so different from a faery after all. He spoke kindly to her and healed her wounds, and offered her refuge among his people on *two conditions: she must remain invisible at all times, as the spriggan-women did, and she must consent to become his wife.*

'I accepted,' she said, 'because I saw no other choice. I had disgraced myself in the eyes of my people, and I thought they would never take me back. And to be the wife of a chieftain and the keeper of all his treasure seemed like a noble thing, even if it did mean staying hidden. I never guessed how heavily that promise would weigh upon me.' She gazed down at her bracelet-covered arms. 'In more ways than one.'

The Grey Man had never treated her unkindly, she said. He had even worked spells on the treasure she carried to make it a lighter burden, and every few days he allowed her to lay it aside and make herself visible for a time – as long as the two of them were alone. But keeping up the invisibility glamour drained her, she said, and she could not sustain it all day unless she let it down at night. So it hadn't been long before the spriggan-wives who shared her sleeping chamber discovered that the Grey Man's wife was a faery – and they had been using that knowledge against her ever since.

'I thought they would treat me more kindly when you were born,' she said. 'I thought they would see, then, that I was truly one of them. But it only made them more jealous.'

The boy was silent, searching her face. He only half-understood the story she had told him, but he knew what it was to feel lonely and unwanted. No wonder she had been crying, if this was what her life had become. How many other nights had she wept in the darkness, and he had never known it?

'And I am never alone,' she murmured. 'In my home wyld lived eighty faeries or more, but there was room for all of us. Here there are

59

scarcely twelve of us – yet everywhere I go I am surrounded. If I could cast off this weight of treasure and run free under the open sky, for just one hour…' Her shoulders sagged. 'But I cannot.'

Cast off her treasure? Faery or not, how could his mother even dream of such a thing? A wife's duty was to know her husband's trove down to the last copper, and hold it safe for him. Even the beauty of the spriggan-women was said to be a treasure in itself – and though the boy had sometimes been tempted to doubt that rumour, in his mother's case he could well believe it.

'Please,' she whispered, folding his hand between her own. He could feel the weight of the bracelets she wore, the cold bands of her rings pressing into his palm. 'Help me.'

'How?' asked the boy, bewildered. He didn't have the power to change his people's laws: he hadn't even earned a name yet. He might be the Grey Man's son by birth, but in his own right he was nobody at all.

'You are my only child.' Her grip tightened, urgent. 'Your father's wealth is as much yours as it is mine. Guard it for me, just a little while, and I will reward you.'

The boy licked his lips, half in fear and half in longing. 'What kind of reward?'

'Anything that I can give you,' she said. 'Food, if you are hungry. Or I could teach you spells, faery spells, that none of the others know… you would like that, wouldn't you?'

Yes, he would. Hunger was bad, but being powerless was worse, and to be ignorant was worst of all. 'When?' he asked.

'When I return.' She must have seen the uncertainty in his eyes, but

she smiled as though he had already answered. 'I knew I could trust you. Help me with these.' She lifted her hair away from her shoulders, raising her chin to expose the mass of chains about her neck. 'Quickly. There isn't much time...'

Sunlight crept across Ivy's eyes, and somewhere close by a thrush was singing. Mumbling annoyance, she rolled away from the window and pulled the covers over her head. She could never get a decent sleep above-ground, no matter how comfortable the bed might be...

Then it dawned on her that she was lying in a bed, in a room with a window, and that it didn't hurt to move at all. Startled, she bolted upright and found Martin sitting in a chair across from her with one ankle crossed over the other knee, cleaning his nails with the point of a small silver knife.

'You,' he said without looking up, 'have a positively supernatural gift for getting yourself into trouble. Next time I go to London, I'm taking you with me. By train, if necessary.'

Ivy ran her hands through her dark curls, feeling disoriented. She'd been so caught up in her dream about the boy and his mother that she'd never guessed Martin was looking for her, let alone that he'd found her. He'd treated her wounds and carried her to this place – a small hotel or village inn of some sort. Yet in all that time, she hadn't wakened once...

'You put a sleeping spell on me,' she blurted. 'And then you healed me again. Without even asking.'

His brows lifted in mild surprise. 'You mean you had other

plans? A raging blood infection, perhaps, with a touch of hypothermia? In any case, you were asleep already. I just made it easier for you to stay that way.'

Ivy opened her mouth, then shut it again. She hadn't meant to sound ungrateful, but she wasn't exactly happy, either. When Martin had saved her life the first time, she'd never imagined that he could heal her wounds and drive the poison from her body with nothing more than his bare hands. Piskey healers worked with herbs and powders and painstakingly brewed potions, not raw magic. So being restored to health so quickly had seemed a wonderful thing to Ivy...until she'd learned how much Martin's impulsive gift had changed her. How in some unsettling way it had made her less like her old piskey self, and more like him.

'I would have healed on my own,' she said at last, quietly. 'You didn't have to do that.'

He flicked the knife closed and tossed it on the table, where it turned into an ordinary-looking pen. 'You're welcome,' he said. 'Now would you care to tell me why I found you lying unconscious on a hillside miles from where we were supposed to be meeting, with bloody clothes and claw-marks all over your body?'

Ivy ran a hand down her side, feeling the newly healed skin through the smooth, clean knit of her jumper. So he'd fixed her clothes with magic too. Part of her was glad, but another part found his generosity unsettling, especially when she remembered the things she'd learned about the Grey Man and his faery bride last night...

But she couldn't say that to Martin. She'd tell him about the dream later. 'A hobby attacked me,' she said, and went on to explain how it had happened, from the time Mattock had hailed her at the Delve to the time she'd fallen bleeding into the heather.

'The bigger bird sounds like a peregrine,' said Martin, frowning. 'And you say it attacked the hobby? That's unusual. It must have been a female, protecting her nest.'

'It was beautiful,' said Ivy, and meant it. The two falcons didn't look that different at first glance – and yet she felt a cold clench in her stomach at the thought of the one, and only admiration for the other.

'Maybe,' Martin said, 'but I'm sure it would have been equally willing to eat you. You were lucky – albeit in a backhanded way. Just enough luck to survive, not enough to keep you from getting hurt in the first place.' He ran a finger thoughtfully across his chin. 'That's very interesting.'

To Ivy the idea of sharing Martin's unpredictable spriggan luck was less interesting than disturbing, but she wasn't about to insult him by saying so. 'I was careless,' she admitted. 'I should have been watching. And I didn't realise how much I'd stand out, now that most of the other swifts are gone.'

'It's a problem,' agreed Martin. 'And it's only going to get worse as the year goes on. That's probably why I've never met anyone else who takes the shape you do. Swifts are common enough between May and August, but beyond that…'

'It's too risky,' said Ivy. She threw back the covers and swung her legs around. 'Especially if I want to go back to the Delve. But I don't know what else I can do.'

'I know. Don't go back to the Delve.'

'You don't understand.' She got up and moved to the window, rubbing her arms distractedly. 'I can't leave all my friends and neighbours to die, just because Betony won't admit she was wrong. She's convinced herself that the poison in the mine was all Gillian's doing, and that she can get rid of it with just a few spells and a bit of patience. But the air in the mine's not getting any better. If anything, it's worse.'

'Why is she so determined to keep her people underground?' asked Martin. 'Even if she grew up hearing the same horror stories you did about spriggans roaming the surface, she must know better now she's seen the upper world for herself.'

'She does know better,' said Ivy. 'When I first went to talk to her about it, Nettle said that nobody in the Delve had seen a spriggan in thirty years, and Betony didn't even pretend to be surprised.'

'Then who does she think is going to hurt you? The humans?'

'No. The Empress.'

Martin frowned. 'But your aunt's a piskey. How would she even have heard of the Empress?'

'The old Joan knew about her somehow,' said Ivy. 'And before she died, she warned Betony not to let the Empress capture even one of our people, or we'd all end up under her power. I tried to tell Betony that the Empress is dead, but as soon as she guessed that I'd heard that news from you...'

'Ah,' said Martin. 'Of course. She thinks I'm the Empress's spy, trying to trick you – or rather, her – into letting down her guard.' His expression turned rueful. 'Clever of her to think of that.'

'Yes,' replied Ivy, 'but the problem is, now she can't think of anything else. I think deep down she knows the mine isn't nearly as safe as she pretends, but she still thinks our people are better off dying as free piskeys than living as faery slaves. And she won't believe there's any other option.' She thumped her fist on the bedpost. 'It's so frustrating!'

'Well,' said Martin, studying his steepled fingers, 'if you're determined to keep beating your head against that particular wall, at least you'll have somewhere decent to stay while you're doing it. I've booked this room for a week.'

Ivy sank onto the window ledge, her anger fading. 'You sold the treasure?'

'It wasn't easy to find a human who'd give me a fair price without a lot of tedious paperwork, but yes.' He pulled a cream-coloured card from his pocket and squinted at it. 'Thom Pendennis, Dealer in Antiquities, London. Not the most attractive human I've met, especially since he kept gaping at me like a fish and asking impertinent questions about my family. But his money seems genuine enough.'

Ivy blinked. 'Why would he ask about that? You don't have any family, do you?'

'It seems I reminded him of someone. Some old schoolmate or former customer, perhaps: he didn't say. But he started to sweat and babble apologies when I hinted I might take my business elsewhere, and he all but begged me to come back again, if I ever had more to sell.' Martin's gaze turned distant with thought. 'It's an odd thing. Even though I'd barely touched the treasure, it was surprisingly hard to let it go. I'd always wondered why my ancestors didn't just sell off their hoards and live like kings, but now…'

'That reminds me,' Ivy began, but then her stomach gave a thunderous rumble. She reached for a packet of biscuits, but Martin stopped her hand.

'We have money now. That means a proper breakfast… assuming you don't mind turning invisible until we're away from the hotel.'

Ivy's hands clenched on the windowsill. 'Invisible?' she asked, trying to sound casual. But it wasn't easy, with the dream about the Grey Man and the faery woman still fresh in her mind. 'Why?'

'Well, technically speaking, there's only supposed to be one person in this room. I would have booked us a double, but as you said yourself, you're a little young to be my wife.'

Martin's mouth curled slyly as he spoke, and she knew he expected her to blush. But Ivy was in no mood to be teased.

'You don't look that much older yourself,' she retorted, heaving the window open. 'I'll see you outside.' Then, mustering her courage, she took bird-shape and dropped to the pavement below.

SIX

An awkward hop across the veranda and several minutes of hiding in the shrubbery later, Ivy was starting to think she should have turned herself invisible after all. But at last the man who'd been reading his newspaper in the garden went inside, and she seized her chance to turn back into human shape. She hurried to the front of the hotel, Martin joined her, and the two of them continued down the narrow, sloping road into the village.

When they came to the bakery, Ivy stayed outside to wait while Martin bought their breakfast. Not until they were sitting together on the bench beneath the town clock with pastries in hand did he break the silence.

'So,' said Martin. 'I take it my jest was in poor taste?'

There was a harbour visible between the white-and-cream buildings, a small crescent of wet sand lined with bobbing sailboats. Ivy watched the gulls wheeling above it as she answered, 'I know you didn't mean anything by it. You couldn't have known. But...' She took a bite of the crescent-shaped roll and chewed, giving herself time to think. 'Last night, I had another dream.'

'About the spriggans?' Martin sat up, alert. 'What was it?'

Ivy explained how the boy had met his mother in the darkness of the fogou, and the things she'd told him about the Grey Man. 'But the dreams are out of order,' she said. 'They seem to be going backwards in time instead of forward, and I don't understand why.'

'I don't know either,' said Martin. 'Except that perhaps you dreamed about the knockers attacking the fogou first because it was such a powerful memory, and because you were sleeping in the place where it happened. And now you're picking up the rest of the story, one piece at a time.'

Ivy's pastry had gone cold. She swallowed the last dry bite with difficulty and said, 'You think there are more dreams coming, then?'

'Wherever these visions of yours are coming from, they must have a purpose. Maybe there's some clue in this story that will lead us to the spriggans, or at least tell us what happened to them. We know they didn't all die out four hundred years ago, so there has to be more to the story.' He gazed thoughtfully into the distance, then got to his feet. 'Come on.'

'Where are we going?' asked Ivy.

'Down to the coast. I spotted a cave when I was searching for you last night, and I want to check it out.' He set off towards the harbour. Ivy got up, brushing pastry crumbs from her fingers, and followed.

Together they made their way across the boat-littered sand, onto a winding footpath that rose steeply towards the cliffs. Halfway up the slope a middle-aged couple walking a dog hailed them with smiles, and awkwardly Ivy smiled back as she stepped aside to let them pass. Like most piskeys she had no fear of humans, but she had never felt at ease with them as her mother and Martin did. But after that they found themselves alone, and for a long time the only sound was the sea washing against the rocks below.

'There,' said Martin, and pointed to the cliffs ahead, where a dark gap yawned above a shore scattered with broken rocks and slabs of granite. 'We'll have to fly down to it, but—'

'I can't go that far.' The words came out before she could stop them, uneven and too loud. 'Not after… I don't want to.'

Martin went still, the wind ruffling his pale blond hair. Then he turned to her, his expression unreadable, and asked, 'Why?'

'I don't want to be a swift,' said Ivy, dashing angrily at the tears that had leaped to her eyes. 'Not right now. So –' She jerked her chin towards the cliffside. 'Go on without me. I'll wait here.'

She thought Martin would be impatient with her, but if anything he looked relieved. 'Is that all?' he asked. 'Well, in that case, there are other ways of flying.' He shifted fluidly into his barn-owl shape, white wings beating the air in front of her, then back to himself again. 'Make yourself small and climb on my back. I'll fly you down.'

*

Once Ivy had got used to the strangeness of burying her hands in Martin's soft feathers and gripping his sides with her knees, the flight down to the cave was exhilarating. But in the end, it proved no different from any of the other places they'd explored: if spriggans had ever lived there, they'd moved on without leaving any hint of their presence. She followed Martin back to the mouth of the cave, where he sprang down onto a flat-topped boulder and sat looking out at the ebbing tide. After a brief hesitation, Ivy joined him.

'Do you think,' she said, picking at a bit of seaweed stuck to her shoe, 'that I could learn another bird-shape?'

Martin considered this. 'Possibly,' he said. 'Most male faeries I know can become a bird and an animal. I've mastered three forms myself, but I've never met anyone who could do more.'

'Why is that?'

'Because you need to feel a strong connection to the creature you're becoming,' said Martin. 'Remember how long you had to spend bird-watching before you saw your first swift? And when you saw it…'

'It felt right,' said Ivy.

'Exactly. But sometimes, no matter how many birds or animals you look at, that connection isn't there. And if you're comfortable in one form, it's not always easy to adjust to another.' He spoke casually, but Ivy sensed the warning behind the words. *Don't get too attached to this idea of yours. It might not work*.

But he'd been wrong about her abilities before; Ivy could only hope he was wrong now. 'You say you've learned three forms?' she asked. 'House martin, barn owl…what's the other?'

'My animal-shape is an ermine.' He gave a half-smile. 'Only an ermine, mind. Which is even less practical most of the year than your swift-form, seeing as stoats only become ermines in deep winter. But I'm partially colour-blind, so when I tried to turn my fur brown I ended up dark green instead. And once Rob and the other faeries stopped laughing, I decided to leave well enough alone.'

Had he mentioned Rob's name before? Ivy didn't think so. 'Was Rob the one who taught you to change shape?'

'No,' said Martin. 'But Rob and I grew up together, after a fashion. He was the Empress's adopted son, while I was…' He paused, considering. 'I suppose you would call me her protégé. There were a few unusually gifted faeries that she marked out for special attention, all of us young and stupid enough to believe it was an honour. Corbin and Byrne Blackwing were expert trackers, and Veronica…'

His expression darkened, as though the name had stirred some bitter memory. Then he went on, 'Veronica had a talent for manipulating minds. We worked together for a time, as the Empress's lieutenants. But though we were allies, we were never friends.'

'Where are they now?' asked Ivy. 'The others?'

'Rob turned against the Empress the minute he got the chance, and joined forces with a band of faeries down in Kent who'd somehow managed to escape her control – the Oakenfolk. He seemed to think they might actually have a chance of beating the Empress, even though they were outnumbered twenty to one.' He picked up a bit of shale and flicked it out over the waves, watching it sink before he went on, 'I told him he was insane, and I wanted nothing to do with it. But I imagine he's feeling quite smug now about having picked the winning side.'

One day, Ivy would have to get him to tell her the rest of that story – how such a small group of rebels had succeeded in defeating the most ruthless tyrant the faery world had ever known. 'What about the rest?' she asked.

'The Blackwing brothers stayed loyal to the Empress until the very end, or as near as makes no difference. And everyone who'd worked with them knew they'd served her more willingly than not. So after she was defeated, they were sent to a magical prison somewhere off the coast of Wales as punishment, with no chance of release.' He picked up another rock, weighing it in his hand. 'I'd most likely have ended up in that prison myself, if I hadn't taken off before Rob and his allies could catch me.'

Ivy had already seen for herself what being cooped up in a cell did to Martin: the days he'd spent trapped in the Delve had nearly driven him mad. No wonder he'd fled to Cornwall rather than risk being imprisoned, and yet…

'But you said yourself that nobody would mourn the Empress,' she said. 'And Rob had already turned against her. So why would he want you punished?'

'Maybe because the Empress was the closest thing to a mother he'd ever known?' asked Martin rhetorically. 'By the time the battle was over she'd been stripped of her powers, and looked like a frail old woman who wouldn't live much longer. I could see the pity in Rob's face, and I knew he had no idea how dangerous she still was, especially with Veronica by her side.' He gazed back at the harbour, where a lone sailboat had slipped free of the crowd and was gliding out into open water. 'Besides, Rob has...other reasons to hate me.'

Ivy would have asked what those reasons were, but something in his face warned her against it. For some time they sat without speaking, until Martin got up, brushed himself off, and said, 'Well, no sense in hanging about here any longer.'

Ivy waited, expecting him to change into a barn owl and carry her as before. But he only arched his brows at her, an unspoken question in his gaze.

'No,' said Ivy.

Martin stepped closer, taking her hands in his. 'I know you're afraid,' he said. 'I don't blame you. A hobby came after me once when I was running from the Empress, and by the time I'd collected my wits enough to switch to owl-shape I thought my heart was going to explode.'

'But?' Ivy asked flatly. Her pulse was beating fast already, and she wanted to snatch her hands away. But she didn't want him to think her a coward, either.

'It's only a short flight back to the hotel. And I'll be right beside you.' His grey gaze held hers. 'Will you at least try? Because I don't think you have much chance of ever learning another bird-shape, if you're too afraid to fly at all.'

Ivy's lips felt dry. She licked them, then forced her chin up and said, 'All right.'

Martin released her and stepped back. Ivy stared up at the cliffs, clenching and unclenching her hands, then took a running jump off the boulder and hurled herself into swift-shape.

It had been scarcely twelve hours since she last took flight, yet her wings felt shaky and unfamiliar, and the touch of the sea-breeze on her feathers made her small body tremble. The memory of struggling in the hobby's talons leaped into her mind, and she felt sick at the thought of flying the two miles that lay between her and the town.

Yet if Martin was right, she had to do this, no matter how much she dreaded it. And now he'd darted into position beside her, the slim black-and-white shape of his house martin-form even tinier than her own. Swallowing her fear, Ivy forced herself onward, riding the sea-breezes towards the jumbled white blocks of the town. The cliff curved; automatically she followed it…

Then she glanced up, and her concentration shattered. A dark falcon perched on an outcropping, staring at her with yellow, unblinking eyes.

It was too much for Ivy. She doubled back and shot for the first patch of shore she could find, stumbling onto the shingle in her own shape. She was breathing into her hands, trying to calm herself, when Martin landed beside her.

'It's all right,' he said. 'It's only a small peregrine, and it's got half a pigeon up there on the rocks, so it's not hungry.'

All the tension rushed out of Ivy, leaving her light-headed.

Not a hobby, a peregrine. Of course. If she'd dared to fly a little closer, she'd have seen that for herself; but instead she'd bolted at the first hint of danger, like the cowardly little swift she was. Shielding her eyes, she gazed up at the falcon on its rocky perch. *I'm sorry*, she thought. *I should have known better…*

And with that, the peregrine's head swivelled towards her and it gave a loud, keening cry.

For an instant Ivy stood transfixed. Then she spun back to Martin and seized him by both arms.

'That's it,' she blurted. 'That's the bird I want to be.'

seven

'But that doesn't make any sense,' Martin said as he followed her across the rocky beach. Between the sea-wind and the waves breaking against the cliffs Ivy could hardly hear him, but she didn't slow down. 'Why are you doing this to yourself?'

'Because I have to,' she said, not taking her eyes off the peregrine on its cliffside perch. She stopped at the foot of a boulder, leaped for a finger-hold and swung herself up onto the rock, clambering up its broken face as resolutely as she had once climbed the Great Shaft. When she reached the top, she had a much better view of the falcon.

'Tell me everything you know about them,' she said to Martin.

He sighed, but he told her. The peregrine was somewhat larger than a hobby but even faster in the dive, capable of hitting a moving target at up to two hundred miles per hour. They nested on uplands and rocky cliffsides like this one, feeding on pigeons and other small game. And though *peregrine* meant *wanderer*, they often stayed in the same hunting grounds all year, migrating only if food became scarce or the weather too harsh for comfort.

As he talked, Ivy traced and retraced the falcon's shape with her eyes, memorising every detail: its hooded cloak of blue-black feathers, its gold-rimmed eyes, the belly and underwings of dappled grey and white. When it launched itself from the cliffside Ivy turned automatically to follow it, nearly falling off the top of the boulder in her haste.

'Don't go!' she shouted after it, scrambling to climb down before it sailed out of sight. 'I'm not finished yet!'

Martin cleared his throat. 'You do realise that back at the Delve, when I told you to learn as much about swifts as you could before trying to turn yourself into one, I was stalling for time?'

Ivy stopped halfway down the rock and looked down at him. 'What?'

'I had no idea how to teach you to change shape,' he said. 'I didn't even think you'd be able to do it. But I was afraid that if I didn't say something you'd leave me to starve, so I improvised.'

'You mean you lied,' said Ivy. She'd almost forgotten Martin could do that, even though he'd admitted as much himself. *I've never lied to you yet*, he'd told her once. *Not that I expect you to be impressed by that, but you should be, because I'm one of the few faeries who can.* 'And then you lied to me about not lying. How am I supposed to trust anything you say?'

'It wasn't a lie.' His words were edged with impatience. 'I misled you, yes, but hardly with malicious intent. What I'm saying *now* is, you've studied that peregrine long enough to know

77

what it looks like, and have a rough idea of how it behaves. There's nothing to stop you trying to take its shape, if that's really what you want.'

She did want it, more than anything. As a swift she'd been fast and nimble, but as a peregrine, she'd also be fearless. She could fly all year round, day or night, without having to worry about being attacked by other birds; she could visit the Delve whenever she pleased and no one, not even Mica, would recognise her. And if she could master falcon-shape, she might even be able to enjoy flying as a swift again, knowing that she could change forms in midair if need be. She climbed to the top of the boulder, spread her arms wide—

And let them fall again, self-conscious. 'Could you go somewhere else?' she said to Martin. 'I can't concentrate with you watching me like that.'

'Should I watch you like this instead?' asked Martin, tilting his head sideways. But when Ivy glared at him, he relented. 'Fine. I'll go.' He vanished, and reappeared a second later at the top of the cliff.

Ivy was tempted to try copying his example, just to see if she could do it. It didn't look that hard... But no, that could wait until she'd finished here. She closed her eyes, summoning the image of the peregrine to her mind. *Picture the falcon*, she told herself. *Focus on the falcon. Become the falcon.* Then with a rush of determination she launched herself off the rock—

And became a swift.

Cursing her failure, Ivy swooped back to the rock and landed in her own shape. She'd try again, and this time she'd get it right. She'd picture the peregrine as she'd last seen it, flying out over the ocean, and copy it exactly…

But it was no use. Again and again Ivy tried, but each time she transformed she ended up in the tiny grey-brown shape she already knew, not the majestic falcon she longed to become. What was wrong with her? Was her magic too weak to master more than one form, or was the real barrier in her mind?

Whatever the obstacle, Ivy was determined to overcome it. If she couldn't fly as a peregrine, she'd soon be unable to fly at all. So she made yet another effort, and then another. But by the fifteenth attempt her head was pounding like a thunder-axe, and her legs trembled so much she could barely stand. She'd transformed back and forth so many times she was nearing the end of her magical strength.

Despair filled Ivy, eclipsing her fears. Blindly she changed shape one last time and shot straight up the cliffside, then dropped onto the grass beside Martin and buried her face in her arms.

'Don't lose heart,' he said. 'As I recall, you didn't find it easy to take swift-form the first time, either. If you want to have your best chance of succeeding, wait for a clear night with a full moon, and try again.'

He had a point. Over the past few weeks she'd become so confident in her swift-shape, she'd forgotten what a struggle it had been to learn it in the first place. She pushed the damp curls from her brow and gave a reluctant nod.

'A peregrine.' Martin shook his head. 'Why that, of all birds? Why do you want to be something that terrifies you?'

'I don't,' she said thickly. 'The hobby terrified me. I want to be something stronger.'

Martin was silent. At last he stretched out his arm and put it around Ivy's shoulders.

'Then you will be,' he said.

Even after several minutes of lying on the grass with her eyes closed, Ivy felt as though she'd been wrung out and hung up to dry. But at least by then she'd recovered enough strength to get up and follow Martin back to the harbour – though when she saw how steeply the street twisted upward towards the hotel, her spirit failed.

'I'll never make it all the way up there,' she said, dropping onto the sea wall and rubbing her aching calves. 'Go on, and I'll join you later.'

'I have a better idea,' he replied, holding out his hand. With a sigh, Ivy let him pull her upright, then followed him down behind the wall, where the shadows lay deep and none of the humans milling about the harbour could see them.

'Close your eyes,' Martin told her, 'and make your mind as blank as you can.'

Wondering what all this was about, Ivy shut her eyes and thought about the inside of the Delve at midnight, the darkest place she'd ever seen. Martin's grip on her hand tightened for an instant, and then he said, 'Done.'

Ivy opened her eyes – and there they stood in the hotel room, with the curtains blowing on the wind. 'How did you do that?' she asked, kicking off her shoes and dropping gratefully into the armchair.

'Easily enough, since we'd both been here before,' said Martin. 'Last night was a bit more tricky – I had to turn you small and carry you here in my barn-owl shape, then slip you into my pocket before I paid for the room.'

No wonder he'd put a sleeping spell on her first. If she'd woken up in his talons mid-flight, Ivy would have died of heart failure. 'Is it difficult?' she asked. 'Travelling by magic?'

'Not especially, once you've got the knack of it,' said Martin. 'You only need to picture a place or a landmark in your mind, and will yourself to go there. Though it has its limitations.'

'Such as?'

'Well, as I said before, you can't go anywhere you haven't visited already. If it's a long journey, like my trip to London, you have to do it in stages and rest a while in between. And every now and then, you end up somewhere where it's impossible to do it at all.'

'Like underground,' said Ivy, remembering how Gillian Menadue had tried to vanish after she'd dropped her smoke-spell down the Great Shaft, and failed. 'Is there anything else I should know before I try it?'

He gave her a sharp look. 'You're not serious.'

'I don't mean right now. I mean later.' After all, she had to get back to the Delve somehow for her meeting with Jenny, and it was painfully clear that she wouldn't be flying any time soon. 'When I've got my strength back.'

Martin relaxed. 'Well,' he said, 'it's obviously not a good idea to Leap in and out of places where you're likely to be seen.' He picked up the electric kettle from the tea tray and sloshed it experimentally, then plugged it in. 'And if you're fighting someone, it's better not to use it for anything but a quick escape. In battle it's easier to jump a mile away than to move a few feet to the side, and an enemy can still hit you as you're fading out.'

'Battle?' Ivy asked, not sure if he was serious. She knew Martin could be deadly with a knife, but she'd never thought of him as a soldier. 'Have you been in many of those?'

'Three, actually,' said Martin. 'They're noisy and confusing and entirely tedious, and if there's anything heroic about them I haven't seen it. I'd stay away from them, if I were you.' He held up a packet of tea. 'Mint?'

'Yes, please,' said Ivy, subdued. She was remembering her last desperate struggle with Gillian in the Delve, the way they'd grappled and clawed at each other as the faery woman fought to get away. She hadn't meant to kill Molly's mother, hadn't even thought she could, but...

She dismissed the dark memory with a shake of her head. That was all in the past now, and there was no sense dwelling on it. The important thing was that despite all the fear and pain and grief it had cost her, she'd saved the Delve.

She could only hope it wouldn't take another battle to save it again.

'You came back.' Jenny lighted on the lip of the Great Shaft, smiling with relief. 'I was afraid you might not be able to get away.'

'I was more worried that you wouldn't,' said Ivy. She glanced behind her, but there was no sign of Martin: true to his word, he'd vanished before Jenny could see him. After a cup of tea, a sandwich, and an hour's rest Ivy had felt strong enough to try her first travelling spell, but Martin had insisted on accompanying her to make sure she arrived safely.

'What happened with Nettle?' she asked. 'Did she tell Betony she'd seen you?'

Jenny shook her head, golden hair tossing. 'She only wanted to know if I'd seen Quartz, because the Joan wanted him to run a message. That boy!' Her expression wavered between fondness and exasperation, as it always did when she talked about her younger brother. 'He's never where you want him to be.'

Well, that was good news at least, if Nettle didn't think Jenny had done anything wrong. But Ivy still felt uneasy about meeting in such a central location.

'Jenny,' she said, 'we can't talk here. Will you come outside?' She stretched a hand through the bars. 'Please. We won't go far.'

Jenny glanced at the shaft beneath her. Her uncertainty was plain: she longed to do as Ivy asked, but feared to take the enormous step of defying her Joan's decree.

But just as Ivy was about to give up and draw back her hand, Jenny gripped it. Gingerly she climbed through the bars, emerging flushed on the other side. Ivy hugged her, then led her down the narrow, gorse-shadowed path that twisted away from the engine house. Jenny crept after her, shading her eyes with one hand.

The jutting rock halfway down the hill wasn't the best hiding place, but for now it would have to do. Ivy crawled in beneath the overhang, and awkwardly Jenny tucked her skirts beneath her and followed.

'Why are you dressed like a human?' she asked, as the two of them sat down.

'Because I've been living like one,' said Ivy, and went on to tell Jenny the rest of her story. She said nothing about Martin or her shape-changing, for fear of testing Jenny's loyalties too far. But she explained how she'd found her long-lost mother living in the human world, and that since then Ivy had spent more time disguised as a human than as her own piskey self. She told Jenny why Marigold had run away from the Delve five years ago, and why she'd never been able to return – because Betony had sworn her to silence and sent her into exile for claiming that the Delve was poisoned.

'But she was right,' said Ivy, her fists clenching on her knee. 'My dad didn't believe her at first, any more than Aunt Betony did – they both thought Mum's sickness was some trouble of her own, and that the rest of us had nothing to worry about. But after she left and he started working longer and longer in the diggings, he started to get sick too.' She looked up at Jenny. 'That's why he ran off to destroy Gillian's smoke-spell, while the rest of us were fleeing the Delve. He had nothing to lose, don't you see? He was dying already.'

Jenny's face cleared – then she frowned, as though she'd just had a disturbing thought. 'But Flint...your dad was the Joan's brother. Surely she must have noticed what was happening to him?'

'Of course she did,' said Ivy. 'Everybody did. But they all put it down to grief over losing Mum, and not having anyone to take proper care of him, and all sorts of other things.' She swallowed, remembering how many times she'd lain awake listening to her father's coughing in the night. She'd urged him to see Yarrow the healer about it, but he never would. 'Even I thought he'd stopped caring, and was trying to work himself to death. I didn't realise he was deliberately poisoning himself until it was too late.'

'Deliberately?' Jenny looked aghast. 'Why?'

A ladybird had waddled under the overhang, big as Ivy's thumbnail at piskey size. She brushed it away, and it whirred off into the sunlight. 'He could never forgive himself for letting Mum go. But mostly I think he believed it was the only way to convince Betony and everyone else that the poison was real. If the strongest knocker in the Delve could get sick from it, sick enough to die...'

'Then the Joan would have to do something about it,' finished Jenny softly.

'But he never got the chance to show Betony what the poison had done to him. And I'm not sure my aunt would have listened, anyway. She'd probably just have blamed his sickness on my mother.' She could just imagine Betony standing by Flint's deathbed, saying coldly, *You brought this on yourself. I warned you not to marry that woman.*

Jenny covered her mouth as though she were shocked, but broke into a barking cough instead. 'Sorry,' she whispered. 'I was trying to hold it in, but—' She coughed again, and wiped her mouth on her apron. 'But if your mum was right, there's been poison in the Delve for years and years. Why are the rest of us only getting sick now? Shouldn't we all have noticed it sooner?'

'It's not just happening now,' said Ivy. 'Look at me, born without wings. How often have you heard the younger children complaining that their stomachs hurt, or the aunties grumbling about an ache in their bones that won't go away? And the old uncles, who've spent years working in the diggings – is it natural for them to wither up and die before they're even a hundred, with yellow teeth and their grey hair falling out?'

Jenny kept her eyes on her lap, and made no answer.

'I'm not saying my aunt's evil,' Ivy went on, 'or that she doesn't care. But I think she only sees what she wants to see, because if she admits the Delve's not safe, then—'

A shadow fell across their hiding place. She saw Jenny mouth *spriggan*, scramble back and cover her face in terror. But Ivy's heart was pounding for entirely different reasons as a firm hand seized her arm, pulling her out from beneath the rock, and she looked up – and up – into a face she knew all too well.

'Then what?' asked Mattock.

eight

'Matt!' exclaimed Ivy, pulling free of the young hunter with an effort – an effort that would surely have failed, if he hadn't been willing to let her go. 'What are you doing here?'

It was a ridiculous thing to say, but her wits had scattered like windblown feathers at the sight of him. Had he come alone? How much had he overheard of her conversation with Jenny?

'I was coming back from Redruth,' Matt replied, his blue eyes searching hers. 'I heard someone cough, and I went to see...' Then a grin broke over his face like the sunrise, and he snatched Ivy up and whirled her around. 'I knew it was you! I knew you'd come back, no matter what Mica said.'

'Mica?' gasped Ivy, smothered against his chest. 'What – did he say?'

'I told him I thought I'd seen you yesterday. He told me... Well, anyway, he said I was wrong.' He must have noticed he was crushing Ivy, because he released her and stepped back, his colour rising. 'Sorry. I'm just glad you're here.'

Ivy dared a glance at Jenny, but the other girl had vanished into the shadows beneath the rock. 'I don't know why,' she said.

'Because you saved my life, that's why. You saved everyone in the Delve from that faery's curse, and I don't care how many old traditions you had to break to do it.' He took her small, thin hand between his big ones, clasping it like something precious. 'You always wanted to fly. I'm glad you found a way.'

Ivy's throat tightened. 'Mica told you.'

'Only because I got him drunk and dragged it out of him. After all you'd done for the Delve, I couldn't believe you'd just take Cicely and disappear. I couldn't understand why he let you.'

'So…' She was afraid of the answer, but she had to know. 'What else did he tell you?'

'Not much.' Mattock scratched at the collar of his shirt, as though it were itching him. He was dressed in a loose jacket and jeans held up by braces, the same clothes he wore on every trip to the human world – though the outfit had never looked quite natural on him, and at piskey size it looked stranger than ever. 'When I asked him what made you leave, he said he was sick of thinking about it. Then he fell asleep on the table.'

So he'd given away Ivy's most damning secret, but he couldn't be bothered to explain to Mattock that she'd been forced to leave the Delve against her will. That sounded like Mica, all right. 'Where is he now?' she asked.

'He didn't want to come.' Mattock's expression turned bleak. 'He's…not been the same since you and Cicely went away.' He paused, stooped under the rock and added, 'Isn't that right, Jenny?'

Ivy's heart skipped. 'It's not her fault—' she began to protest, but Jenny interrupted her.

'Never mind, Ivy. Mattock won't tell.' She clambered to her feet, brushing off her long skirt. 'Will you, Matt?'

'You shouldn't be out here, Jenny. It's not safe.' His gaze flicked to Ivy, reproachful. 'You both know that.'

'If it's safe enough for Ivy,' Jenny retorted, 'it's safe enough for me. Anyway, what's going to hurt us this close to the Delve?'

As though she hadn't been terrified, only a minute ago, that Mattock was a spriggan come to carry her away.

'Besides,' Ivy added before Matt could argue, 'Nettle told me there hasn't been a spriggan sighted near the Delve in over thirty years.'

There was a stunned pause. 'What?' Jenny whispered, and Matt cut in like an echo: 'What? That's ridiculous! Mica and I caught a spriggan just a few weeks ago!'

'You mean the stranger you beat senseless and chained up at the bottom of the Shaft?' Ivy knew she was flying in stormy weather by speaking so frankly, but Jenny needed to hear the truth. 'He didn't even know what a spriggan was. He'd only come to the Delve because my mother sent him to find me.'

'You *talked* to him?' Mattock's face darkened, then went pale. 'You're the one who let him go. And he was the one who—'

'Led me to my mother, yes,' cut in Ivy. She knew he'd been about to say *taught you to change shape*, but Jenny was shocked enough already. 'The point is, he wasn't a threat to the Delve. The real threat was Gillian, and she's dead now. There are no spriggans or evil faeries hunting us any more, and that means—'

'We don't have to stay underground.' Jenny sank back onto the rocks, staring. 'We've been trapped down there all this time, breathing poison, for *nothing*.'

Mattock cast Ivy a hard look, then crouched in front of Jenny. 'It's not nothing,' he said. 'There are more dangers on the surface than spriggans. Why do you think we hunters train for months before we're even allowed to go outside? There are wild animals out there, and…and all kinds of other things. It's not safe to let everyone go wandering about, don't you see?'

'Oh, I see,' said Jenny, with a cracked laugh. 'I see that you hunters have no reason to want anything to change. You're free to go outside whenever you please, because you're so *big* and *strong* and what you do is so *important*. We girls can stay below and rot, for all you care.'

'That's not true.' Matt spoke evenly, but his jaw was tight with anger. 'And you're wrong to think we hunters have nothing to lose. What do you think happens to us once we get too slow to hunt any more, or have sons old enough to do the hunting for us? We go straight down to join the knockers in the diggings, where the air's worst of all.'

'But by then you've had twenty or thirty years of fresh air and freedom,' Jenny said. 'And even as a knocker, nobody's going to stop you going above for a pipe or a stroll. Nobody's going to say,

"You can't do that, it's not safe for the likes of you." But we women have to hear that all our lives.' She pushed him away and rose, turning appealing eyes to Ivy. 'When Cicely went missing the first time, and you went to look for her, I thought the spriggans had got you for sure, and I'd never see you again. But when you came back to help us fight Gillian and I saw how healthy you were, how *alive*... I wasn't sure what to make of it. But now it makes sense.'

'Jenny,' said Mattock, but she ignored him and clutched Ivy's hand.

'I understand now why you had to leave. And why you had to come back, no matter what Betony said. Because we needed you. We needed someone to tell us the truth.'

Mattock muttered a curse and sat down on the rocks, dragging his hands over his face. 'All right,' he said, 'let's say it is the truth. The surface is safe, or at least safer than we've always thought, and the Delve is poisoned. But if the bit of your conversation I overheard is anything to go by, the Joan doesn't see it that way. So what can any of us do about it?'

'She won't listen to me,' said Ivy. 'She thinks I'm trying to stir up trouble in the Delve. But if someone can make her see that it's not just the weak ones or the old ones who are getting sick, but all of us, and that the best way to cure it is to get our people outside...' She walked a few steps down the trail, frowning in thought. Then it came to her, and she whirled on the others in excitement. 'Yarrow! She's the Delve's healer: she knows how many piskeys have come to her complaining of one thing or

91

another. She could talk to Betony for us.'

Mattock looked dubious, but Jenny's face brightened. 'Yes, of course!' she said. 'The Joan would listen to her, I'm sure. But do you think she'll do it? Yarrow's very…quiet.'

Ivy knew what the other girl meant. No one would question the healer woman's skills, or complain of the way she treated her patients. But she was unusually reserved for a piskey, and she was also young – only a few years older than Ivy and Jenny. It was hard to imagine her even approaching the Joan without a summons, let alone arguing with her.

'Maybe not alone,' she admitted. 'But if we could convince a few of the sicker ones to go along with her and tell their stories to Betony, she might.' She turned to Mattock. 'Would you do that? Keep an eye out for piskeys who seem especially unwell, and see if they'd be willing to talk to the Joan about it?'

'I don't know, Ivy.' He spoke without looking up. 'People can be touchy about these things. Nobody likes to admit they're not as strong as they used to be, or that there might be something wrong with them that they can't fix. It's not the piskey way to complain.'

'You mean it's not the way of the menfolk,' said Jenny. 'The women and children aren't so proud as all that. Or at least they have enough common sense to know when they need help.' She looked at Ivy. 'I'll ask my mum. And maybe one or two of the neighbours, if they're willing to talk about it.'

'Will you talk to Yarrow too?' asked Ivy. 'I know it won't be easy to get her alone, especially if there are so many piskeys coming to see her. But if you offered to grind herbs for her, or help her with the records…'

Jenny nodded. 'I'll try.'

'But you'll have to be careful,' Ivy warned. 'If any of this gets back to my aunt before we're ready, she might think we're plotting against her.' And if Betony felt threatened, she would act quickly – and ruthlessly – to eliminate the threat.

'I know.' Jenny gave a tiny smile. 'Don't worry. I'm always careful.'

'Not careful enough, if I could hear your coughing halfway across the hillside,' said Mattock. 'If you want to meet again, we'd best find a safer place to do it.'

'We?' asked Ivy. 'I thought you were against this idea.' In fact, she'd begun to fear he'd try to stop them. He'd seemed thrilled to see Ivy at first, willing to overlook any transgression she committed. But all that had changed when she confessed to letting Martin go.

'I don't much like it, I'll admit.' Mattock pushed himself to his feet, his face sombre. 'But I've seen enough to know that you and Jenny are right. The Delve's not safe any more. And if all we need is a bit more evidence to convince the Joan…' His mouth curled ruefully. 'Then I'd be a fool not to help you.'

Relief swept through Ivy like a cleansing breeze. She threw her arms about Mattock and hugged him. 'Dear old Matt,' she said. 'I should have known I could count on you. There's just one thing.'

Mattock looked at her.

'You can't tell Mica about any of this. Not that you've seen me, not that we've talked, not what we're doing. Please.'

'Ivy...'

'I know.' She lowered her eyes, not wanting to see his disappointment. 'I know he's your best friend. But he wouldn't understand, Matt. He doesn't understand anything about me.'

Matt was quiet so long that Ivy feared he would refuse. But at last he said, 'If that's what you want.'

Ivy broke into a smile. 'Then it's all settled,' she said, hooking an arm around his waist and reaching out to draw Jenny into their circle. 'Where shall we meet next time?'

When Ivy returned to the hotel she expected to find the room empty, and Martin out on some errand – or else that he'd be lounging in the armchair, awaiting her report. But there he lay atop the unmade bed, fully dressed except for his shoes, curled in on himself with his jacket clutched tight to his chest. His teeth were gritted, his breath came in shuddering gasps, and when the floor creaked beneath Ivy's cautious step, he flinched as though she had struck him. But his eyes stayed closed beneath the drift of his hair, and when she whispered his name, he did not answer.

He'd told her that he didn't dream, and maybe it was true. But whatever was happening in his mind right now, he wasn't enjoying it. Ivy hesitated, wondering if she ought to shake him, then thought better of the idea. She'd waked Mica once in the middle of a nightmare, and he'd flailed out and smacked her in the face. Instead, Ivy took the coverlet from the foot of the bed, and drew it up over Martin's shivering body. Then with the lightest of touches she brushed the hair back from his brow and let her hand rest there, as she used to do for Cicely when her little sister had a bad dream.

Martin relaxed. For several heartbeats he lay unmoving, then rolled over in a languid movement and stretched. He gazed drowsily at Ivy – then jerked upright, his face hardening to anger.

'How long have you been here?' he demanded, flinging away the coverlet as though it disgusted him. 'How long was I asleep?'

'I don't know,' said Ivy, taken aback. 'I just got here.' She stepped hastily out of Martin's way as he leaped from the bed. 'Where are you going?'

Martin stopped, fingers hovering above the doorknob. Then his hand dropped to his side. 'My apologies,' he said, turning back to her. 'I didn't expect you back so soon.'

His expression was calm now, detached. He was trying to save his dignity, and Ivy knew she ought to let him, but her curiosity was too strong. 'What was all that about?' she asked.

'All what?'

She gestured to the bed. 'Is it always like this, when you sleep in your own shape? Is that why you fly off every night?'

'I have no idea what you mean.' He spoke calmly, but every line of his body was tense. 'I don't like people staring at me when I'm asleep, that's all.'

Ivy sat down on the end of the bed, unsure whether to believe him. Could he really be so oblivious to what was going on in his own mind?

'You looked like you were having a nightmare,' she said. 'A bad one. Are you sure you've never been able to dream? Even when you were a child?'

Martin folded his arms and leaned back against the doorframe. 'I don't remember much of anything about being a child,' he said. 'The first memory I have is of walking along a road at night, and getting hit by a car.'

He must have seen the shock on Ivy's face, because he went on more mildly, 'Not badly. It was only a glancing blow. But the police came to investigate, and when I wouldn't – couldn't – tell them where I lived or who my parents were, they put me in foster care.'

Ivy had learned about *police* during the weeks she'd spent with her mother in Truro, but she'd thought they only punished lawbreakers. 'What does that mean?'

'Well, in my case, it meant that for nearly a year I was shuffled from one human family to another, until I ended up with an old woman who called me a devil and gave me the same food she fed her cats. I think,' he added reflectively, 'that I might have scared her to death.'

'Stop trying to frighten me,' said Ivy. 'If you don't want to talk about it, just say so. What happened?'

'She accused me of stealing her money,' he said, 'and came after me with a wooden spoon. I flung up my hand to ward her off, and all her dishes flew out of the cupboard and smashed to bits on the ceiling. She turned grey and clutched her chest, and I ran. The last I saw of her was the ambulance taking her away.'

His tone was neutral, but the line between his brows said otherwise. 'It wasn't your fault,' said Ivy.

'Not the heart attack, perhaps,' said Martin. 'But she wasn't wrong about the money.' He gave a thin smile. 'Not that it lasted long, once I was on my own. I ended up living in an old crate in one of the grimier parts of London, and by the time the Empress found me, I'd have done just about anything for a hot meal and a pair of clean sheets.'

'How old were you then?' Ivy asked.

'Thirteen, maybe? I couldn't tell you. All I know is that I'd been on the streets for well over a year.'

So he'd been eleven or twelve when the humans found him. Still more a child than a man, but surely old enough to remember *something* about his past? Either he'd lost his memory in the accident, or perhaps...

'I can hear you thinking,' said Martin. 'Whatever it is, you might as well say it.'

Ivy looked at her hands, small and pale against the dark fabric of her jeans. 'The night before my mother disappeared,' she said carefully, 'she had an argument with my father. I overheard her crying, and I asked what was wrong.'

Or at least, that was what Mica and Marigold had told her. Ivy herself had never been able to remember anything about that night, no matter how hard she tried. 'She'd started coughing up blood, and she knew she had to leave the Delve before the poison killed her. But she didn't know where she was going, or whether she'd even survive. She didn't want me following her onto the surface, so she…she wiped my memory.'

'And that's what you think someone did to me?'

'Maybe. All I know is, whoever did it, they must have cared about you.'

He gave her a derisive look. 'Why on earth would you think that?'

'Because,' said Ivy with forced patience, 'if they only wanted to keep you quiet, it would have been simpler – and probably safer – to kill you outright. And if they wanted to make you suffer, they'd have left at least some of your memory intact, so you'd know you were being punished.'

Martin frowned, and she could tell he was thinking. 'That's assuming it was deliberate,' he said at last, 'and not some kind of accident. I'm not ready to jump to conclusions yet.' He pushed himself away from the door and walked to the armchair, sitting down and throwing one leg over the other. 'Anyway, enough about that. How did your meeting go with Jenny?'

Resigned to the change of subject, Ivy told him the whole story. 'We're meeting again in three days,' she finished. 'Matt knows a place in the wood, an old adit, where we'll be hidden from both the Delve and any humans who might wander by.'

'I know exactly the one,' said Martin dryly. 'It's not a bad place to camp, provided you don't mind being set upon by piskey thugs in the middle of the night and dragged underground without so much as a by-your-leave. Not that I'm bitter, mind. But if you happen to see your brother again, you might consider punching him in the face.'

'Not Mattock?' asked Ivy.

'As I recall, he was fairly restrained by contrast. You're welcome to box his ears, though, if you can reach that high.' Martin drummed his fingers on the arm of the chair. 'But seriously – do you think this plan of yours is going to work?'

Ivy's smile faded. 'I hope so,' she said. 'Because if Betony still won't listen, even after we've shown her the evidence…I'm not sure what else we can do.'

'Why waste time trying to convince her?' asked Martin. 'From what I know of your aunt – and after spending several days in her dungeon, it's a good deal more than I'd like – she's as hard as the Delve's own granite, and just as impossible to move. You've gone against her wishes before; what's stopping you now?'

'You don't understand,' said Ivy. 'Even if I could find somewhere else for our people to live, even if I could convince them that leaving the Delve would be for the best, they'd never agree to it unless Betony does. They believe in her, right or wrong, and they'll follow her to the death if she says it's the piskey thing to do.'

'You mean she controls them.'

'No, nothing like that. She doesn't need to compel people to obey her, the way your Empress did. They obey her because she's the Joan.'

'I don't understand.'

Of course he wouldn't. He hadn't grown up in the Delve. 'Nobody knows where the Joan's power comes from,' Ivy explained. 'It isn't passed down from mother to daughter, or anything so obvious. But when a Joan grows too old and feeble to rule any more, she calls all the grown piskey-women to her, and tests them one by one. The woman who can draw fire into her hands and wield it without being burned – she's the new Joan.'

'What if there's more than one?' asked Martin.

'There never is,' said Ivy. 'As soon as the new Joan touches fire, the old Joan's power goes out. It's the proof she's our rightful queen.'

'That's convenient,' said Martin. 'For the woman with the power, anyway. It seems remarkably inconvenient for everyone else.'

'Maybe. But since we piskeys don't choose our Joan or give her the power she holds, we can't un-choose her or take away her powers either. The best we can do, even if she's dim-witted or selfish or cruel, is wait for her to die.'

'Or kill her.'

Ivy's head snapped up. 'That's not funny, Martin. Even from you. *Especially* from you.'

'You're right.' He pressed his fingertips together and studied them. 'It wasn't funny.'

But he did not apologise, or look as though he was sorry. And there was no hint of a smile on his face at all.

A chill rippled through Ivy, and all at once the room seemed darker and smaller than before. If he was saying what she thought he was saying…

No, never. No matter how angry Betony made her sometimes,

no matter how unfairly she'd treated Ivy's mother or even Ivy herself, there was no way Ivy could raise her hand against her aunt. It was impossible. Unthinkable.

Yet if it came down to a choice between one woman's life and the lives of every piskey in the Delve...

'I have to go,' Ivy blurted, leaping off the bed. The last thing she glimpsed was Martin's startled face before she willed herself away.

nine

Ivy walked across the sand, shivering in the afternoon breeze. When she'd Leaped away from the hotel she'd pictured the nearest safe location that came to mind, the corner behind the sea wall where Martin had taken her that morning. But though she'd been wandering about the harbour for half an hour now, watching the gulls circle and listening to the soothing murmur of the waves, her thoughts were no less turbulent than before.

How could Martin suggest such a thing to her? Did he really imagine Ivy would consider murdering her aunt? Such an act would fly in the face of everything she stood for as a piskey – the simple honesty and bold courage that Ivy's people valued most. Even if she could muster the will to do it and the conviction that there was no other way, she'd never be strong enough to challenge Betony face to face: all the Joan had to do was raise her hand, and Ivy would burn up like a dry leaf in a bonfire. So she'd have to sneak into her aunt's bedchamber and stab her while she slept, or some other horrible, deceitful, *sprigganish* trick…

No, it was out of the question. Even thinking about it made Ivy feel as though worms were eating at her insides, and she wished she could scrub Martin's words out of her brain. She'd talked to Jenny and Mattock, which was as much as she could do to help her people at present; she had to trust that her friends knew what they were doing, and leave the matter in their hands.

A pair of gulls flapped overhead, and Ivy gazed after them in longing. Flying would be the perfect distraction, if only she could shake the memory of the hobby's talons piercing into her last night. But no matter how hard she tried to convince herself that she'd learned her lesson and it would never happen again, the thought of taking swift-shape made her shudder. Perhaps she'd overcome her fear in time, but not today.

And that meant she was stuck here, or at least limited to the few places in Cornwall she knew well enough to picture in her mind. There would be no more exploring or making new discoveries for her, unless she walked – or asked Martin to carry her, and right now she didn't like that idea much, either…

'There you are.'

Ivy stiffened, then turned. Martin had come out from behind the sea wall and was walking towards her. A group of children had been tossing a ball back and forth by the stairs, but at the sight of him they stopped and edged away.

'What do you want?' Ivy asked, resisting the temptation to do likewise.

'You should have some money of your own,' he said. 'So you

can buy food, or anything else you might need when I'm not here.' He pressed a square of hard leather into her hand. 'Take as much as you want.'

So he was already itching to find more spriggan haunts to investigate, and since Ivy couldn't fly he'd decided to leave her behind. Ivy looked at the wallet, stiff with newness and closely packed with bills – and all she could think about was the faery woman in her dream, bowed beneath the weight of the Grey Man's hoard. She pulled out a few banknotes, then thrust the wallet back at Martin.

Martin's brows pinched together. 'You're sure that's enough?'

Ivy wasn't, not without counting it first. But she wasn't about to do that in front of him. 'It's enough for now,' she said.

'As you wish, Lady Disdain.' He put the wallet away, then said more quietly, 'I didn't mean to suggest that you personally murder your aunt, you know. You didn't give me a chance to explain.'

'Oh?' asked Ivy, stung into defensiveness. 'Then what were you suggesting? That I should ask you to do it?'

Martin's grey eyes became cold as pebbles. 'I wouldn't if you begged me,' he said, and vanished.

The beach seemed even emptier after he had gone. Ivy turned and walked back towards the town, picking her way between the boats left stranded by the ebbing tide and the cars parked along the edge of the sea wall. She was already regretting her harsh words, but there was no taking them back now. She wished she had someone else to talk to, someone solid and practical and kind, who knew how things stood between Martin and herself and could help her make sense of it all...

Ivy stopped short. How could she not have thought of it before? She'd been so caught up in her worries about piskeys and spriggans that she'd almost forgotten about Molly, the one friend she had who was neither. Gillian's daughter had known Martin even before she'd met Ivy: they'd bonded over their shared love of the theatre, and he'd encouraged her to pursue her dream of becoming an actress. But while the girl might be grateful to Martin she was by no means blind to his faults, and Ivy knew she could count on Molly to listen to whatever she might say.

She'd been hesitant about visiting Molly before, not wanting to intrude on her grief. But surely it was time to look in on the younger girl and see how she was doing, if nothing else?

Hope renewed, Ivy hurried up the rest of the steps into the town. She'd buy herself a change of clothes, something that didn't look like she'd been sleeping in it for a week. Then she'd have a quick bite of supper to keep up her magical strength, and will herself to Molly's cottage.

When Ivy materialised in the yard behind Molly's house, she was relieved to find everything as she remembered it – the stone-walled square of the cottage before her, and the narrow barn behind. Two horses grazed in the nearby field, a dapple-grey mare and a stocky bay gelding. Ivy lifted her hand to them, and they tossed their manes and whickered back.

Ivy would have liked to go down and greet Duchess and

Dodger properly, but she had no treats to give them, and she was mindful of her new shoes. The woman in the shop had assured her they would go perfectly with the dress, but Ivy was already regretting the heels. She hurried over the cobbles, careful to keep her weight on her toes, and made her way to the front of the house.

She'd never seen Molly's father before, not even in a picture. But when the door opened, Ivy recognised him at once. He had the same dark hair, sturdy bones and sun-browned skin as Molly, the same lively intelligence in his eyes – dimmed though it was by weariness, and the lingering shadow of grief. 'Can I help you?' he asked.

'Is Molly here?' asked Ivy, resolved not to be shy. She'd been intimidated by Gillian's cold manner even before she knew Molly's mother was a faery, but the same instinct told her that Mr Menadue was human, and not unkind. 'I'm…an old friend of hers.'

'Oh?' His shaggy brows lifted. 'Well, you'd best come in, then.'

He held the door wide for her, and Ivy stepped inside. A surprising number of things about the cottage had changed since her last visit – furniture moved or removed, pictures missing from the walls. But what struck her most was how different the air smelled. Not only because of the slightly faded flower arrangements that filled every shelf and table, but because there was no trace of the cloying perfume that Gillian had worn to mask her natural faery scent.

'I'll see if Molly's up to a visit,' said the man. 'Sorry, I don't think we've met before – what's your name?'

'Ivy.'

'Right.' He strode down the corridor, calling, 'Molly! Your friend Ivy's here!'

'*What?*' came a muffled shriek, and Ivy's heart started thumping. What if the younger girl had changed her mind, and decided she couldn't forgive Ivy for her mother's death after all? What if she regretted helping the piskeys of the Delve, and no longer wanted anything to do with—

A door banged open, and footsteps pounded. Molly burst out of the hallway, skidded past the kitchen, and flung herself at Ivy.

'There you are!' she exclaimed, hugging her. 'I rang your mum's place a few days ago trying to get hold of you, but she didn't know where you were or when you'd be back, and I was starting to worry—' She took a step back, looking Ivy up and down. 'Why are you dressed like that?'

'I...I wanted to wear something nice,' said Ivy. 'To show my respects.'

'Well, you would have fitted in all right at the funeral,' said Molly with a dubious wrinkle of her nose, 'but that was a week ago. Now you just look like my dad's secretary.'

'Executive assistant!' shouted her father from the corridor, and Molly yelled back, 'You're not an executive!' and grinned, as though it were an old joke. But there were strained lines about her eyes and shadows underneath them, and Ivy sensed that she wasn't her old exuberant self quite yet.

'I'm sorry I didn't come before,' she said, squeezing Molly's hand. 'If I'd known you wanted me, I would have come right away.'

And she meant that literally. Not long ago she had *thanked* Molly for helping her free the piskeys Gillian had trapped, and while humans might see that as a simple expression of gratitude, it had a far more potent meaning to magical folk. By saying *thank you* to Molly, Ivy had declared herself forever in debt to the other girl, ready to do whatever she asked and give her any help she needed – no matter how difficult it might be or how high the cost.

'Oh, I'm all right,' Molly said. 'It wasn't that important. But ever since Martin broke out of the Claybane and turned up here looking for you, I've been dying to know what happened.' Her eyes lit up with eagerness. 'Have you seen him? What did he say?'

Well, at least she didn't have to wonder if Molly would be interested. 'Is there somewhere we can talk in private?' Ivy asked. 'This might take a while.'

'We can say anything we like in here,' said Molly as she opened the door of her bedroom and led the way inside. 'Dad's got his music on, so he won't—' She stopped. 'What are you staring at?'

Ivy had paused in the doorway, speechless. The basics of the room were much as she remembered from her last visit: bright purple walls, four-poster bed, bookshelves in the far corner. But otherwise, the place looked completely different. Gone were the faery-printed coverlet and curtains, the piskey statuettes that had once crowded the window-ledge, the pile of bright-winged dolls in the corner. And all the pictures had been taken down, leaving only bare hooks and forlorn strips of tape behind.

'Oh, that,' said Molly. 'I did that when we got back from the funeral. All that faery stuff…it didn't feel right any more.' She sat down on the end of the bed, and after a moment Ivy joined her.

'I'm sorry,' she murmured.

'It's not your fault.' Molly spoke quietly, her eyes on her feet. 'I know you would have saved Mum if you could. It's only… I thought I knew her, and I never really did at all. She gave birth to me and raised me and everything, but…' Her shoulders slumped. 'I keep wondering, did she ever love Dad and me even a little? Or was she just using us all along?'

Ivy put an arm around her. 'I think she did love you, in her way,' she said. 'The look on her face when I talked about you, especially near the end…I could tell that she cared, even if she wasn't very good at showing it.'

'She was *terrible* at showing it,' said Molly with a choked laugh, and turned her face against the bedpost. She sniffed and swallowed, then went on hoarsely, 'But never mind that. Martin did find you, didn't he? Did he tell you how he got out of the Claybane?'

'Not exactly,' said Ivy, with some reluctance. Only the blood of a close relative should have been able to free Martin from the curse, and Ivy had only tried using her own blood because Molly had insisted. She'd never expected it would work, but it had –

and she still wasn't sure what that meant. 'Did he say anything to you about it?'

'He didn't stay long enough. He was so dead set on talking to you, he took off as soon as I told him you'd gone back to the Delve.' She paused, drying her wet cheeks on her sleeve, then added, 'I've never seen him so worked up about anything. You'd almost think...'

'What?' asked Ivy, but the other girl only smiled.

'Never mind,' she said. 'It's probably nothing. So what happened after that?'

It took some time for Ivy to explain how she and Martin had ended up travelling together, and all that had happened since. But Molly listened to the whole story with no sign of impatience, and the look she gave Ivy at the end was as sympathetic as she could have wished for.

'For a clever faery – or spriggan, I suppose – Martin can be awfully thick sometimes,' she said. 'I'm sure he meant to be helpful, but what a thing to say!' She wormed her way up the mattress to the headboard, propping one pillow behind her and piling the others around her. 'No wonder you were upset with him. I would have been too.'

Ivy twisted the copper bracelet around her wrist, feeling its warmth. Wherever Martin had gone, he couldn't be far away. 'Maybe. But I shouldn't have said what I did to him, either. He talks as though killing the Empress was just something that needed to be done, but the first time I met him, he was quoting some speech from Shakespeare about guilt and murder and...I don't think he was acting.'

'I know what you mean,' said Molly. 'He tries to act like nothing bothers him, but I've never really seen him happy, either. And he can't seem to settle down in any one place for long. It's like he's looking for something, but he doesn't know where to find it.'

'I think I know,' said Ivy, and when Molly gave her a curious look she added, 'I mean his people. The spriggans. But the only trace we've found of them so far has been in dreams, and I'm the one having those.'

Did Martin envy her those visions – perhaps even resent her for them? He'd never said that he felt that way, but it must be frustrating for him to realise that a piskey-girl who'd spent most of her life underground knew more about his people than he did. No wonder he'd felt compelled to keep searching, even once it was clear that Ivy could no longer fly...

'You're probably right,' said Molly, and sighed. 'I wish I could help both of you. But everything's changed now Mum's gone.' She hugged her pillow close and propped her chin on it. 'Soon I won't even be here any more.'

Ivy was startled. 'What do you mean?'

'Can't you tell? We're packing up. Dad has to travel so much for his work, it doesn't make sense for him to live this far from London. The only reason we stayed here at all was because of Mum. So he wants to sell the house, or let it out to someone. And in ten days I'm going away to Hampshire, or Hertfordshire, or...I don't remember, but Dad says it's a really excellent school with one of the best theatre programmes in the country. Just like I always wanted, only Mum never—' She broke off, and buried her face in the pillow.

Gillian Menadue had discouraged her daughter's interest in acting, because she feared it would take Molly away from her. Ivy had never expected that one day she would feel the same.

'Aren't you happy about going?' she asked, to hide her dismay.

'I am,' mumbled Molly. 'It's an amazing chance, and I want it a lot. But I can't take Dodger to school with me, so Dad says we'll have to sell him – he's already found a buyer for Duchess. And I know this cottage isn't anything special, but I've lived here my whole life.' She surfaced from the pillow, her dark eyes haunted. 'I begged Dad to keep it so we could come here on holidays at least, but he says it's foolish to pay someone to clean house and look after Dodger if we can only be here a fortnight or two out of the year.'

Ivy could see Mr Menadue's point. But the pain of losing her own home in the Delve was still fresh in her mind, and she would do anything to spare Molly that grief if she could. Perhaps after a year away at school she'd feel happier about the change, but it seemed too harsh a loss for a young girl who had endured so much already.

Could Ivy use magic to influence Mr Menadue into changing his mind? Perhaps, but there was no guarantee he wouldn't change it back again, and anyway it felt wrong to manipulate people that way. It would be better if she could find a more piskey-like solution to the problem, some honest and sensible arrangement that would satisfy everyone involved. Creative thinking didn't come easily to magical folk, but Ivy set her jaw and closed her eyes in concentration. There had to be an answer, if only she could think of it...

Her eyes snapped open. 'Molly,' she said, 'could you ask your father how much money it would cost to rent the cottage? I know someone who might be interested.'

ten

The boy crouched at the end of the passage, alone except for a tiny glow-spell to keep back the dark. He tried not to look too closely at the chains and bracelets piled in his lap, but he couldn't help lifting a handful of treasure now and then to wonder at its heaviness. Even in this dim light he could tell that there was more silver in the hoard than there was copper, and more gold than either – a hoard that any spriggan would envy.

Yet dazzling as all this wealth might be, it wasn't even half of what the Grey Man owned; according to the boy's mother, he had secret troves near every cave and fogou they'd ever visited. Swords in jewelled scabbards, crowns and circlets, even a golden drinking-cup that had once belonged to King Arthur himself. And it would all be his one day, if he proved himself brave and strong and clever as a chief's son ought to be...

His chin bumped his chest and he blinked awake, berating himself for dozing off. Yet dawn would come soon, and his mother had not returned. Perhaps he should go out and look for her, in case she'd lost *her way.*

But what to do with the treasure? He couldn't leave it lying here for anyone to see. The boy hesitated, then pulled off his cloak and bundled the jewellery up in it, dropping the coin purse on top. He tied up the makeshift sack and pushed it to one side of the tunnel, then crept up the slope to the fogou's exit.

He was squinting out at the darkened valley, wondering where his mother might have gone, when he heard footsteps in the tunnel behind him. Relieved, he turned to greet her – and a rough hand seized him by the throat.

'Fool of a boy,' came a harsh whisper, pitched low so that only the two of them could hear. 'You think I don't know the sound of my own treasure?'

It was the Grey Man.

The boy stood rigid, speechless with terror. He'd thought the spell of silence he'd cast over the tunnel would protect him, but it must have lapsed while he slept.

'Where was she going?' the chief demanded. 'How long since she left you?'

'I…' stammered the boy. 'I don't…'

The Grey Man growled. Kindling a glow-spell just bright enough to see by, he dragged the cloak-bundle out of the shadows and dropped it at the boy's feet. 'Is that all of it?' he demanded.

The boy nodded, his gaze downcast. He couldn't bear to look at those cold grey eyes and sharp-chiselled features, didn't want to see his chief's hand come down for the inevitable blow. But there was only silence, and finally the boy could bear it no longer and glanced up.

The Grey Man didn't look furious, not any more. He only looked tired, and grim, and a little sad. He lifted the bundle of treasure, gave it a jingling shake, and lowered it again. Then he gripped the boy's arm and asked, 'What did she say to you?'

There was no use explaining how bewitched he'd been by his mother's luminous beauty and coaxing words, or that he'd never imagined it possible for a faery to break her promise. He knew better than to make excuses for his foolishness, or even beg forgiveness for it. So in halting words the boy told him the story, from the moment he'd wakened at the sound of his mother's sobbing to the time she'd cast off her last bracelet and danced out of the fogou, light-footed as a girl.

When he had finished, the Grey Man was quiet for a long time. At last he said, 'So. She told you that you are my son.'

The boy's mouth went dry. Had she deceived him about this as well? He started to stammer an apology, but the chief stopped him. 'No, lad. She may have tricked you, but she spoke the truth. Though it was not my wish that you should know it – but ill done or not, 'tis done now.'

The boy hung his head, cheeks hot with shame. It was bad enough that he'd failed his chief, but to have betrayed his father was even worse. He should never have left his bed tonight, even if all the women in the world were weeping; he should have hardened his heart and stopped his ears, as a man and a warrior ought to do. What good was it to have found a mother, if she only meant to use and abandon him? And what joy was there in forcing the Grey Man to acknowledge him against his will?

'Look at me, boy.'

It was a command, and disobedience was unthinkable. He looked up miserably into the Grey Man's face.

'She may not be lost to us yet,' said his father. 'Perhaps she meant to keep her word, but some mishap has kept her from returning. I will go out now, and find her if I can. As for you...' He gave the boy a shake. 'Say nothing of this to anyone. Now back to bed with you.'

So he wouldn't be beaten, or cast out of the fogou – or at least, not yet. He seized the Grey Man's hand and kissed it, then fled before his father could change his mind.

Ivy woke with a start, dazed by the vividness of her dream. When she'd returned from her visit to Molly last night, she'd been thinking so hard about what to say to Martin that she hadn't expected to sleep at all. Yet she'd barely got her shoes off before exhaustion claimed her, and she'd tumbled into yet another vision.

Why it had happened, and kept happening, Ivy wasn't sure. But she was certain of one thing now: the boy in her dreams was Martin's ancestor. She hadn't seen the boy's face yet because there were no mirrors in the fogou, but the Grey Man's narrow, hard-chiselled features and the faery woman's pale, silky hair were Martin all over again. In fact, the resemblance was so striking that if Ivy hadn't known better, she'd have thought the boy might be Martin himself.

But that was impossible. Not even the most powerful faeries could expect to live much longer than three hundred years; four was out of the question. And though the faces of adult faeries like

Marigold and Gillian showed few signs of age, Martin's features had yet to take on that same timeless quality. He couldn't be much older than Mica.

So where were all these dreams coming from? Could it be the bracelet Martin had given her? She'd seen the boy's mother wearing the same bracelet in her dreams; perhaps the boy had put his memories of her into it somehow. In which case all Ivy needed was to take it off before she went to sleep, and the dreams would go away...

But if she did that, how would she ever find out the rest of the story?

Ivy groaned, furrowing her fingers through her hair. On top of everything else, she'd fallen asleep in her new dress, and now the dark green linen was full of wrinkles. But it had been a waste of money anyway. It might be piskey custom to wear one's best when visiting a grieving family, but it seemed humans – or at least Molly – didn't expect anything of the kind.

Stiffly Ivy got up and made herself a cup of tea. She was taking it back to bed when the curtains rippled, and the ghostly shape of a barn owl appeared on the other side of the glass.

'Back already?' said Ivy in surprise, and opened the window. The owl bobbed inside, dropped to the carpet – and became Martin, staring at her with an extraordinary look on his face.

'What?' she asked.

'You're...' He gave his head a shake, as though he couldn't credit what he was seeing. 'Why are you wearing *that*?'

Ivy glanced down at herself. The sleeveless, close-fitting dress was different from anything she'd owned before, but the woman in the shop had told her it was perfect.

'I went to see Molly,' she said defensively. 'Why? What's wrong with it?'

'Nothing,' said Martin. 'You look very...grown-up, that's all.' He studied her one last moment, then walked to the armchair and sat down. 'How is Molly, then?'

'Well enough,' said Ivy, reaching into her bodice for the paper Molly's father had given her. 'But she'd be a lot happier if we helped her with this.'

Martin took the page from her and unfolded it, frowning, as Ivy launched into her explanation. 'If we rent the cottage,' she finished, 'Molly's father won't have to sell it. And if we offer to take care of Dodger too—'

'Wait,' said Martin. 'Who is the *we* in this plan? You and your piskey friends?'

'Don't be a buffle-head,' said Ivy. 'I mean you and me, of course. Wouldn't it be better than sleeping in the open, or moving from one hotel to another?' She sat down on the arm of the chair, pointing to the sum written on the paper. 'We have that much money, don't we? Or we could get it, if we sold a bit more of the treasure.'

He tilted his head to look up at her, blond hair drifting across his brow. 'A few hours ago you didn't want anything to do with my money. Now all of a sudden its *ours* and you're making grand plans with it?'

'It's not the same,' Ivy said testily. 'This isn't for me, it's for

119

Molly. And considering she's saved your life at least twice, don't you think you owe her something too?'

Martin folded the paper and laid it aside. 'I'm not certain this is the best idea—' he began, but Ivy interrupted him.

'I'll look after the house, if that's what you're worried about. But think, Martin. This isn't just any human cottage, it's *Molly's* cottage. It's perfect, don't you see?'

He did: she could tell. Gillian had laid charms around the house to keep unwanted magical folk at bay, and the only reason Martin had found it in the first place was because Molly had invited him in. Of all the places in Cornwall that a fugitive and an exile might seek refuge, the Menadues' cottage was surely the safest.

'I'll keep the barn clean as well,' Ivy added quickly, before Martin could raise another objection. 'And look after Dodger – I know you're not fond of horses. All you have to do is—'

'Convince Molly's father that the two of us are responsible adults with enough income to pay the rent?' asked Martin. 'I don't think that's going to work. I may be an actor, but I know my limitations. And elegant as that dress of yours may be, it doesn't make you look *that* much older.'

He rose and paced to the window, twitching the curtain aside to peer at the brightening sky. 'Besides, you don't look like my sister, and you're too young to be…well, anything else. It's all very suspicious, from a human point of view.'

Ivy slid down onto the seat of the armchair, her confidence waning. 'But surely, when he sees we have the money…'

'Then he's going to wonder where it came from,' said Martin. 'Some humans might be willing to accept a large pile of banknotes from two mysterious young people with no family and no references, but I doubt Mr Menadue is one of them.'

Ivy put her head in her hands. She'd been so positive that her idea would work, if only she could persuade Martin to help. Perhaps she could disguise herself and Martin with glamour, and make them appear older than they were? But she had never been skilled at crafting illusions, and there were too many things that could go wrong. Or she might ask Molly to put in a good word for them, but if Mr Menadue asked how she knew Ivy and Martin so well, what could the human girl say?

No references. Too young. No family…

Ivy's face cleared, and she sat up. 'But I do,' she said aloud.

Martin gave her a quizzical look. 'Do what?'

'Have family,' said Ivy. She sprang up from the chair, snatching up her old jeans and jumper from the bureau, and disappeared into the washroom. Talking to her mother was going to be tricky, and she had no idea how it would turn out. But for Molly's sake, she had to try.

Ivy knocked at the door of her mother's flat, heart pounding in time with her knuckles. It was still early in the morning, perhaps too early, but…

The door creaked open, one wary brown eye peering through the gap. Then came a gasp, a cry of 'Ivy! Ivy's back!' and her little sister dragged her inside.

'Where did you go?' she demanded, shoving Ivy onto the sofa and dropping down beside her. 'I can't believe you just went off like that, without even—'

'Cicely,' said Marigold. 'Let Ivy speak.' She crossed the bare floorboards with a dancer's grace and sat down on the foldaway bed where Cicely had been sleeping. 'I can see that she has something important to tell us.'

Ivy glanced around the flat – the bedroom so small that only one person could sleep there, the modest square of the sitting room, the narrow strip of kitchen just visible around the corner. It had never been intended for a family, which was one of the reasons Ivy had been glad to get away from it. She could only hope that after two weeks of living practically on top of one another, her mother and Cicely would feel the same.

'Molly is going away to school,' she said, 'and with her mother gone, there's no one to look after their cottage. Her father's looking for someone to rent the place, and…I thought of you.'

Marigold blinked in surprise. But she did not interrupt, and that gave Ivy courage. Quickly she went on to explain the situation, emphasising how much more comfortable Molly's cottage would be for them to live in, and that she'd worked out an arrangement that should make it possible for them to afford the rent. By the time she finished Cicely's face was shining, and she looked ready to pack up her things right away.

'Mum!' she exclaimed. 'Molly has a *horse*. I've always wanted to ride one. Please, can we?'

'I don't know, Cicely.' Marigold sounded troubled. 'My work is here, and Molly's cottage—'

'Isn't that far,' interrupted Ivy. 'You could Leap there and back three times a day if you had to, and not feel any more tired than you do walking here.'

Marigold gave her a sharp look as if to say, *How do you know about that?* But she must not have wanted to talk about travel-magic in front of Cicely, because she let it pass.

'I've been to Molly's house,' she said. 'I know what a place like that must cost to rent, especially with all the furnishings. Even if we agreed to keep it tidy and look after Molly's horse as well, I can't imagine her father would let it for so little money. What kind of *arrangement* did you make?'

'I know someone who's willing to share the cottage with us,' said Ivy. 'He found some buried treasure and got a good price for it, so he can afford to pay most of the rent. It's—'

'*Mica!*' squealed Cicely, and jumped up from the sofa. 'I knew it! He was only pretending to be on Aunt Betony's side, he was planning this all along!'

She started eagerly towards the door, but Ivy stopped her. 'It's not Mica,' she said. 'I'm sorry, Cicely, but I haven't seen him since we left the Delve.' She turned to Marigold, hoping she didn't look as nervous as she felt. 'I left Martin waiting outside. Is it all right if I ask him to come in?'

eleven

As far as Ivy knew, her mother had no objection to Martin – in fact, quite the opposite: after the Empress was dead she'd gone out of her way to hide him from the faeries who were chasing him, and then she'd sent him to find Ivy on her behalf. So while her mother would doubtless be surprised to see Martin alive and free of the Claybane, Ivy had good hope that the shock would be a pleasant one.

She'd been wrong. As soon as Martin walked in Marigold rose to her feet, back stiff and mouth set. 'Ivy,' she said, 'please take Cicely outside.'

'I don't need her to take me anywhere!' Cicely was indignant. 'Why can't I stay? I'm old enough.'

Ivy hesitated, not sure that leaving her mother alone with Martin would be a good idea. She might look gentle and speak softly, but in Martin's memories Ivy had seen her fighting in one of the Empress's battles, eyes blazing and hands alight with magical power.

'I think—' she began, but Martin caught her eye and tipped his head towards the door. *Go on. I'll be all right.*

Resigned, Ivy took her sister's arm. 'Come on, Cicely. If they want to talk in private, we should let them.' She led the younger girl, still protesting, out the door and down the steps to the street. Then she turned to her and said, 'I don't like being sent away either. But we're not going to change Mum's mind by making a fuss, so we may as well sit down and wait.'

Cicely's expression was mutinous, but she sat. A minute went by in fuming silence, while Ivy watched a car thread its way up the narrow street and vanish over the crest of the hill. At last Cicely said in a small voice, 'I really thought it was Mica.'

'I know,' said Ivy.

'I just don't understand how he could turn his back on us. I don't—' She pulled her knees close to her chest and dropped her chin onto them. 'I don't understand him at all.'

Ivy put an arm around her, and they sat without speaking until Martin came out onto the step. 'Your mother wants you,' he said to Cicely, and she leaped up and ran inside.

'What did she say?' Ivy asked, when the door had shut.

'Well,' said Martin, 'she wasn't entirely pleased with the idea of us sharing Molly's cottage, since she's worried that Rob and the other faeries are still hunting for me. And she wasn't convinced she could depend on me to keep paying my share of the rent. But in the end, I talked her around. She's going to ring David Menadue this morning—'

Ivy flung her arms around him and hugged him. 'You did it!

I'm so grateful, Martin!'

Martin went rigid. Then his fingers closed on her shoulders, pushing her away. 'Enough of that piskey nonsense, please,' he said roughly. 'I owed Molly a debt, so I took the opportunity to repay it. There's nothing special about that.'

He was so close that she could see the faint sun-flare of yellow around his pupils, and the flecks of darker grey in the silver of his eyes. He looked shaken – no, more than shaken: he looked terrified. Ivy drew back. 'What kind of "nonsense" do you mean?' she asked. 'Gratitude?'

'Cultural differences,' he said, avoiding her gaze. 'Faeries may be grateful, but they aren't usually so…demonstrative about it, in my experience. I'd appreciate a warning next time.'

'I see,' said Ivy, her colour rising. 'Well in that case, you needn't worry. I won't do it again.' She stepped around him, heading for the door.

'Where are you going?' asked Martin.

'Back inside,' Ivy said. 'I want to be there when Mum calls Mr Menadue.'

True to her word, Marigold telephoned Molly's father later that morning, and chatted to him for some time in a very human-sounding way about what good friends their daughters were and how sorry she was to hear that Molly had lost her mother, until Ivy thought she would go mad with impatience. But by the time the conversation turned to business, Mr Menadue seemed more than willing to consider the idea. In fact, he suggested that they visit the cottage that very afternoon, to see if it would suit them.

'But you've already seen it,' said Cicely, after Marigold had rung off. 'Why can't we just tell him we want it now?'

'Because he doesn't know that I've seen the house before,' replied their mother, 'and it's only polite to accept his offer. Humans aren't the same as piskeys, my darling. They have their own way of doing things, and it's important to respect that if you want them to trust you.'

So when Marigold, Ivy and Cicely arrived at the cottage some hours later, they had to follow David Menadue on a tour of the house and barn and try to look interested in all the details, when the whole time Ivy was chafing to know whether he'd agree to their terms or not. Only Molly's presence at her side made the waiting bearable.

'I hear you have a cousin who'd like to share the rent as well,' David Menadue said to Marigold as they came out of the barn. Molly had stayed behind to saddle the horses and take Cicely out for a ride, but Ivy was determined to stay close to their parents until she knew what the outcome would be. 'Apparently Molly did some sort of drama training with him last year? It's a small world.'

Marigold gave a vague smile – the safest response for someone who, unlike Molly, couldn't actually lie. 'Martin is an accomplished actor,' she said.

'The only thing is,' Mr Menadue continued with a hint of apology, 'I'm afraid you'll find the cottage a bit tight for four.

There's only the two bedrooms, you see. So perhaps you'd be better looking elsewhere.'

Ivy held her breath, but Marigold stayed serene. 'Oh, that wouldn't be a problem,' she said. 'Martin told me he doesn't expect to be with us often, or stay for more than one or two nights at a time. I'm sure he'll be quite happy in the study.'

'Well, as long as that's settled,' said Molly's father. He jingled something in his pocket and glanced around the yard, then turned back to Marigold. 'Shall we continue this over tea? Molly's made some rather drippy jam, and I think she'll be disappointed if we don't try it.'

'That would be lovely,' said Marigold, and the two of them walked off together. As soon as they disappeared, Ivy dashed back into the barn.

'Foot in the stirrup,' Molly was telling Cicely, 'and swing your leg over. There you go!' She waited until the younger girl had settled herself onto Dodger's back, then looked at Ivy. 'Well?'

'They've gone for tea,' said Ivy. 'That's good, isn't it?'

Molly broke into a grin. 'Knowing my dad, it's as good as done. He never invites *anyone* for tea.' She hugged Ivy. 'This is brilliant. I can't thank you and Martin enough. Where is he, anyway?'

Ivy took Dodger's bridle and led him out into the yard. 'Here, Cicely,' she said, handing her sister the reins even though she probably wouldn't need them – piskeys had a natural rapport with horses, so the two of them would be galloping about in no time. She watched as they trotted down the slope into the field, then turned to Molly.

'Martin's all right,' she said, 'but he's been…odd. I think something's bothering him.' Following the other girl back into the barn, she went on to tell Molly all that had happened since Martin's return that morning.

'And when I hugged him,' she finished as Molly tightened Duchess's saddle girth, 'he reacted like I'd done something horrible. He's never behaved that way before.'

Molly tilted her head to one side, considering. 'It's hard to know with Martin,' she said. 'But he does seem to enjoy catching people off-guard, and he doesn't like it at all when they do the same to him.'

True, thought Ivy. Perhaps it was that simple.

'Or maybe,' Molly continued in the same musing tone, 'he's in love with you.'

'*What?*'

'It was just an idea.' Molly slipped the bridle over Duchess's nose and patted the mare reassuringly. 'Don't you think it would explain a lot, though?'

'*No*,' spluttered Ivy. 'Martin? It's ridiculous.'

'Why? Because he's never said anything about it?' Molly folded her arms. 'My mum never said she loved me either. But you told me you were sure that she did.'

Ivy looked at the cobbles, unable to meet the other girl's accusing eyes. How could she explain her certainty about Martin's feelings – or lack of them – without calling Gillian's into question?

'That's not what I meant,' she said at last. 'It's just that Martin and I are different. Too different to be anything more than friends, and sometimes I'm not even sure we're that.'

And besides, the idea of *anyone* being in love with her was ridiculous. Growing up she'd been reminded at every feast and festival, if she hadn't known it already, that a scrawny, wingless piskey-girl wasn't even fit for dancing, let alone wooing. Keeve had joked at Ivy's fifteenth-year Lighting that not even a spriggan would want her…

'Anyway,' Ivy added more firmly, 'he's much too flighty to settle down with anyone. It was all I could do to talk him into renting your cottage, and he's already told my mother he doesn't plan to be here any more than he has to.' And it was hard to imagine how Martin could possibly care much for Ivy, if he found it so easy to leave her behind. 'Not to mention that he's—'

'Well, it's obvious you don't think much of the idea, at any rate!' Molly sounded exasperated, but when she caught sight of Ivy's face she relented. 'Never mind. I just worry about Martin sometimes, and I think it would be nice if he had someone to look after him.' She handed Duchess's reins to Ivy. 'Go on, then. Your sister's waiting.'

When Ivy returned to the hotel that evening she found Martin pacing the room. Surely he hadn't been waiting for her all day? She thought of asking, but decided she'd better not.

'It's all settled,' she said. 'We're moving into Molly's cottage this Saturday morning.'

'All right. I'll be there.' He pulled a thick envelope from his pocket and tossed it on the table. 'You can give that to your mother, when you next see her. It should be enough for now.'

'Where are you going?' Ivy asked.

'Well,' said Martin, 'since I've just given your mother all the money I had, it's back to the carn for me. Then I'll pay another visit to Thom Pendennis. He'll be delighted, I'm sure.'

He spoke lightly, but Ivy felt a stirring of unease. 'I thought you said you weren't going back to London without me,' she said.

'That was when it was just the two of us. You have your family now.' He pulled out his wallet and peered into it, then put it back in his pocket. 'But you needn't worry about Rob and the others, even if your mother does. They won't catch me.'

'Are you sure? You've been caught before.'

'True. But I didn't have you looking out for me then.'

Ivy stared at him. 'Are you mocking me?'

'Absolutely not. Believe me, after the way I've spent the last few years, having someone I can actually trust to watch my back is a revolutionary experience.' He glanced in the mirror and flicked a strand of hair out of his eyes. 'Besides, there's no use wasting jokes on someone with no sense of humour.'

'I do so have—'

'You do not. Not that I've ever seen, anyway. But that's all right.' He quirked a smile at her. 'There are worse faults. I'll see you on Saturday, Ivy of the Delve.'

Then he was gone.

twelve

'She's not coming back, boy.' The Grey Man crouched close to him in the twilight, his expression grimmer than ever. 'Our luck's run out.'

The rest of the search party – old Helm and a young tracker named Dart – had already headed into the fogou for a meal and some well-earned sleep. It had been Helm who'd told the boy that the chief wanted to see him, but one look at the old warrior's face had warned him the news would not be good.

The boy swallowed. 'Is she… ?'

'Dead? No.' The chief straightened, folding his arms and gazing out across the valley. 'Though it might be better for all of us if she were. Her trail crossed the path of some knockers bound for their diggings, and that was the last we could find of her.'

Knockers. Sturdy, pickaxe-wielding miners who also served as the piskeys' soldiers and enforcers, they feared and hated spriggans as much as the boy's people hated them. If the knocker-men had captured his mother, they'd never get her back without a fight…

But that battle would never come. How could the Grey Man ask *his warriors to risk their lives and the lives of their families, all for the sake of a faery woman who'd despised his treasure and deliberately run away?*

'Our best hope now,' his father murmured, 'is that they don't question her too closely about where she came from. Because if they do...'

The boy didn't have to ask what he meant. Nomads though his people were, it was no small matter to move their clan from one wintering place to another. By now all the other carns and caves large enough to hold such a band had already been claimed by other spriggan tribes, so if they lost the fogou they'd have nowhere else to go.

'Let this be a lesson to you, boy.' The Grey Man spoke coldly, his features hard as granite. 'Aye, a lesson for us both. Never give your heart to a woman, even if she begs for it. And never trust a faery's bargain...'

Ivy blinked against the pillow, then rolled over with a groan. Last night she'd taken off the copper bracelet and left it on the tea tray, clear across the room. Yet the instant her eyes closed, she'd been back with Martin's ancestors again. And if the boy's last conversation with the Grey Man hadn't been depressing enough, she'd gone on to relive his rough awakening later that night, his desperate escape with the treasure, and all the same horrific details of the fogou's destruction she'd witnessed before.

Had the dreams come full circle, and this was the end? Or were there more memories that Ivy had yet to witness? Either way, Martin would want to know about the things she'd seen.

She'd been too preoccupied with Molly to tell him about her previous dream, and now he was gone. But when he returned – *if* he returned – she would remember.

Ivy climbed out of the bed and put on the fresh set of clothes she'd brought from her mother's house, revelling in their cleanness. She hadn't realised how much simple pleasures like warm baths and clean clothes meant to her until she'd started travelling with Martin and had to go for days on end without them. Though it had been easy enough to forget all that when she was in bird-shape…

And now she had no bird-shape to hide in, no matter how much she missed the comforts of flight. After Martin left her yesterday she'd walked along the beach until the moon rose and tried turning herself into a peregrine again – but like all her previous attempts, it had failed. She'd rallied herself for a second try and then a third, but each time she found herself in swift-form the terror that gripped her was so overwhelming that she'd dropped back into her own piskey shape at once. And on her fourth attempt, she'd been so determined not to let herself turn into anything but a falcon that she'd tumbled onto the shingle without changing shape at all.

It was no use telling herself she was being a fool, or a coward: she'd called herself all those names and more, but it hadn't given her back her courage. Perhaps when the other swifts returned next April she'd feel confident enough to fly again, but for the time being, Ivy was grounded.

And maybe that was for the best. Now that Martin had shown

Ivy how to travel by magic, she didn't actually *need* wings unless she wanted to go somewhere new, and she had too many responsibilities to go exploring in any case. She'd promised to meet Jenny and Mattock this afternoon, for one thing. Perhaps they'd have good news for her about what was happening in the Delve.

'Sorry we're late,' said Jenny as she and Mattock climbed down to join Ivy in the shelter of their meeting place, the old mining adit Matt had shown them before. The opening was shallow, the passage behind it caged off to keep humans from wandering into the abandoned tunnels. But there was ample room for three piskeys to shelter beneath the overhang – if they didn't mind sharing the space with a few cigarette stubs and discarded beer bottles. 'It was my fault. Yarrow asked me to deliver something to the Joan.'

'What was it?' asked Ivy, sitting up. If Betony was starting to feel ill, perhaps she'd be more sympathetic to her people's plight.

'Just a sleeping potion,' said Jenny. 'Seems you aren't the only one in the family who finds it hard to settle.'

Ivy hadn't found it hard at all, lately. But with all these dreams she'd been having, she wasn't sure whether the extra sleep was worth it. 'So you've been helping Yarrow, then,' she said, trying to stay hopeful. 'Did you ask if she'd be willing to talk to the Joan?'

'I tried,' Jenny said, 'but she gave me a strange look, and then she asked where I got that idea. So I told her I've been worried

135

about Mum's chest, and thinking more fresh air would be good for her. And she said that might help a little, but it wouldn't solve the real problem, and we just have to be patient until the Joan's finished dealing with it.'

'But that's nonsense,' said Ivy. 'If Betony's spells were working, our people would be feeling better, not worse.'

'I know. But when I suggested that to Yarrow, she…' Jenny paused to cough into her sleeve. 'She said that if I was going to talk instead of work, she'd find another helper. She was practically rude, and that's…'

'Not like Yarrow at all,' finished Ivy, as Jenny coughed again. 'But she's still got you running errands?'

'Oh, yes,' Jenny said. 'Really, she can't afford to lose me. I've been taking medicine to all the old aunties and uncles for her, and even with my help she's busy most of the day.' She sighed. 'I don't think she was angry, anyway. I think she was frightened.'

'We can't count on her, then,' said Mattock. He sat down heavily, wiping his arm across his brow. 'That's much the same as I found, when I talked to the knockers. They all said there was nothing odd about feeling a bit under the weather sometimes, and that the important thing was to keep busy and not let it get you down. And when I asked whether they didn't think that there was more sickness in the Delve now than before, they blamed it all on Gillian.'

Ivy was not surprised. When Marigold had first become ill, she'd faced much the same resistance from her neighbours. There were a hundred excuses and explanations for the sicknesses and premature deaths that had touched nearly every clan among them, from spriggan mischief to old faery curses to 'a bit o' what they call rheumatism, it runs in the family, you know'.

'I asked my mum to talk to our neighbours too,' said Jenny, 'but they said they were sure the Joan knew all about their troubles already, and was doing the best she could.' She sighed. 'And then Mum said they were probably right, and that piskey folk ought to stay cheerful and not fret over things we can't change. She won't even let me take her to the Great Shaft now.'

Ivy pushed the heels of her hands against her eyes. How could they prove to Betony that their people's way of life needed to change, if they couldn't even convince the piskeys who were suffering the most?

'Then we'll have to try something else,' she said at last. 'If the older ones are too afraid or too set in their ways to help us, we'll have to go to the younger piskeys instead. They may not be sick enough to change Betony's mind, but if we can make them understand the danger our people are in, they might be willing to do something about it.'

'Do something?' asked Jenny. 'You mean…without the Joan?'

'Yes,' said Ivy. 'That's exactly what I mean.'

'You can't be serious,' said Mattock. 'You want us to go behind your aunt's back? There's no way, Ivy.'

'Why not? Don't you think saving our people is worth the risk?'

Matt made an impatient gesture. 'It's not about risk, it's about what's right! I know Betony's not perfect, but she's still Joan the

Wad, the Torch that lights the way for our people. It's our duty to follow where she leads—'

'Even if she's leading us off a cliff?' demanded Ivy. 'We've been fooling ourselves, Matt. If Betony could watch her own brother getting sicker every day and put it all down to brooding and overwork, what kind of evidence do you think is going to convince her? She's not a torch leading us out of the darkness, Matt. She's more like – like a great stubborn boulder, blocking out all the light.'

The minute she finished speaking, she knew she'd gone too far. Jenny had turned so pale that even her lips were ashen, while Mattock's face was darker than she'd ever seen it.

'I'm going to pretend I didn't hear that,' he told her. 'This time. But don't ever say it again.' He climbed to his feet. 'Come on, Jenny. We're done here.'

'Matt,' pleaded Ivy, but he shook his head.

'I can't listen to treason, Ivy. Not even from you. Jenny, are you coming or not?'

Jenny smoothed her crumpled skirts, not looking at him. Then she said quietly, 'No. You can leave if you want, but I'm staying.'

'You can't do that!'

'Yes, I can, and I will.' She got to her feet. 'Ivy's right, Matt. The Joan may be powerful, but she's only one woman, and there are over two hundred piskeys in the Delve who deserve better than she's willing to offer them. If we can't move Betony, then we need to go around her. It's the only way.'

'It's too dangerous. If you're caught speaking against the Joan—'

'I'm not a fool, Matt. I know what happens to people who cross her.' She moved closer to Ivy and took her hand. 'But that's why I have to do this, don't you see? After all Ivy did to save the Delve from Gillian, and all she's suffered because of it – no one could blame her if she'd gone off to join the faeries, or even the spriggans! But here she is, risking her life to help us. Don't you think that should count for something?'

Mattock didn't answer.

'We owe her, Matt. We can't let her do this alone.' She spoke softly now, with a hint of reproach. 'And you don't really want to, do you?'

Mattock shoved his hands through his hair. He paced around the fire, stood a moment staring out of the adit, then turned back. 'I've done my best to talk you both out of this,' he said. 'I don't want to see a noose around your necks, any more than I want it around mine. But…all right.'

'So you won't try to stop us?' asked Ivy.

'I should hope I'm good for more than that,' said Matt. 'I may be cautious, but I'm no coward.' His hand dropped to the hilt of his hunter's knife. 'If you're really convinced that going against Betony's the only way to do this…then I'm with you.'

'There's nothing written on this. Where do I put it?' Ivy's little sister blew a stray curl from her forehead and hefted the box in her arms, looking unsteady enough to drop it any minute. Hastily

Ivy set down her own load and moved to help her.

'Those are *plates*, Cicely,' she chided. 'You shouldn't be carrying anything so heavy. Here, give that to me.'

'Why? I'm as big as you are, or nearly.' She twisted away before Ivy could take the box from her. 'Just tell me where to put it. I'm fine.'

She was in a snappish mood, and Ivy couldn't blame her: the two piskey-girls had ended up doing all the work of carrying things into the cottage, while their mother and David Menadue stood by the moving van and talked. But Molly's father looked even more sombre than usual and Marigold was wiping her eyes, so it didn't seem right to interrupt them.

'Take it to the kitchen, then,' said Ivy resignedly.

Tired as she felt, she couldn't really complain; the move had gone quite well on the whole. Mr Menadue had called Marigold halfway through the week, offering to rent a mover's van and drive it over for them. Molly had spent most of yesterday afternoon with Ivy and Cicely, showing them how to look after Dodger while she was gone; the only reason she wasn't helping them now was because she was in the barn with him, saying goodbye.

Fortunately, it wasn't long before Molly returned, and with her help the work was soon finished. 'They're talking about Mum, you know,' she said to Ivy as they stood at the front window, watching their parents walk slowly across the garden. 'And your dad.'

'I know,' said Ivy. Marigold and Gillian had been friends once, so she would understand David Menadue's grief better than most. And she was good at talking to humans – *really* talking, as though she was one of them herself. 'I don't mind.'

The front door opened, and the two adults came in. Marigold's eyes were still a little red, but she smiled as she made her way around the boxes to join them. 'Where's Cicely?' she asked.

'In my room,' Molly told her. 'I think she's trying to decide which half of the bed she likes best. Have you seen Mar— I mean Mr—' She stopped, flustered, and shot Ivy a pleading look. Apparently she had no idea what name Martin was using.

'Richards,' supplied her father. 'I suppose he had you call him by his first name in class?' He turned to Ivy's mother. 'Do you do that with your dance students, Marigold?'

'No, indeed,' she said with a little laugh. 'They call me Mrs Flint. And that must be Martin now.'

Ordinarily Ivy would have been sceptical, since all she could see through the front window was a car, and she was sure Martin didn't know how to drive. But the copper bracelet had been growing warmer all morning, and when the back door of the cab opened and that silver-blond head appeared, there could be no doubt.

'Well, that's it then,' said David, managing to sound both cheerful and faintly disappointed. He took a pair of keys from his pocket and handed them to Marigold. 'There's the house and the barn for you.'

Not even five years of living among humans could make a faery comfortable saying *thank you*, but Marigold managed to convey her gratitude with a smile. 'We'll take good care of the place,' she said.

Martin leaped lightly onto the step and stood in the open doorway, surveying them all with interest. 'I didn't expect such a large welcoming party,' he said. 'Have I been especially good, or especially wicked?'

There was something different about him, and Ivy wasn't sure she liked it. Not that she could find any fault with his appearance, in fact quite the opposite: he looked as healthy and well-groomed as she'd ever seen him. His eyes sparkled like piskey-wine, and a smile teased about his lips. But instinct warned her not to be fooled by first impressions.

'Not especially either,' said Marigold. 'Just late enough to avoid all the hard work, as usual.' That surprised Ivy: her mother didn't usually speak so bluntly, or show such a dry sense of humour. 'Where are your things?'

'I have no things,' Martin replied, gesturing grandly. '*I eat the air, promise-crammed. You cannot feed capons so.*'

'You've been to the theatre!' exclaimed Molly. 'Was it *Hamlet*? Where?' But her father tapped his wristwatch.

'I told Harry I'd have his van back by noon,' he said, 'and we've got a seven-hour drive ahead of us. Say goodbye to your friends, Molly.' He shook Martin's hand, clasped Marigold's, and went out.

Cicely came galloping out of the bedroom. 'You're leaving? Already?'

'I'm afraid so,' said Molly. 'I've already missed a week of school as it is.' She turned to Martin. 'I really appreciate all you've done for me,' she said. 'I'll never forget it.'

Martin dismissed this with an airy wave. 'It was Ivy's idea,' he said. 'I just went along with her, as usual.'

'Not just that,' Molly said. 'I mean everything. If you hadn't told me I was a born actress, and that I shouldn't let anyone, not even Mum, tell me otherwise…' She stretched up and kissed him on the cheek. 'Take good care of yourself. I don't want anything to happen to my faery godfather.'

Cicely giggled, but Martin did not smile. He made Molly a slight, respectful bow, and stepped back to let her pass.

'Come to the van with me?' Molly asked Ivy, and the two of them headed outside. The human girl paused, watching the cottage until the front door shut. Then she said, 'I wasn't sure whether I should say anything about this. It's probably nothing. But the last few days, I've had a feeling that someone's looking for me.'

That was odd. 'Is it a good feeling? Or a bad one?'

'I couldn't really tell at first,' Molly said. 'That's why I didn't mention it before. I thought it might be something to do with Mum, you know…missing her, and wondering if…' She cleared her throat. 'Anyway. But now I don't think that's what it is. It feels more like – like somebody creeping up on me from behind.'

'You mean to hurt you?'

Molly nodded. 'I'm probably being silly, but—'

'No, you were right to tell me.' Ivy frowned, thinking. Molly had no particular magic of her own, but being half-faery made her more perceptive than the average human. She might be sensing some ill intent directed towards her – an envious schoolmate or mean-spirited neighbour, for instance. But if so, her unease would surely go away once she'd put some distance between herself and the cottage.

'Could you send me a message, once you're settled at school?' Ivy asked. 'And let me know if you still feel the same way?'

The human girl nodded eagerly. 'I'll ring you. First chance I get.'

'Molly!' shouted David. 'Hurry up! It's almost twelve!'

Molly made a face. 'I'd better go.' She gave Ivy a hug. 'Take care of yourself. And *him*.' Then she ran and jumped in beside her father. The last Ivy saw she was leaning out the window, waving madly with both hands, as the van drove away.

thirteen

When Ivy came back into the cottage Martin was lounging in the front room, surveying the boxes scattered about the floor. 'Your mother and sister appear to have accumulated a surprising number of *things*,' he said. 'More trouble than they're worth, I'd say. Where are you going to put them all?'

There wasn't that much clutter: in fact, Mr Menadue had been surprised at how few belongings Marigold possessed. But Ivy could tell Martin wasn't really interested in the question.

'Where have you been?' she asked, trying not to sound accusing. He still had that strange, flighty air about him, and if she pressed him too hard he might disappear again.

'Here and there.' He waved a hand in the same vague, theatrical gesture as before. '*Where the bee sucks, there suck I*. Why, did you miss me?'

Ivy decided to ignore that. 'I have something to tell you,' she said, pulling a box close to the sofa and sitting down on it. Marigold and Cicely were banging about in the kitchen looking for the kettle, so they wouldn't be likely to overhear. 'I had two more dreams about the spriggan-boy. Martin, I think he must be your ancestor.'

The lazy humour vanished from his face. He sat up, intent as a hunting ermine. 'Tell me,' he said, so Ivy did.

'But since I saw the fogou destroyed the second time,' she said, 'I haven't had any more dreams. So maybe that's the end.'

'I wonder,' murmured Martin. 'Maybe that was all I needed to know, but…' He shook himself back to attention. 'Well, if you do start dreaming again, tell me.'

'That might be difficult if you plan to go on being *here and there*, as you put it.' This time she didn't hide her impatience; if he'd had time to see a play and get his hair trimmed, he could have at least let her know he'd got back safe from London. 'But *if* it happens, and *when* I see you, I'll try.'

'Do they upset you? The dreams?'

He spoke gently, and Ivy was disarmed. 'Not…exactly,' she said. 'I've seen a few things that made me uncomfortable, but…' She hesitated. Had she ever put it this way before, even to herself? 'I'm not afraid of spriggans any more. I just wish I knew why my people hate them so much.'

'So do I,' said Martin. 'In the past three days I've spent more time in pubs than I care to think about, listening to every droll-teller and yarn-spinner I could find. But all they could tell me about spriggans was that they're ugly little dwarfs who bring bad luck and bad weather.' He drummed his fingers on the arm of the sofa. 'That, and a few mildly diverting tales about someone's great-great-granduncle who went treasure-hunting by moonlight, or just took an ill-advised shortcut after a few pints, and ended up with a spriggan horde chasing him all the way home.'

Guilt pricked at Ivy. Even if he had gone to the theatre once or twice, she should have known Martin hadn't been idle. He couldn't forget his people, any more than she could forget hers. 'I'm sorry,' she said. 'But at least you were able to sell the treasure – or were you?'

'What? Oh. Yes.' He seemed preoccupied now, flicking loose threads off the upholstery. 'Yes, the trip was…fairly profitable. You should have enough to keep you for another two months at least.'

He always said *you* when talking about the cottage, never *us*. Ivy had to wonder if he meant to spend any time there at all. 'I talked to Matt and Jenny again,' she began, 'but—'

'Did somebody say *Jenny*?' Cicely poked her head around the corner, brown eyes wide. 'You saw her? When?'

Ivy cast a desperate look at Martin. She couldn't lie to her little sister, but she didn't want her getting involved in the conspiracy either. And if Cicely guessed that Ivy was meeting Jenny and Mattock outside the Delve, it would be next to impossible to keep her away.

'Your sister was telling me about a friend of hers back in the Delve,' said Martin mildly. 'Tell me, sweetling, is eavesdropping a family tradition, or just an unfortunate personal habit?'

Cicely turned pink, and immediately withdrew. Ivy let out her breath. 'Come on,' she whispered. 'I'll tell you the rest outside.'

*

'If you ask me,' said Martin, 'you and your friends are far less likely to succeed in leading a revolution than you are to get yourselves killed.'

He was leaning against the wall of the barn, well away from Dodger – the bay gelding had no love for Martin, and the feeling was mutual. Ivy stopped combing the horse's mane and started braiding it. 'Why? Because you don't think my people are capable of thinking for themselves?'

'I have no idea what they're capable of,' Martin replied. 'Apart from murdering my ancestors in droves, apparently, but you tell me piskeys don't do that sort of thing any more.' He plucked a bit of straw from his sleeve. 'But you underestimate how little imagination most magical folk have, and how reluctant they are to change. Why do you think the Empress was able to seize power so quickly, and hold onto it for so long? The first generation of faeries she conquered couldn't adapt quickly enough to stop her, and the generation that grew up under her rule didn't know how to live any other way.'

'But someone did rise up against her in the end,' said Ivy. 'Rob and his rebels. You told him he'd never succeed either, but he did.'

Martin pushed himself off the wall with an impatient thrust of his shoulders. 'Only because he and all his followers agreed that the Empress was a cruel, selfish tyrant, and that they were prepared to fight her to the death. You don't have that advantage, and from what you've told me, it sounds like you never will.'

'So what are you saying?' demanded Ivy. 'That I should just sit back and watch my people die?'

'What I'm saying is, don't set your heart on saving them. They may not want to be saved.'

Ivy clenched her jaw. 'I think you give up on people too easily.'

'And I think you don't give up on them even when you should.' He walked closer, careful to stay out of Dodger's reach as the horse snorted and bared his teeth. 'The problem is, your plan's too weak. Even if your friends manage to convince a few piskeys – or a few dozen – to sneak outside behind Betony's back, it's only going to be a matter of time before she finds out and puts a stop to it.'

'Not if there are enough of us,' said Ivy.

'It'll never be enough, unless you're ready for a battle. As long as your Joan is alive, she will always be the most powerful piskey in the Delve, and there will always be at least a few people who are loyal or fearful enough to do whatever she tells them. You can't change your people's whole way of life just by *talking*.'

'I am not going to kill my aunt,' said Ivy angrily. 'Or ask anyone else to kill her, either. She's arrogant and stubborn and judgmental, and she's hurt people I care about, and I hate – I hate the choices she's made. But she hasn't done anything to deserve that.'

'Maybe not,' said Martin. 'Yet. But as soon as she suspects someone is plotting against her, she'll do whatever it takes to weed out that treachery and make sure it doesn't happen again. In which case exile will be the best your friends can hope for. But

I doubt she'll settle for anything less than execution, especially if she finds out you're involved.'

Ivy clutched at Dodger's mane. 'What? That doesn't make sense. Why would she kill Matt or Jenny because of me?'

'Because you'll have proven to her that a banished enemy can still be a threat. You really ought to read *Richard II*, you know, or better yet see it performed. Shakespeare can be quite illuminating when it comes to politics.'

Shakespeare again. Ivy had never heard of the man except from Martin, but she was already sick of him.

'Even if you're right,' she said, swinging her leg over Dodger's back and dropping to the straw, 'there's nothing I can do. I can't go into the Delve myself, so I have to let Matt and Jenny do as they think best, in their own time and in their own way.'

'You're not doing them any favours,' said Martin. 'They need a strong leader.'

'I am not anyone's leader!' Ivy snapped. She unlatched the half-door and shut it behind her. 'Yes, the other piskeys followed me once – *just* once – when I led them all out of the Delve. But only because Betony was trapped in the Claybane, and they could see the smoke coming, and they were desperate enough to follow the first person who offered to help them. It had nothing to do with me!'

'And yet,' said Martin, 'even in exile, you've managed to talk at least two piskeys into conspiring against their Joan and risking their lives to start a rebellion on your behalf. Do you think they'd do that for just anyone?'

Ivy slumped against the box, weary of the whole conversation. 'They're my friends,' she said. 'And they care about the Delve as much as I do. Of course they would.'

Martin leaned closer, bracing his palm on the post above her head. His breath warmed her lips as he murmured, 'I think you're wrong.'

Then he pulled back and walked away.

'Another sandwich, Martin?' asked Marigold.

Outside the kitchen window the sun was setting, slanting between the curtains and laying a golden stripe across the table. Martin slid his chair sideways, out of the light. 'I appreciate the offer,' he said, 'but no. I've had enough.'

He'd avoided Ivy all afternoon – not that she'd made any real effort to seek him out after their conversation in the barn, but somehow he had managed to keep his distance from wherever she happened to be. Yet he'd smiled at her when they sat down to dinner, so she didn't think he was holding a grudge. He seemed more preoccupied than anything else, and she wondered what was on his mind.

'I'm going to make up a bed for you in the study,' Cicely announced with pride. 'Ivy and I are sharing Molly's room, and Mum gets the big room across the tunnel – I mean the corridor. That's fair, isn't it?'

'Quite fair,' agreed Martin. 'But there's no need. I won't be staying tonight.'

'Why not?' asked Cicely.

'Cicely,' murmured Marigold, but Ivy's little sister kept looking at Martin, expectant.

'As it happens,' Martin said, 'I've been investigating a mystery of sorts. I've just been offered a potentially valuable clue, and I've decided it's worth pursuing. But I might be gone for some time.'

Had he made some new discovery about the spriggans while he was away? Or had her dreams told him more than she'd thought? 'For how long?' Ivy asked.

'I'm not sure yet.' Martin rose and inclined his head to all of them in turn. 'Good night, sweet ladies. Enjoy the cottage.' He took a step back, measuring the open window with his gaze – and only then did Ivy guess what he intended.

'Wait!' she cried, but it was too late. His form blurred, and Cicely let out a squeak of astonishment as the ghostly white shape of a barn owl flapped across the kitchen and vanished into the yard.

'Did you see—' she spluttered. 'How did he *do* that?'

'All male faeries can take bird-shape,' said Marigold, picking up Martin's plate and carrying it to the sink. 'They don't have wings like…like most females, so that's how they fly.'

And knowing Martin, he'd taken owl-shape in front of Cicely just to provoke this conversation. He knew Ivy hadn't told her family about her shape-changing; apparently he'd decided it was time she did. But what would be the point of Ivy talking about it now, when she could no longer bear to take swift-shape, and she was too weak and clumsy to change into anything else?

'I wish I could become a bird,' said Cicely wistfully.

'Why?' asked Ivy, rising to help clear the table. 'You have perfectly good wings of your own.'

'Only when I'm piskey size, though, and it's not like I've ever had much chance to use them. Down in the Delve, they mostly just got in the way.' She rested her chin on her hand. 'It doesn't seem fair that boys get different magic from girls.'

'Piskey magic and faery magic is different too,' Ivy reminded her. 'We can do some of the same things, but every group of magical folk has their own specialties. Isn't that right, Mum?'

Marigold turned on the water and began filling the sink. 'So it seems,' she said. 'Even different faery wylds sometimes have different approaches to magic – and some faeries are better at certain spells than others. But I wonder if that's more a matter of exposure and confidence than anything else. It's hard to cast a spell successfully unless you've watched another faery or piskey cast it first. And if you don't believe you can do something, you probably won't.'

Perhaps that was why Ivy couldn't turn herself into a peregrine. Because deep down, in spite of her longing, she didn't really believe. How could a small, skinny piskey-girl become something so fierce and powerful?

'Could Mica learn to turn himself into a bird, then?' asked Cicely. 'If he saw Martin do it?'

'He wouldn't even if he could,' said Ivy. 'He told me once that piskeys don't do that kind of thing.'

'Why not?' When Ivy didn't answer, Cicely turned to Marigold. 'Mum, do you know?'

'I'm not certain,' Marigold replied, reaching for a dishcloth. 'But I think it might have something to do with the spriggans.'

Ivy nearly dropped the cutlery she was holding. 'Spriggans? What about them?'

'When I was growing up in the Delve, I heard a droll-teller say that spriggans could change their form at will,' Marigold said. 'It was one of the things that made them so terrifying, because there was no way to tell what they really looked like. But piskeys were different, he said, because they were true to their own nature. They might grow larger or smaller, but their bodies would always look the same.'

True to their own nature. Mica had said something like that too, the first time Ivy had asked him about shape-changing. Was that why he'd turned his back on Ivy when he realised she could take swift-form? Because in his eyes, that made her no better than a spriggan?

'Ugh.' Cicely made a face. 'I never thought of *that*. Do you mean spriggans could even disguise themselves as piskeys, if they wanted?'

'I don't know,' said Marigold. 'Perhaps. Maybe that's why the Joan put so many wards around the Delve – to keep anyone who wasn't a true piskey from getting in.' She took the dishes Ivy had stacked and slid them into the dishwater. 'But I've never seen a spriggan, and I doubt they still exist. Now both of you, clear out and leave the washing-up to me. You've done enough work for today.'

*

Hidden behind the carn, the boy wrapped his thin arms around himself and wept until he felt hollow. But the tears had dried on his wind-burned cheeks before the knocker-men sheathed their knives, shouldered their thunder-axes, and disappeared.

Once the quietness of the valley had seemed comforting, like a well-kept secret. Now it was deathly, and the boy had no desire to stay there any longer. But where could he go? His old foster-clan might take him back, but first he'd have to find their winter lodgings, and that would be far from easy. Travelling on foot with little magic to protect himself, he'd fare no better than his mother had, and likely worse.

Perhaps he could hide among the humans for a while. He'd heard of spriggans who'd slipped their hungry babes into human cradles, and others who disguised themselves as wandering crowders to beg meals and shelter. He had no fiddle and not even a blind woman could have mistaken him for a baby, but perhaps some kind-hearted humans might take pity on him nonetheless.

Of course the carn held wealth aplenty, but the boy knew better than to use it. The coins in the Grey Man's hoard were ancient, and the humans would be sure to ask where he'd come by them. No matter how the boy hedged, it wouldn't take them long to guess he'd found treasure – and then they'd never let him go until he'd led them to the rest of it. That would not only be a betrayal of his father's last wish, it would be the worst disgrace that any spriggan could suffer, and no clan would ever welcome him again.

So his pockets would have to stay empty, even if his belly did too. But he should at least look over the ruins of the fogou before he left.

Not that he had any hope his people might still be alive, but he might find a weapon or some provisions to take with him. The boy pushed himself upright and started down the slope into the valley.

If the destruction had looked horrifying from above, it was even worse at close quarters. The once-solid roof of the tunnel had shattered into cracked slabs and jagged shards plunging deep into the earth, and the twisted bodies of spriggan warriors lay tumbled among the wreckage. Telling himself not to look at their faces, the boy clambered down into the pit and began his search.

It didn't take him long to find a knife, though it wasn't easy to pry it out of the dead warrior's hand and even longer to undo the sheath that went with it. The boy was so thin that he had to wrap the belt around himself twice, but the leather was only slightly torn, so it should hold. He tugged his ragged shirt down over it and kept searching.

He was picking his way among the rocks, his eyes on a dusty scrap of fabric that looked like a cloak, when something shifted beneath his feet. He tried to leap clear as the stone tipped over, but his feet skidded out from under him, and with a cry he tumbled into the dark.

He landed hard on the floor of the tunnel, dirt and pebbles showering around him. Instinctively he flung his arms over his head, expecting to be crushed. But the rock had stuck fast on an outcropping, and moved no further. The boy uncurled, licking blood from his bitten lip, and clambered to his feet.

He'd landed on the floor of the passage, but there was no easy escape from this level: both ends of the fogou had collapsed. His best chance was to climb the jagged pile of rocks in front of him, if it *would hold. The boy spat into his palms, rubbed them together, and stepped forward.*

The first stone he stepped onto held firm, as did the next. But he'd scarcely put his weight on the third stone when it dislodged in a heart-juddering shower of rubble, leaving him dangling by his fingertips. Gritting his teeth, he toed around for another foothold...

And a hand closed around his ankle.

fourteen

The boy clung to the rock pile, too shocked to move. Terror seized him as the hand groped up his leg, and he bit his lip to stifle a scream. Then a groan floated up from below him: 'Help…me.'

He'd seen the fogou collapse in on itself, dust billowing from the wreckage. Surely no spriggan born, no matter how strong or cunning or even lucky, could have survived such devastation. Yet even as he wavered those fingers clutched at him again, weak but undeniably real.

Swallowing back his fear, the boy dropped to the floor and began digging at the pile with both hands, pulling out rocks and tossing them aside. Before long his fingers were bleeding and his back ached with the strain, but he kept working doggedly until he'd cleared a space large enough for the trapped warrior to crawl out.

Something inside him had hoped, against all reason, that his father had survived. But as soon as the man's head and shoulders emerged and he saw that blunt-featured face with its bristling black beard, he knew better. It was Helm, the Grey Man's oldest and most trusted companion.

'So, lad,' Helm wheezed, heaving the rest of his body free. 'You got away. Anyone else?'

The boy shook his head.

'Aye. Well.' Helm coughed again. 'We can't all be lucky at once.' He dropped his forehead against his blood-streaked arm and lay there panting a moment. Then he gripped the stones with one big hand and pushed himself to his feet.

His hair and beard were grey with rock-dust, and there was an ugly gash across his brow. His sleeves and trousers were ripped in several places, showing bloody scrapes and cuts beneath. But his stout leather jerkin was intact, and his limbs looked whole.

'The Grey Man's dead. Shaper rest him.' Helm fell back against the wall of the tunnel, gazing up at the light filtering through the rocks above. Grime had settled into the lines of his face, making him look craggier than ever.

'He shoved me away, when the roof cracked,' he said. 'Then he used the last of his power to shield me, so I wouldn't be crushed with the rest. The greatest spriggan chief in all Kernow, giving up his life for an old soldier with barely any treasure to his name. And do you know why?'

The boy shook his head.

'I asked him – begged him – to let me go.' Helm's eyes were dark beneath his bushy brows. 'It was my place to die with my chief, and I thought the knockers would finish me off anyway. But he told me I had to live, and look after his son.'

Heat pricked at the boy's eyes, though he'd thought all his tears long spent. He'd failed in nearly every way a son could fail

159

his father, but still the Grey Man had died thinking of him.

'That would be you, lad,' said Helm gruffly, clapping him on the back. 'A sorry little mouse as ever ate crumbs, but we'll make a man of you yet.' He jerked his head towards the shifting heap of rubble. 'We'll give our folk a proper farewelling, and then be on our way.'

'Ivy.'

The whisper was so soft that she would never have heard it, if it hadn't been a hand's breadth from her ear. Ivy's eyes flew open and she rolled over – to find Martin stooping over her in the darkness, holding a finger to his lips.

'We need to talk,' he said, glancing at Cicely's blanket-huddled shape on the far side of the bed. 'Get dressed and meet me outside.' Then he vanished.

Ivy slid out of bed, her heart hammering, and pulled on a long-sleeved shirt and slim trousers. The cottage was dark and utterly still, the sky outside so thick with cloud that not a single star shone through. She combed her curls with her fingers, shook off the last foggy remnants of sleep, and willed herself out into the night.

Martin was standing by the corner of the barn, waiting for her. He straightened as she approached, and it struck her that he seemed ill at ease – almost, if she hadn't known him better, shy.

'I thought you'd gone,' she said.

His smile was half grimace. 'So did I, at first. But then I thought…it was only fair to tell you.'

'Tell me what?'

'I think I may have found the other spriggans. Or at least, one of them.'

'What? Where?'

'I'm not sure yet,' Martin admitted. 'It may be a trick, or even a trap. That's why I didn't say anything before. I hadn't decided whether it was worth the risk.' He leaned against the stone wall, gazing across the field to the dark line of trees beyond. 'But this time when I went to see Thom Pendennis, he asked me straight out if I was human. And when I asked what sort of question that was, he told me I wouldn't be the first spriggan who'd come into his shop to sell treasure.'

Ivy drew in her breath. So Thom had known, or at least suspected, all along. 'Go on.'

'He told me there's an older spriggan named Walker who's been bringing him bits of his family trove for years. He wondered if I knew him at all, and when I said no, he looked surprised. 'I thought he must be an uncle of yours, or some sort of relative at least,' he said. 'You look so much alike—'

His voice cracked on the last word, and he turned his head away. He had to clear his throat before he spoke again. 'He offered to arrange a meeting, but I said I'd think about it. Thom's a shifty sort of fellow, and I had a feeling I might be better off trying to find this Walker on my own.'

No wonder he'd been gone so long. 'But you haven't?' Ivy asked.

'No. So I've decided to take my chances with Thom after all,' he said. 'No doubt he'll want a bribe of some sort, or at least a reward if all goes well. But if Walker can tell me what happened to the other spriggans, or lead me to them...then it'll be worth it.'

The leaves stirred, and an apple fell with a thump from the tree at the corner of the barn. The clouds thinned and frayed apart, revealing the flashing lights of an aeroplane gliding westward towards the sea. Ivy watched until it vanished, then said, 'Well, I'm glad. I hope you find them.'

'Come with me.'

She looked at him, startled. He sounded serious, but surely he couldn't mean it?

'What I said this afternoon – it was something splenitive and rash, as Hamlet would say.' His mouth bent wryly. 'It would be foolhardy to attack your aunt, and you'd have little chance of surviving if you did. But if you've already warned your friends in the Delve about the poison, and they're already doing all that they can or should to help...' He spread his hands. 'Do they really need you any more? And now that Molly's gone and your mother and sister are settled in her house, do they really need you either?'

He *did* mean it. 'But I can't go to London with you,' Ivy stammered. 'I'm supposed to meet Jenny and Matt again in two days' time, and Molly's promised to ring and tell me...something important. And anyway, I can't fly.'

'Are you certain?'

'*Yes*,' Ivy said in frustration. 'I've tried everything. It's no use.'

'Then ride on my back, like you did before.' He took her hand.

'But I need your eyes, Ivy. I need your dreams. I need someone to help me know the truth when I find it. I don't want to do this alone.'

Ivy felt as though the Great Shaft had opened beneath her, and she was falling into it stomach-first. 'Martin, I'm sorry. I can't.'

He released her abruptly and stepped back, his jacket rasping the stones. 'What you really mean,' he said, 'is that you don't want to.'

'It's not that – I have responsibilities! There are people counting on me, people who care about me, and it wouldn't be right to—' She broke off, then added heavily, 'I'm not like you, Martin. I can't drop everything on a whim and run away.'

His expression turned icy. 'My apologies,' he said. 'I shouldn't have troubled you with my *whim*.'

Oh no. Had she really put it that way? 'I didn't mean—' she began, but Martin cut her off with a gesture.

'It doesn't matter; I understand. Your loyalties are with your own people, as they should be. Steady and constant as the earth itself.' He clapped a hand to his heart and bent in a cool mockery of a bow. 'Farewell, fair cruelty.'

'Martin, wait!' cried Ivy. 'I haven't told you –'

But he was already gone.

When Ivy woke the next morning she felt hollow inside, as though a cold wind were whistling through her bones. She'd never had the chance to tell Martin about her latest dream, and now he was gone – perhaps only for a few days, but it might also be weeks, or even forever. After all, what reason had she given him to come back?

She could only hope that in finding Walker and perhaps the rest of his fellow spriggans, Martin would also find rest from his wandering. Because if he knew what it felt like to have a home and a people, maybe he'd understand why Ivy had made the choice she had.

Resolving not to brood over it, Ivy threw herself into unpacking, organising and putting away her family's belongings with such determination that Marigold and Cicely soon retreated and left her to it. She worked hard all that day and slept that night without dreaming, and when Molly rang the following day with a triumphant report of her first day at school, she listened with as much interest as a friend should.

'So everything's all right, then?' Ivy asked, when Molly had run out of stories to tell her. 'You haven't had any more feelings of being watched?'

'Not a one,' Molly said. 'They went away as soon as I got here – maybe even sooner. I'll let you know if they ever come back... but I really don't think they will.'

Ivy was relieved to hear that the other girl was doing so well, and when their conversation ended she felt better than she had in a long time. Surely she'd done the right thing by staying here, and there was no need to wonder what else might have been.

Still, she couldn't bring herself to stop wearing the copper bracelet. It had turned cool with Martin's absence, but not uncomfortably so, and Ivy had grown so accustomed to having it around her wrist that she felt naked without it. But late that night as she lay listening to her sister's gentle snores, the metal suddenly flared hot enough to make her gasp, then turned icy cold. And when Ivy snatched off the bracelet, there was a red mark all around her wrist.

'What do you think it means?' she asked, sitting on the edge of her mother's bed as Marigold examined the burn. Ivy didn't expect her to heal it: only male faeries could do that particular kind of spell. But Marigold knew more about magic in general than she did.

'I'm not sure,' said Marigold. She picked up the bracelet and turned it over in her fingers. 'But if you hadn't told me Martin had put a spell on this, I'd never have guessed it had ever been magical at all. Where did it come from?'

Ivy hesitated. She hadn't told Marigold that she and Martin had found the treasure together, much less that he'd given her a half-share. 'I think it belonged to his family,' she said, as truthfully as she could.

Marigold went still. Then she set the bracelet down on the nightstand, out of Ivy's reach. 'I didn't realise you'd become so close.'

Ivy sighed. 'Mum, it's not…whatever you think it is. But Martin's done a lot to help me. All of us. If he's in trouble—'

'I doubt that,' Marigold said. 'I think it more likely that he broke the spell himself, so that no one could use your bracelet to find him.'

Or because he no longer trusted Ivy to watch his back. 'Maybe,' she said. 'But what if we're wrong, and he needs our help?'

'Martin can look after himself. He always has. But there are things I need to ask you, Ivy.' She smoothed the blankets over her knees, an oddly self-conscious gesture. 'You never told me how Martin escaped the Claybane. Was it your blood that freed him?'

'Yes,' said Ivy, 'but I—' She was about to say *I don't know why it worked*, but Marigold cut her off.

'And that week you spent away, before you came back to offer us Molly's cottage. Were you with Martin then?'

'Yes, but it wasn't like—'

'Oh, Ivy.' She sighed. 'I know what it's like. You believe he needs you, cares for you, that he would never willingly hurt you. But you wouldn't be the first to believe that. Or the first to be wrong.'

'What are you saying?'

Marigold put a hand over her eyes, as though even the light of Ivy's skin-glow was too much for her. 'He's an actor, Ivy,' she said. 'He can pretend to be anything he wishes, or thinks you want him to be. And I know you may find this hard to believe, but…he can also lie.'

'I know that,' Ivy said. 'He told me himself.'

Her mother looked startled, but she was quick to recover. 'Yes, but don't you see? If Martin can lie to other faeries, he can also lie to you. You can never trust him, because you can never know who he really is.'

Which was the same thing she'd said about spriggans. 'But you trusted him once,' Ivy said impatiently. 'You must have, or you wouldn't have sent him to the Delve to find me.'

'Only because I was desperate,' Marigold said. 'And I knew he would do as I asked him, because he owed me a great debt. I risked my own safety to hide him from his enemies, even though he had once betrayed me—'

'Betrayed *you*?' Ivy's resentment dissolved into shock. 'Why?'

'To save his own skin, of course.' Her mother's lips thinned bitterly. 'We were both fleeing from the Empress at the time – me to Cornwall, he to Wales. When our paths crossed on the way out of London, he made me believe I could trust him, and that we would be safer travelling together. But once the Empress's hunters caught up with us, he led them onto my trail so he could escape.'

Martin had confessed to being a liar, a spy and even a murderer, but he'd never told Ivy that. Probably because he knew how angry she would be if she found out. All the years Ivy had thought her mother dead, Marigold had been fighting to escape the Empress's power and get back to her family. And just when she finally got her chance, Martin had stolen it from her.

'And I wasn't the only one he betrayed,' Marigold said sadly. 'There was a faery girl named Rhosmari, not much older than you, who Martin promised to guide to safety – but instead he handed her straight over to the Empress. And one of the first things he did as the Empress's servant was to kill a helpless old man, a human, who didn't even know he had offended her.'

Ivy swallowed the sickness that had risen in her throat. Even though she had no doubt that her mother was telling the truth, part of her still wanted to protest that Martin had only acted in ignorance, or because he had no other choice. She knew him too well to believe him entirely selfish, or that he felt no remorse for the wicked things he'd done...

But what if she'd only ever seen what Martin wanted her to see? What if all his actions towards her, even the most seemingly noble and self-sacrificial ones, had been part of some cunning deception?

Marigold brushed a stray curl back from Ivy's face. 'I don't blame you for taking pity on him,' she said. 'You have a caring heart, and he knows all too well how to turn that to his advantage. He can make himself seem honest, sincere – even vulnerable, if need be. But he has no loyalty to anyone but himself, and his own freedom, his own desires, will always be more important to him than yours.' She cupped Ivy's chin in her hand. 'I know it's hard for you to believe right now, but you're better off without him. Let him go.'

Ivy closed her eyes, wrestling with her conscience. She'd misjudged Martin once, to her own shame, and she didn't want to make that mistake again. Yet even if she could be sure he hadn't meant to sever the link between them, what could she do? Without the finding spell on the bracelet, she had no way to track him. And he'd warned her, however teasingly, that if the bracelet went cold he was probably dead…

'You're right,' she said at last, though every word made her feel sick and heavy inside. 'I have work to do here, and people who need me. Martin can take care of himself.'

part two

The striving of birds to kill, or to save themselves from death, is beautiful to see. The greater the beauty, the more terrible the death.

– J. A. Baker, *The Peregrine*

fifteen

The last leaves of autumn had fallen, stripping the wood below the Delve into a skeletal tangle of wet grey trunks and crooked branches that offered little shelter from the November wind. Even the greenery that had once grown thick around the adit had died into sodden heaps of brown, and there were no birds or animals in sight.

Ivy crouched by the small fire she'd built inside the adit, feeding twigs into its crackling mouth. She was glad of the wool coat her mother had bought for her on their last trip to Truro, but in the chill damp of the tunnel, it hardly seemed warm enough. It was a good thing Martin had taught her how to make a campfire, or today's meeting with Matt and Jenny would be miserable indeed…

She sat back, absently turning the copper bracelet around her wrist. The burn it had given her was long healed, but the memories it brought back to her were still bittersweet, and she wondered if she would ever know what had become of her old companion. Had Thom Pendennis kept his word and led Martin to his fellow spriggans? Was Martin with his own people now, safe from Rob and the others who'd been pursuing him? Perhaps happiness was more than he deserved: certainly Marigold seemed to think so. But Ivy couldn't help hoping that he'd found a little peace at least.

She'd built the fire up into a discreet but cheering blaze, and was holding out her hands to its warmth, when Mattock's crunching steps sounded at the mouth of the adit. She rose, expecting to see Jenny behind him. But he was alone.

'Jenny's going to be late today,' he said, before Ivy could ask. He kicked a stone closer to the fire and sat down on it, blowing into his cold-numbed hands. 'She had an errand to run for Nettle, so she told me to go ahead.'

That was nothing unusual these days. Like so many of the older piskeys, Nettle lived deep in the Delve where the poison was thickest, and she'd grown too feeble to keep up with all her duties as the Joan's attendant. Over the past few weeks she'd been relying on Jenny's assistance more and more, which sometimes made it difficult for the piskey-girl to get away.

'Did she say whether she'd had the chance to copy out Yarrow's records?' Ivy asked.

'I doubt it,' said Mattock, taking off his flat miner's cap and pushing a weary hand through his hair. 'Between looking after her mum and the other aunties, she's not had much time to spend with the healer during the day. And after that business with Copper and his "little bit o' medicine", Yarrow's taken to locking up the infirmary whenever she isn't there.'

Ivy couldn't blame her. The stubborn old knocker had decided that if his cough hadn't gone away it was only because Yarrow was being stingy with her doses, so he'd marched into the healer's cave and helped himself to a whole bottle of her strongest remedy. His wife had found him unconscious on the floor of their cavern, and he'd nearly died.

'What about you?' she asked Matt. 'Did you get anywhere with Hew and Teasel?'

Matt grimaced. 'I thought it was a sure thing, when I overheard Hew grumbling to her about Betony. But when I got them alone and mentioned that I'd been having a few doubts about the Joan myself, they looked horrified and said I shouldn't talk that way. They've been avoiding me ever since.'

Ivy's heart sank. The older couple, who'd lost their only son when Betony refused to let a search party travel more than a half-day's journey from the Delve, had been their best hope yet of starting a resistance against her. But like all the other opportunities that they'd pursued, it had evaporated like a will-o'-the-wisp as soon as they tried to seize it. What would it take to make their fellow piskeys realise the danger they were in? Even with so many sick and weak among them, they still clung to their belief that their Joan knew what she was doing, and that they had nothing to fear.

'And Betony?' Ivy asked, without much hope. 'I suppose she's still as healthy as ever.'

'Of course.' Mattock picked up a stick from the woodpile and began whittling it with his hunter's knife. 'She's outside as often as not, these days – Gossan too, now that she's got him training the young hunters.'

'Well, could we use that? Ask people whether it doesn't seem unfair that the Joan and her consort can go above whenever they please – or at least point out how much healthier they are because of it?'

'I tried that,' said Matt, tossing a curl of wood shaving onto the fire. 'But you know what everyone thinks? The Joan and Jack have more magic than the rest of us, so of course they don't get sick. And the reason the Joan's been spending so much time on the surface is because she's looking for the spriggan that put a curse on us.'

Ivy let out a groan. Of course. Martin had escaped from the Delve, much to the Joan's displeasure; now that Gillian was dead, he was the obvious scapegoat for the piskeys' troubles. Maybe it was a good thing he'd disappeared before Betony could find him…

'Ivy?'

She looked up.

'I know you had a lot on your mind when you came back to the Delve last time,' Matt said, his blue eyes intent. 'And what with Gillian and…everything else, maybe you've forgotten. But do you remember—'

'I'm here!' Jenny popped up at the mouth of the tunnel, breathless and windblown. She hurried to the fire, hugging her rabbit-wool shawl about her, and Mattock stepped back to give her room. 'Ugh, it's cold out there,' she said. 'But wait until you hear what just happened.'

'What?' asked Ivy.

'Nettle's too sick to attend the Joan any more. So Betony's letting her go.'

The news shouldn't have surprised Ivy as much as it did. The old woman had been unwell for some time, after all. But Nettle had always had such a firm, no-nonsense air about her, with her bright black eyes and wits as sharp as her tongue, that she'd seemed practically immortal to Ivy.

'Do you think she's dying?' she asked.

'I don't know,' said Jenny. 'But Nettle seems to think so. Because when I was tidying up for her after lunch, she called me over and told me she'd had her eye on me for a long time now, especially since I started helping Yarrow in the healer's cave. And then she said...she'd like to mention me to the Joan.'

'Mention you?' Mattock dropped the stick he'd been holding. 'Jenny – you mean she wants you to take her place?'

Jenny gave a wavering smile. 'I think so.'

'But can she do that?' asked Ivy. 'Isn't it the Joan's right to choose her own attendant?'

'She can refuse Jenny if she wants,' Matt said, 'but Nettle's served too long and too well for Betony to ignore her dying wishes. It would be an insult, and people would wonder. Especially since any fool can see Jenny's a better choice than any of the other girls our age.'

He had a point. There were only two other unmarried

piskey girls in the Delve old enough to take on such a responsibility, and neither of them had anything like Jenny's reputation for hard work, unselfishness, and good common sense. There was just one problem, as far as Ivy could see.

'But if you're attending the Joan,' she said, 'then you'll have to stay by her all the time. You won't be able to meet with us any more.'

Jenny's smile faded. 'I know. That's the part that scares me. I'll have to be so careful. I don't think I'll be able to come outside any more at all.'

Mattock and Ivy looked at each other. Losing Jenny would be a blow, but it could also be a tremendous opportunity. And if Jenny refused Nettle's offer, it would look even more suspicious – after all, why wouldn't she want one of the most prestigious positions in the Delve?

'It's not so bad,' Matt said at last. 'If you have a message for Ivy, you can always send it through me. Besides, winter's coming soon, and then you won't want to be outside anyway.'

Jenny nodded, but the worry on her face remained. Ivy slipped her arm around the other girl's waist. 'There's nobody I would trust to do this more than you,' she said. 'Betony likes you, I think. More than she's ever liked me.'

'Oh, Ivy.' Jenny pressed her fingers against her eyes. 'That's only because I've never stood up to her, like you have. She might like me, but she doesn't respect me. Let alone fear me, like she fears you.'

Ivy gave a startled laugh. 'Fear me? I'm only one piskey-girl, half her size and with less than half her power. Why would Betony be afraid of me?'

'I don't know,' said Jenny. 'But I know she does, at least a little. If she didn't think you were a threat to her, she wouldn't have exiled you from the Delve.'

'So? She exiled my mother too.' And Marigold had been so timid back then, so uncertain and easily cowed, that she couldn't convince her own husband to take her seriously until it was too late. 'I think Betony just doesn't like people telling her things she doesn't want to hear.' Ivy stepped away, glancing at the low-burning fire. 'I should go. It's getting late, and Cicely's going to wonder where I am. When do you want to meet again?'

'This time tomorrow,' said Jenny. 'Nettle's going to talk to the Joan tonight, so I'll know by then if she's approved me or not.' She looked at Mattock. 'Will that be all right for you? I know Mica's expecting you to go to Redruth with him, but—'

'I'll deal with Mica,' said Mattock firmly. 'Tomorrow it is.'

As usual, Ivy waited until Jenny and Mattock had left the adit before willing herself back to the cottage – or rather, the barn, since that was where Cicely would expect her to be. For weeks her little sister had been begging to help look after Dodger, promising to clean out his box every morning and make sure he was groomed and fed. But Ivy preferred to work in the barn alone, glad for the excuse it gave her to slip away without her family wondering where she'd got to.

So once she'd landed in front of Dodger's box, she headed for the barn door without a second thought. But then Cicely spoke up behind her:

'Where did you go?'

Ivy spun around. Her sister stood there with flushed cheeks and accusing eyes, the phone receiver clutched in one hand.

'Molly rang a few minutes ago,' she said. 'And I came out to bring you the phone, only I couldn't find you and you didn't answer when I shouted, so I told her to ring later. But then you just popped out of nowhere, and *where have you been?*'

'Not far,' replied Ivy, her mind scrambling for how to answer without rousing Cicely's suspicions. The last time her little sister had guessed Ivy was sneaking off without her and decided to investigate, the results had been disastrous. She paused, then went on in a kinder, almost pitying tone, 'I'm sorry you were frightened. I only meant to be away a little while, and I thought you were old enough not to worry.'

Colour flooded back into Cicely's face. 'I wasn't scared!' she said hotly. 'And I am old enough. But you could have told me you'd learned that – that jumping thing.' She folded her arms. 'It's not fair. Mum said I couldn't try it until I was older. But she lets you do anything you want.'

'That's because I *am* older,' said Ivy, relieved that her sister had taken the bait. It was as devious a trick as Martin had ever played, and she was half-ashamed of herself for doing it. But at least she'd distracted Cicely from asking any more questions. 'Did Molly say when she'd ring back?'

'Later,' Cicely said resentfully. 'I don't know when. And Mum said to tell you she'll be late tonight, so we should have dinner without her.'

Again? Ivy thought as she walked out into the yard, Cicely hurrying after her. A cold drizzle was falling on the cobbles, and the sky above was the colour of old tin. A jackdaw perched on the corner of the roof, regarding them with bright black eyes.

'Mum's been working a lot lately,' Ivy said as they came up to the front door. 'Some days it seems like she's hardly home at all.'

Cicely opened her mouth to reply, and her face crumpled. She plunged past Ivy into the house and fled down the corridor, sobbing.

Ivy unlaced her boots and hung up her coat, giving her sister time to calm herself. Then she walked into their room and sat down on the edge of the bed. 'What did I do wrong?'

Cicely's answer came thickly, muffled by the pillow. 'It's not you. It's only—' She turned over, rubbing her eyes. 'I know I shouldn't have been listening, but nobody ever tells me anything, and I'm tired of being treated like a baby. And now we're going to lose the cottage.'

'What?' Ivy was startled. 'Why?'

In halting words Cicely spilled out her story: a few days ago, their mother had taken a call from her human friend Serita, the owner of the Rising Star Dance and Theatre Academy where Marigold worked. She'd gone into the study and shut the door, but Cicely had crept up and listened at the keyhole – which was when she found out that Serita had recovered from her long illness, and was coming back to teach at the school again.

'And that means she won't need Mum any more,' said Cicely, 'or at least not nearly as often. We've used up all the money Martin left us – I know, because I looked – and when I asked Mum if he was coming back, she said she didn't think so. Oh, Ivy, what are we going to do?'

Ivy heaved an inward sigh. Cicely had always been fretful and prone to worry, but back in the Delve she'd at least had her chores and her friends to keep her distracted. Since they'd come to live in the cottage, however, she'd had little of either. There were no children nearby for her to play with, and after one of the neighbours had asked why she wasn't at school, she'd become nervous about leaving the cottage alone. No wonder even the smallest troubles seemed so large to her, when she had nothing else to think about.

'Cicely, there's no reason to be anxious,' she said. 'Mum's been in the human world long enough to know how it works, and she can find another job if she needs to. I'm sure Mr Menadue will understand—'

'He won't,' wailed Cicely. 'I know he won't, he doesn't at all, because last night he rang and Mum talked to him for *ages*, and I heard her saying "Be patient with me, give me more time," and when she came out of the study, her eyes were all red. And you saw what she was like this morning.'

Marigold had seemed preoccupied, true. She'd put the milk in the cupboard and the sugar in the refrigerator, and then gone for a long walk without inviting either of the girls to come. And she'd looked paler than usual, as well. Perhaps she'd just slept poorly, but…what if Cicely was right?

She would have liked to believe Molly's father could never be so unkind. But when she thought back, he'd called at least twice in the past few weeks, and the one time Ivy had answered he'd asked her a number of pointed questions about how Dodger was doing, as well as whether the house was still in good repair and everything was still working correctly. If he didn't trust them to take care of his property and they couldn't pay the rent on time, he might decide to sell the place instead…

Ivy straightened in determination. She wouldn't let it come to that, not when she had the power to stop it.

'Don't worry,' she told Cicely. 'If money's what we need, I know where to get some. Just give me a few days, and you'll see.'

When Marigold returned to the cottage that evening, Ivy studied her mother's face closely for signs of strain. She seemed tired and distracted, but after four hours of teaching dance classes, that was nothing unusual. Still, even if Cicely was wrong about the cottage, they'd need more money soon. Ivy waited until Cicely was asleep and Marigold had retired to her bedroom, then took an old rucksack Molly had left in one of the cupboards and willed herself to the carn.

An icy wind raced across the hilltop, nipping at Ivy's cheeks and tossing her hair in all directions. The clouds had fled before it, and now a thousand stars glittered like gemstones in the black vault of the sky. Ivy gazed up at the moon, coin-round and swollen with power – and a faint, almost forgotten hope stirred inside her. She dropped the rucksack and climbed up the rocks to the carn's summit, shivering with anticipation.

Make me a peregrine, she pleaded silently. *Let me fly.* Then she spread her arms, leaped onto the wind—

And tumbled to the base of the rocks in her own shape, wingless as she'd been before.

For a moment Ivy lay there winded and gasping, clutching her bruised elbow against her chest. Then she picked herself up and limped over to the carn.

Unsurprisingly, it still refused to open to her touch. But Ivy had her own way of getting inside – or hoped she did. She closed her eyes, forming a picture of the carn's interior in her mind. Then she willed herself into it.

She'd never tried to travel such a short distance before, let alone into a confined space, and she'd been half-afraid of bouncing right back to the hillside again. But the wind died at once, and when she opened her eyes there were stone walls all around her and a rectangle of darkness at her feet. Ivy kindled her skin-glow, pushing up her sleeves to let the light radiate from her arms and hands. Then she picked her way down the stairs to the treasure chamber – and stopped dead.

The Grey Man's hoard had been ransacked.

A few coins lay scattered across the floor. The bulkier armour and pieces of jewellery had been tossed in a heap to one side of the crock, weapons piled up like so much rubbish on the other. And the crock that had once overflowed with necklaces, brooches, and other small items was now less than half full.

Ivy paced around the room, her mind churning. If she hadn't known better, she might have thought some greedy stranger had done this. Yet what thief would leave so much of the treasure behind? Whoever had done this had been in a tearing hurry, and taken as much as he could…but he hadn't touched Ivy's share.

A tide of relief flowed over her. So Martin was still alive – and he hadn't forgotten her, either.

Yet it wasn't like Martin to be so careless, especially with treasure. What could have driven him to raid the hoard so ruthlessly? He'd hinted that Thom might expect some reward for leading him to Walker, but surely not even the greediest human would demand so high a price…

Well, whatever the answer, she wouldn't find it here. The night was getting colder, and if she didn't get back to the cottage soon, Cicely might notice her missing. Ivy flexed her bruised elbow, wincing at its stiffness. Then she opened her rucksack, and began scooping treasure into it.

She'd taken as much as she could comfortably carry, and was turning to leave, when her toe bumped the short sword she'd admired before. Ivy stooped and picked it up. It was too big to fit in her pack, and too awkward to easily sell…but perhaps it wouldn't hurt to keep just one thing for herself? Carefully Ivy buckled it at her side, and walked in a circle to make sure she wouldn't trip over it. Then she swung the pack onto her shoulders, and headed up to the surface.

She had more than enough treasure to pay her family's debts. Now all she needed was someone to buy it.

*

When Ivy came to the adit the following day Mattock was already inside, building the fire. She crunched through the debris and sat down next to him, putting her hand over her mouth to stifle a yawn. By the time she'd hidden the rucksack in the rafters of the barn and crept back to the room she shared with Cicely, it had been nearly midnight – and after that she'd lain awake for another two hours, too full of nervous excitement to settle. She hadn't had a single spriggan dream since the night Martin left her, but she hadn't slept half so soundly since then, either.

'Jenny'll be here soon,' said Matt, rummaging in his pocket for tinder and flint. 'Or at least she ought to be. She's been down in the Silverlode all morning.'

The Silverlode was the lowest and most spacious tunnel in the Delve, with the washing-cisterns and Market Cavern at one end, and the Joan's stateroom and private chambers at the other. So there were any number of reasons Jenny might need to go there – but after what she'd told them yesterday, Ivy doubted she was buying vegetables or scrubbing laundry. She could only hope that her meeting with Betony had gone well.

'Can I ask you something?' she said, watching wood shavings curl and blacken in the heat of the newly lit flames.

Matt's body tensed. 'What is it?'

'When we – I mean, we piskeys – need money to buy things from the humans, we sell some of our ore and gemstones to a buyer in Redruth. Someone we trust to handle our business secretly, and not ask too many questions. Isn't that right?'

186

Matt relaxed and sat back. 'That's right. We've been dealing with the same family for nearly a hundred years.'

'So who are they?' asked Ivy.

'The only one I know is Ralph Pendennis,' said Mattock. 'His great-great-grandfather was a miner who made a bargain with the knockers, and as the oldest son of the family, he's the one responsible for upholding it. He keeps a little gem and mineral shop in town. Why?'

Pendennis – the same last name as Martin's dealer in London. That couldn't be a coincidence, surely…but Mattock was waiting for her answer, and Ivy had no time to waste thinking about it.

'I have some coins and jewellery to sell,' she said. 'My mum needs money, and this is the only way I know to get it. So I was wondering if you'd come to Redruth with me, and help me talk to this dealer.'

Mattock looked pained. 'Ivy…'

'I know,' Ivy said quickly. 'We'd be gone for hours, and if you go off without Mica he's bound to wonder where you've got to.'

'It's not that. Mica spends most of his time in the diggings now anyway, so he probably wouldn't even notice.' Mattock sat up and poked the fire, sending up a flurry of sparks. 'But I've already gone to Ralph's shop once this month, and I'm not sure—'

'Ivy?'

The dry brush rustled, and Jenny scrambled into the tunnel. Her eyes looked wild, unnaturally huge and dark, and beneath her woollen shawl she was shivering.

'Jenny!' Ivy jumped up. 'What happened? Are you all right?'

The piskey-girl gave a distracted nod. She allowed Ivy to guide her closer to the fire, but she did not sit down.

'I've just come from seeing Nettle,' she said. 'I went to tell her Betony had accepted me as her new attendant, and—' She swallowed. 'She *knows*, Ivy. She knows I've been seeing you.'

Ivy had thought she was cold already, but Jenny's words froze her to the marrow. If Nettle, the Joan's most trusted servant, had guessed that Jenny and Ivy were meeting in secret…how long would it be before Betony knew as well?

'But she says that's our business, not hers,' Jenny went on. 'All she wanted was for me to give you a message. She says…' She let out a shaky laugh. 'She wants to see you. That her last wish, before she dies, is to talk to you again.'

sixteen

Ivy stared at Jenny, unable to believe what she'd just heard. No matter what everyone else thought, Nettle of all people must know that Betony had declared Ivy a traitor and banished her from the Delve. If Ivy were caught sneaking back into the mine, she could be arrested, imprisoned – even executed. What could the old woman have to say to her that could possibly be worth such a risk?

'I thought at first Nettle was asking me to bring her to you,' Jenny went on, 'but she said no, you have to come down. I told her you couldn't possibly, but she said it wouldn't be the first time you'd disobeyed your aunt when you thought it was important enough. And, well' – she gave Ivy an apologetic look – 'she's right, isn't she?'

Ivy edged closer to the fire, but she still felt cold. Part of her longed to do as Nettle was asking, if only to see the Delve again. But if she went back into the mine, it wouldn't just be her own life she was risking. Jenny, Mattock, Nettle herself – all of them would be at Betony's mercy, if anything went wrong.

Yet she wasn't bound by any oath that would keep her from answering Nettle's summons. And the old woman was no fool: she wouldn't make such a request of Ivy unless it was vitally important.

'All right,' she said at last. 'I'll do it.'

'I don't like this,' muttered Mattock as he strode up the slope to the Delve, Ivy following invisibly at his heels. Jenny had already gone ahead of them, fluttering down the Great Shaft to tell Nettle that Ivy was coming. 'What if it's some trick of the Joan's, to give her an excuse to arrest you? Nettle's been loyal to her all these years – it doesn't make any sense that she'd turn against Betony now.'

'I don't like it either,' said Ivy, 'but I trust Nettle. I'm sure she wouldn't betray me.'

'Why?'

Because I know what she is, thought Ivy, but she could hardly say that to Mattock. Still, the knowledge that the Joan's attendant was a pure-blooded faery like her own mother, taken captive at a young age and raised up as a piskey-woman, gave her confidence. Nettle had spent a lifetime hiding her true nature, so she wouldn't do anything that might tempt Ivy to give that secret away. Especially since Ivy also knew that Nettle was Gillian Menadue's long-lost sister, and that her abduction by the piskeys was one of the reasons Gillian had been so bent on seeking vengeance.

'I can't say exactly why,' Ivy said at last, 'but I have good reasons. If you can get me safely to Nettle's quarters and back, we'll be all right.'

Mattock sighed, but made no further protest. He ducked into the bristling thicket of gorse that hid the Delve's nearest entrance from view, and kindled his skin-glow to light their way into the Earthenbore. This baked-clay tunnel was the hunters' traditional route in and out of the Delve, and every sound they made echoed through its labyrinth of entrances and exits. So Ivy had to tread lightly – and Matt extra-heavily – to make sure no one would hear her.

Soon, however, they left the Earthenbore behind and descended the Hunter's Stair into the Narrows, a thin, sloping passage with smooth granite walls and a pebbled floor. Ivy had passed this way many times, and her chest started to ache with memory. Right around the corner was the chamber where they kept the chickens, with its soft day-lamps and honeycombed roof for ventilation. A few steps to the left lay the Upper Rise, covered in bright mosaics of plants and animals to help the piskey-children with their learning. And beyond that stretched the tunnel that had once been Ivy's favourite, with its sky-coloured tiles of china clay. Even creeping behind Mattock with his skin-glow her only light, the Delve looked more beautiful to Ivy than ever before.

But it wasn't merely craftsmanship that made the Delve special; it was the piskey folk who lived there. Yes, they'd been warlike and ruthless once, but they'd raised their children and grandchildren in peace. And as they walked into Long Way, the door-lined stretch of granite where Ivy's home cavern used to be,

191

her senses wakened and her heart beat faster with the hope of seeing just one familiar neighbourly face. Perhaps it would be Quartz, Jenny's scamp of a younger brother, jumping up to surprise them with his gap-toothed grin. Or Mattock's mother Fern, rosy-cheeked from hauling her laundry basket up the stairs…

'Matt! There you are.'

Oh no. Mica. Instinctively Ivy flattened herself against the wall, willing her invisibility glamour not to falter as her brother strode up the corridor towards them.

'Where've you been, anyway?' Mica asked, pushing the cavern door wide and holding it, so Mattock could go in. 'Seems like half the time I come looking for you these days, you're off somewhere mysterious. If this keeps up, you're going to have to tell me who you're courting.' He lowered his voice in mock menace. 'And it had better not be Jenny.'

'Not on your life,' said Matt, with a feeble attempt at a smile. 'But I've…got something to look after just now, and I'm in a hurry. I'll stop by later, all right?'

The humour in Mica's face faded, and a pang went through Ivy as she realised how much he looked like their father. Not just the broad handsome bones or the dark brush of hair across his brow, but the deep lines about his eyes and mouth that made him seem older than his years. How much time had he been spending down in the diggings?

'Is that so?' he asked flatly. 'What would you say if I decided to come with you, and see what this *business* of yours is about?'

The two boys stared each other down, and Ivy bit her lip. Mica was a hunter, trained to detect any unusual sound or movement. If he insisted on accompanying them even a short distance, it wouldn't take him long to sense that Ivy was there. What were they going to do?

She was on the verge of shrinking herself tiny and creeping into a crack somewhere when Mattock put his hand on Mica's shoulder.

'I'd say that friends ought to trust one another,' he said quietly. 'And that not every secret I keep is mine to share, even with you.'

If Ivy had said anything like that to Mica, he'd have scoffed at her. But faced with Matt's gentle reproach, her brother deflated. He nodded slowly, all the fight gone out of him. Then he went back into the cavern and shut the door.

As Ivy followed Mattock through the Delve the tunnels grew busier, and she spotted more and more people she knew. A knot of piskey-children sat by the gem-studded entrance to the Treasure Cavern, playing with dolls and tin soldiers. As they walked through Potters' End they met Hew and a couple of the other knockers trudging up from the diggings. And when they came down the steps to the Silverlode there were piskeys of all ages scattered about, from the old uncle drowsing on a bench outside the Market Cavern to the young hunters arguing over a game of dice.

It was all much as Ivy remembered, except for two things. One was the bitter, sulphurous taste to the air – she'd barely noticed it when they first came in, but now it was strong enough to make her lungs constrict in protest. The other was how sickly everyone looked, especially the women. They still smiled and laughed, but it looked like a brave effort: their faces sagged beneath the dark hollows of their eyes, and they coughed almost as often as they spoke.

Anger kindled inside Ivy, and she clenched her invisible fists. How could Betony ask her people to endure such suffering, and tell them it was all for their own good? What would it take to shake her from her complacency, and make her understand the evil she'd done?

A distant bell announced the closing of the Market, and the uncle on the bench groped for his cane. Nodding to his fellow hunters, Mattock skirted the dice game and set off along the Silverlode, Ivy a shadow at his heels. They passed the Market Cavern, turned down Elders' Way – and there was Jenny, frantically beckoning them into Nettle's quarters.

'What took you so long?' she whispered as she shut the door behind them. 'I was about to come looking for you.'

'Mica,' said Mattock, and Jenny's mouth framed a silent, sad *oh*. Then she looked around and asked, 'Ivy?'

'I'm here,' Ivy said, turning visible. 'Where's Nettle?'

Jenny led them across the small, stuffy-smelling cavern, drawing aside the curtain to the even more modest chamber beyond. There in her bed-alcove lay the old woman, curled motionless with her back to them and the covers pulled high about her. But when Jenny stooped over the bed and said, 'Nettle,

Ivy's here,' she stirred and struggled upright – and the blankets fell away to expose the wings crumpled against her back.

If Jenny was shocked, she didn't show it. But Matt made a choking noise, and Ivy didn't have to ask why. Like Marigold when she lived in the Delve, Nettle had spent her life using a glamour to change the translucent, fragile-looking faery wings she'd been born with into the broad, moth-like wings of a piskey. But now that she was too ill to keep up the illusion, it was obvious what she truly was.

'Ivy-lass,' Nettle croaked. 'Ah, but it's that good to see you again.' She gripped Ivy's hand with her gnarled, papery one. 'I knew you'd come.'

Growing up, Ivy had never been close to Nettle: she'd found the Joan's attendant almost as daunting as Betony herself. But that was before she'd learned of Nettle's faery origins, or her relationship to Gillian and Molly. And seeing the old woman now with yellowed skin and sunken cheeks, all her protective illusions stripped away – it struck her as deeply, painfully wrong. Even faeries had to die some time, but no one should have to die like this.

'What can I do?' she asked softly. 'How can I help you?'

Nettle sniffed. 'I've no need of fussing. I called you here to—' Then her eyes focused on Mattock, and she said sharply, 'Eh, lad, what are you gawping about? Get away with you.'

'It's all right,' said Jenny. 'He's with us. He brought Ivy down from the surface.'

'Any fool can tell *that*,' Nettle shot back. 'Why he's still

195

dandling after her like a lovesick goose is what I'd like to know.'
She raised her voice again. 'The Joan banished Ivy for a reason,
my lad: she's not going to pardon her for the likes of you. She's
more likely to throw you out of the Delve after her, if she doesn't
hang you first.'

Matt's face turned redder than his hair, but he didn't move.
'I've my own reasons for being here,' he said, 'and with respect,
Auntie, you don't know me as well as you think.'

'Hmph,' said Nettle. 'I knew your father, lad, and you're as
like him as no matter. Soft heart, hard head – they'll both be the
death of you, if you aren't careful.' She leaned closer to Ivy.
'Though you could do worse,' she added in a cracked whisper, 'if
you don't mind thinking for two.'

Matt threw up his hands and stalked out, letting the door-
curtain fall behind him. Ivy's cheeks were burning, as much for
his sake as her own – even if what Nettle had said was true,
which she doubted, it wasn't fair to humiliate Mattock that way.
But the old woman looked more satisfied than sorry.

'That's got rid of him,' she said, and patted the bed beside her.
Cautiously, Ivy sat down. 'Look, my girl, I served your aunt for
nigh on fourteen years, and the Joan before her for sixty. The
Delve is my home, and faery-born or no, I'm as true a piskey as
ever was. You know that.'

Ivy nodded – though she still wondered how Nettle could have
forgiven the piskeys who'd stolen her from her wyld and killed
the rest of her family, let alone chosen to stand with them against
her own sister. When Gillian attacked the Delve, it could have

been the perfect chance for Nettle to avenge herself on her captors, escape to the outside world and reclaim all her lost youth and beauty. But if there'd been any doubt of the old woman's loyalties, her refusal to leave the Joan's side had made them plain enough.

'So what I'm about to say to you, Ivy-lass, you know I don't say lightly.' Nettle let out a rattling sigh. 'Your aunt Betony's not right in her mind. And if you don't stop her, she'll do a terrible thing.'

Jenny clapped her hands over her mouth. Ivy felt stunned herself – if even Nettle dared to speak against Betony, the Joan must be mad indeed. 'What is it?' she asked.

'She wouldn't say whether she means to kill the girl or not,' Nettle said. 'But to her mind, the Delve will never be safe until we piskeys are the only ones who know of it. And even with poor Gillyflower dead and buried, that's not enough for her…'

Ivy's mouth went dry. 'Molly,' she whispered. 'She's after Molly.'

It was so obvious now, she could only curse herself for not having seen it before. Molly's feeling of being watched by unfriendly eyes, Matt's remark that Betony had been spending more time than ever outside the Delve…

'Aye,' said Nettle heavily. 'Molly's a brave girl, a good girl. If she hadn't given her own sweet blood to break the Claybane, your Mattock and our Jack and even the Joan herself wouldn't be with us now. But my lady can't see it. All she sees is that Gillian's daughter knows where to find us, and she's sure she'll come back and destroy us all one day. She's tried every scheme and spell she could think of to hunt Molly down, and it's driving her nigh wild that she still hasn't found her.'

Ivy could guess why she hadn't: the protective charms Gillian had laid about the cottage had shielded Molly as long as she lived there, and for the past two months she'd been at school in Hampshire. No wonder the Joan was frustrated.

'I've done all I could to keep Molly safe without the Joan knowing it – laid false trails aplenty to throw her off the scent. But I'm too weak for spells now, and my lady won't give up, she's that stubborn.' Nettle's hand tightened on Ivy's, imploring. 'That's why you've got to stop her, before she finds Molly and does her a harm—'

'It's all right,' Ivy said, before the old woman could become more agitated. 'Molly's safe. She's far away from here, right outside Kernow, where Betony can't touch her.'

Nettle's rheumy eyes widened. 'You're sure of that? Sure and no mistake?'

'Absolutely sure. And I've sworn to do everything I can to keep Molly out of danger, from Betony or anyone else. You don't need to worry.'

'Ah.' Nettle sagged back against the pillows. 'Thank the Gardener.' Her hand slackened, falling away from Ivy's, and she closed her eyes.

'I don't understand,' said Jenny in hushed tones, as Ivy climbed off the bed. 'Why is Nettle so worried about a human girl? And who is this *Gillyflower* she was talking about?'

'I'm resting, not dead,' Nettle spoke up crisply from the alcove. 'Or deaf, either. Use your eyes, Jenny-girl. I was born a faery, outside the Delve, and Gillyflower – her you call Gillian – was my sister. Which makes Molly my niece, and all that's left of my blood. But I've not told the Joan that, and don't you go telling her either.'

Jenny nodded, but her expression was troubled, and Ivy could understand why. After a lifetime of being taught that faeries were cunning, malicious creatures only slightly less dangerous than spriggans, it was a shock to realise that one of them had been living in the Delve all along, and that nobody had known the difference.

'And speaking of faery folk,' added Nettle, her shrewd black eyes fixing on Ivy, 'how's Marigold?'

Ivy closed her eyes, not wanting to see the dismay on Jenny's face. She hadn't meant to hide the truth from her friends, but their meetings had always been so rushed, and she'd never found the right time to explain. 'She's fine,' she replied bitterly. 'But if you want people to keep your secrets, Nettle, it's not very fair of you to go around telling theirs.'

'Ivy?' Jenny sounded shaken. 'What are you saying? You mean your mother…'

'I'm sorry I didn't tell you before,' Ivy said. 'It's not that I didn't trust you, but I—'

'Never mind that,' interrupted Nettle. 'Jenny's got sense enough to work it out for herself, or she's not the girl I took her for.' She pushed herself up against the pillows. 'But you two had best watch yourselves, and that lad of yours as well. I've done my best to keep the Joan from noticing what you've been up to, and she's been distracted fretting about that Molly business in any case. But all this creeping about asking people how they're feeling and if they think there might be something amiss in the Delve won't end well for you, any more than it did for Marigold.'

'But what else can we do?' Ivy asked. 'When I tried to warn Aunt Betony about the poison, she wouldn't listen. And there's no way the three of us can stand up to her alone.' If it still *was* the three of them, after this.

'Then you'd best bide your time until you find somebody who *can* stand up to her,' said Nettle with asperity. 'But you can't go poking a bees' nest and expect not to get stung.' She pointed a shaky claw at Jenny. 'I've done my best to give you youngsters a chance. Don't go wasting it on foolishness.'

Ivy was about to reply, but the sound of running footsteps and a rattle of curtain-rings distracted her. Matt stood panting in the archway, his eyes wild.

'Betony's coming,' he said. 'She's halfway down the Silverlode already. Ivy, we have to get out of here!'

There was no time to lose. Ivy gripped Nettle's hand, cast a last pleading look at Jenny, then dashed out the door after him.

'It's a good thing you decided to stand guard,' said Ivy in an undertone as she and Mattock crouched at the far end of the passage, shielded by the invisibility charm she'd cast over them. Betony had come striding into Elders' Way mere seconds after the two of them had whisked out of sight, and now she stood before Nettle's door with one foot tapping, waiting for Jenny to answer.

Her aunt hadn't changed at all, at least not that Ivy could see: her dark hair fell thick and smooth to her shoulders, and her skin was only lightly creased by age. She had the same striking bones as Ivy's father and Mica, and her cream-dappled wings were almost as lovely as Jenny's. But her eyes were as cold as the bottom of the Great Shaft, her posture so stiff that she might have been carved from granite. It was hard to imagine what Gossan had ever seen in a woman so harsh and unyielding – yet there he stood behind her, as always.

'Knock again,' he suggested in his deep, mild voice. 'She may be alone, and unable to hear you.'

'I think not,' Betony replied. 'I saw Jenny come this way – ah, here we are.' The door had opened and Jenny appeared, holding out her skirts in a curtsey.

'I'm sorry to have kept you waiting, my lady,' she said. 'I was helping Nettle into her chair. Please, come in.'

And no doubt Nettle had been giving her some last-minute advice, as well. Ivy waited until the cavern door had shut, then tugged Mattock's sleeve and they slipped out of the corridor together.

Getting out of the Delve ought to have been easier than getting in, since by this time many of the piskeys had retreated to the privacy of their caverns and the main passages were all but empty. But though Mattock set an easy pace, Ivy found it hard to keep up with him: her head started pounding before they'd even climbed out of the Silverlode, and by the time they passed the Treasure Cavern it was a constant struggle not to cough. It was a relief when they came out onto the surface, and she could turn visible and breathe fresh air again.

'Are you all right?' Matt asked her.

'I didn't realise – how bad it was – until we started climbing,' Ivy panted, her hands on her knees. 'The air in the Delve's gotten worse since I was here last time. A lot worse.' She exhaled, then straightened up again. 'Anyway. You'd better get back to Mica, before he gets suspicious.'

He took a step back, watching her. 'Are you sure?'

'Yes. But if it's not too much to ask,' she added before he could disappear, 'would you think about what I said before? About helping me find that dealer – Ralph Pendennis?'

Mattock shook his head. Ivy's heart sank – until she saw one corner of his mouth lift in a tiny smile.

'No need to think about it,' he said. 'You heard Nettle: it's your job to do the thinking for both of us. If you don't mind, that is.'

Blood leaped into Ivy's cheeks. 'I don't believe that,' she said. 'Or anything else she said about you. I know you're not – I mean, she was just trying to embarrass you into leaving.'

And part of her was still annoyed at Nettle for that. Mattock had always been such a good friend to her, better than her own brother; it wasn't fair to dismiss his loyalty as some silly infatuation, even if she'd thought it was possible for him to feel that way.

'I'd be glad of your help,' she went on, 'but if you think it's too risky to go together, I'm sure I can manage.'

Matt stopped her with a hand on her shoulder. 'I'm sure you can, too,' he said. 'But there's no reason you should have to. Give me a couple of days, and I'll come to Redruth with you.'

seventeen

The sky was darkening by the time Ivy returned home, and she knew it must be well after tea. Fortunately, Marigold had taken Cicely to Truro with her for the afternoon, and with any luck they wouldn't be back for some time yet...

But she'd barely unlocked the front door before her mother opened it. 'Where have you been?' she asked.

Ivy's mind went blank. She couldn't tell Marigold the truth: her mother knew Betony's ruthlessness too well, and it would only distress her to know that Ivy had dared to go against the Joan's command. And if she found out about her conspiracy with Jenny and Mattock, she might try to stop her going back to the Delve for her own safety. That was a risk Ivy couldn't take.

'I wasn't out looking for Martin, if that's what you're wondering,' she said.

'I'm glad to hear it.' Marigold closed the door behind her as Ivy hung up her coat. 'But Cicely tells me this isn't the first time you've disappeared and not told anyone where you were going.

What have we done to make you feel you can't trust us?'

'I do trust you,' Ivy said slowly, buying herself time to think. 'But it's…awkward, and I wasn't sure how you'd react if you knew.'

Could she do this? The answer that had come to her wasn't a lie in fact, but it was certainly one in intent. Yet she had to satisfy Marigold somehow, and if this kept her from wondering what Ivy was up to, it would be worth it. She looked up, and met her mother's gaze.

'Mum,' she said. 'I've learned how to take bird-shape.'

Emotions chased each other across Marigold's face: shock, disbelief, confusion. It was exactly as Jenny must have looked when she realised that Ivy was half-faery, and a sudden dread that she might lose them both clutched at Ivy's insides. It was painfully hard to stand still, watching tears well up in her mother's eyes, and not run away.

'My own daughter,' Marigold whispered. 'I never imagined…' Then, to Ivy's astonishment, she pulled her into an embrace. 'I'm so proud of you!'

Ivy ducked her head, afire with shame. She'd told the truth in the most deceptive possible way – she didn't deserve to be praised for it. 'Martin taught me to turn myself into a swift, when I was still back in the Delve,' she mumbled. 'So we could fly to see you.'

'No wonder you were travelling together,' said her mother, releasing Ivy to arm's length and smiling at her. 'I couldn't imagine how you'd become so attached to him, or why he'd take such a risk for someone who could only slow him down, unless…'

She gave a little laugh. 'Well, now I see how foolish I was. Can you show me?'

She moved to the door, but Ivy hung back. 'I can't,' she said. 'It's not safe to be a swift at this time of year.' And besides, it had been so long that she wasn't even sure she could do it any more. 'I've been trying to learn falcon-shape instead...but it's harder than I thought.'

Marigold's face cleared, and Ivy knew she understood – or thought she did. 'So you've been practising where no one would see you,' she said. 'Oh, Ivy. If I'd only known!'

'Then...it's all right if I go off by myself sometimes?' She hated herself for asking, but she had to be sure. Especially with Matt taking her to Redruth in two days' time.

'Of course,' said Marigold. She glanced back at the corridor, then added in a hush, 'But I think it would be best to keep this between ourselves. Cicely's going through a difficult time right now, and she might not take it well.'

No, she certainly wouldn't. First she'd be outraged that Ivy hadn't told her, then she'd sulk because Ivy got to do *everything* and it wasn't *fair*, and then she'd pester Ivy to teach her bird-shape as well. And Ivy didn't have time for any of that right now.

'I agree,' she said, forcing a smile. 'It'll be our secret.'

Ivy spent most of the following day with Cicely, as much to ease her conscience as anything else – though when Ivy told her she could take care of Dodger from now on, the delight on her little sister's face only made her feel worse for not giving her the chance before. Looking after the horse would be a good distraction from her worries, or so Ivy hoped.

But when she climbed into bed that night and found Cicely still awake, she knew with sinking certainty what her sister was about to ask. 'Did you get the money yet?'

'I'm working on it,' said Ivy. 'Soon. Maybe tomorrow.'

'Are you going to sell that treasure you hid in the barn?'

Ivy sat up, aghast. 'Cicely!'

'I couldn't help it,' her sister pleaded. 'I saw something sticking out between the rafters and I had to know what it was.'

Well, at least she hadn't found the sword – Ivy had hidden that beneath the wardrobe, where even Cicely wouldn't be likely to notice it. 'All right then, yes,' she said. 'Martin and I found the treasure together, so he gave me a half-share. But Mum doesn't know about it yet, so don't say anything.'

Cicely nodded, satisfied. She wriggled down beneath the coverlet, and soon was quiet.

But even knowing that her sister would be happy to let her leave the cottage tomorrow, Ivy had an uneasy feeling there was something, or someone, she'd overlooked. Not Marigold: she'd just assume that Ivy was off learning falcon-shape. Not Mattock either: he'd promised to take her to Redruth, and it wouldn't be like him to break his word. She had the treasure already, so there was no difficulty there...

So what could she have forgotten? Ivy was still puzzling over it when she fell asleep.

*

As soon as Ivy arrived at her rendezvous with Mattock the next day, she knew something was wrong. It was all there in the slump of his shoulders, his downcast eyes. She gripped the straps of her rucksack and opened her mouth to ask – but he spoke first.

'Nettle died last night,' he said. 'We buried her this morning.'

Ivy looked at the rock-littered floor of the adit, a painful tightness in her throat. She hadn't even said a proper goodbye. 'Did anyone…notice?' she asked, knowing Matt would understand what she meant.

He shook his head. 'She made Jenny promise to wrap her up so no one could see her wings. She wanted to be buried as a piskey.'

'She *was* a piskey,' Ivy burst out angrily. 'In every way that matters. Nettle was honest and hard-working and loyal, and she loved the Delve. She shouldn't have had to hide what she was to get the respect she deserved.'

'You're right,' Mattock said. 'She shouldn't. And neither should you.'

Ivy stopped breathing.

'Mica told me, when he was drunk,' he said, stepping closer. 'I've known all along. I just figured you'd say something when you were ready.'

'But…when you saw Nettle, you were shocked. You—'

'Well, of course I was shocked. I never expected *her* to be a faery.' He took her hand, reassuring. 'But when I thought some more, it made sense. There's a story the hunters tell about a time when there weren't enough piskey-women to go around, so the knockers went hunting for faery brides. I used to think it was just

208

an old uncles' tale, but...I guess not.'

'And you don't hate me?'

'How could I? I know you.' He gave her a faint smile. 'Half-faery or not, you have a true piskey's heart. That's all that matters.'

The knot of tension in Ivy's chest dissolved into grateful warmth. Matt was everything she loved about the Delve: solid, familiar, comforting. She rose up on tiptoe and kissed his cheek.

Matt's hand tightened on hers. 'Ivy,' he began – and thunder rumbled in the distance.

'Oh no.' Ivy pulled away, grabbing her pack and swinging it onto her shoulders. She'd wrapped up the treasure so it wouldn't jingle, but it was still heavy. 'We'll be soaked. Come on!'

Reluctantly Matt followed her out of the adit, then took the lead as they moved through the trees, changing to human size so they could cover more ground. Above the tangled branches the clouds hung low and leaden, and the first raindrops were beginning to fall. Ivy had to hurry to keep up with Mattock's long strides, but she didn't ask him to slow down. She could only hope they'd reach Redruth before the storm broke.

Moving with the confidence of familiarity, Matt led her by a series of footpaths and wooded trails, then to a tree-lined roadway with a pavement running along one side. He kept a brisk pace, and Ivy had to trot to keep up as they left the countryside behind for the stone hedges and slate-roofed cottages of Redruth.

The rain was falling steadily now, flattening Ivy's curls and dripping down the back of her neck. Cars whizzed along the roadway, spraying muddy water in their wake. The houses grew narrower and closer together, penning them in. Ivy's shoulders burned from the weight of her rucksack, but she hefted it and kept walking. It couldn't be much further now.

At last they came to the city centre, where the road shied away from a cobbled avenue watched over by a tall clock tower. Humans hurried in and out of the shops, umbrellas raised and collars turned up against the weather. A statue of a miner stood on a pedestal with his back to them, arms outstretched as though longing to fly; further down a pack of hounds made out of old miners' boots shone wetly in the rain. Mattock led her down the hill to another street, turned right, and finally stopped beneath a worn-looking sign that said GEMS AND MINERALS FOR SALE. He opened the door, and a bell tinkled as he led Ivy in.

The shop was narrow and bare of decoration, apart from the shelves of rock samples and a few scattered cases tilted to display the minerals inside. But the shelves were dusty, the glass smudged with fingerprints, and in the dim light even the crystals looked dull. The whole place had a shabby, neglected air about it, as though its owner had long stopped caring whether anyone came in or not.

A thin, grey-haired man emerged from the back of the shop, rubbing his spectacles clean on a corner of his shirt. At first he looked irritable, but as soon as he put the glasses back on and focused on them, his manner changed at once.

'Welcome, honoured folk of the Delve,' he said, standing to

attention. 'How can I serve you?'

Ivy was taken aback. As she'd understood it, the Pendennis family's agreement with the piskeys should have ensured them a comfortable and prosperous life. But from the look of this place and the man's strained, almost fearful expression, something had gone badly wrong with the bargain.

Still, there was nothing she could do about that now. 'I have some things to sell,' she said, slipping off her rucksack. 'I was hoping you could give me some money for them.'

'Things?' Ralph Pendennis blinked. 'You mean ore? Gemstones?'

'Not those kinds of things,' said Ivy. She walked to the till, turned the pack upside down and let its contents spill across the counter.

Once the clattering subsided, the silence was profound. Ivy could feel Mattock's stare on her back – even he could tell that this treasure was hundreds of years old, and that it hadn't come from the Delve. The older man was staring too, pinching one corner of his spectacles as though he couldn't believe what he was seeing. He moved to the counter, picking up one item after another for examination.

'This is beyond me, I'm afraid,' he said at last, clearing his throat. 'Antiquities aren't my specialty, so I'd hesitate to put a value on them. But these pieces are...quite remarkable.' He peered at Ivy. 'May I ask how you came by them? They aren't piskey-made, surely; the workmanship's not fine enough.'

'No,' said Ivy, 'they're not from the Delve. But I'd like to sell them as quickly as possible, so if you can't help me, can you tell me who can?'

Ralph Pendennis rubbed his chin, as though engaged in some internal debate. At last he opened a box beside the till and took out a small, cream-coloured card.

'Try my nephew Thom,' he said, pushing it across the glass to Ivy. 'He has a shop in London. Make sure to tell him you're one of my customers' – he laid a faint but definite emphasis on the word *my* – 'and that I expect him to treat you fairly.'

Ivy caught the hint: Thom Pendennis wasn't always as honest as he should be. Well, that fitted with what Martin had said about him, so she'd know to stay on her guard. But how could she possibly get all the way to London by herself, when she couldn't even fly? Martin had said something about a train, but she'd still need enough money for a ticket...

'There must be something here you're willing to buy,' she said. 'For the sake of our bargain, if nothing else?'

The older man's lips pursed – calculating, Ivy thought, until she looked closer and saw the unhappiness in his eyes. No, he did not want to give her money; by the looks of this shop, he didn't have much to spare. But either he was too honourable to break his oath to the piskeys, or he was too frightened of what might happen if he did.

'These,' he said, pulling a handful of Roman coins towards him. 'I'll give you forty pounds each.'

Which wouldn't be enough to keep Ivy's family from losing the cottage, but surely more than enough to get her to London.

She'd just have to hope that Thom Pendennis would respect his uncle's advice, and deal fairly with her.

'All right,' she said, scooping the rest of the treasure into her rucksack. 'I'll take it.'

eighteen

Mattock stayed quiet until he and Ivy left the shop. But the minute they were alone, he rounded on her. 'I thought you were selling your mum's wedding jewels. But treasure? That's *spriggan* stuff, Ivy. What are you doing with it?'

'I told you I had some coins and jewellery to sell,' said Ivy, brushing the wet curls out of her eyes. The clouds were still grumbling overhead, and she wished she could will herself home, but that would only upset Matt even more. 'And there's treasure in the Delve too.'

'Treasures made from our own gems and ore, with our own skill, for our own people! Not human treasure stolen from graves and barrows and hoarded away all greedily, so no one else can enjoy it!'

'Well, I'm not hoarding it, I'm selling it. So now somebody *can* enjoy it.'

'You haven't answered my question.'

Ivy set her jaw. 'My business is my own, Matt. As yours is yours.'

She started back up the street, and after a pause Mattock caught up with her. They walked for some time without speaking, and then he said, '*He* gave it to you. Didn't he.'

'Who?' asked Ivy, not breaking stride.

'The spriggan you freed from the Delve. He gave you some of his treasure, to reward you for letting him go.'

Ivy spun to face him. 'Firstly,' she said, 'he told me he was a faery, not a spriggan. Secondly, we found the treasure together, so half of it is mine by right. And thirdly, he's gone off somewhere and I'll probably never see him again. So even if he *was* a spriggan, what difference would it make?'

'It matters,' said Matt quietly, 'because you were travelling with him. It matters because he really was a spriggan, no matter what he said. And it matters because...' He ran a thumb along her cheek. 'You're crying for him.'

'It's *raining*, Matt,' she snapped, jerking away. Yes, an unexpected surge of misery had risen up in her at the thought of never seeing Martin again, but she'd pushed it down before it could show...or at least she thought she had. 'And I can travel with anybody I like.'

'You can't even see it.' Mattock looked nauseated. 'He's bewitched you, deceived you, just like the spriggans did to piskey-girls in the old stories.'

'Don't be ridiculous.' Ivy set off again, stomping through a puddle. 'He did no such thing.'

'What makes you so sure? How would you know if he did?'

Because she'd doubted, questioned, and quarrelled with

Martin too many times to be under his spell. She knew his faults, his sins, his most infuriating traits – all the things he would have hidden from her if he had the power, which made her all the more certain that he didn't. But how could she explain that to Mattock, without telling him their whole story?

'I just know,' she said. 'Trust me.'

Matt winced as though she'd struck him. 'This is why the Joan doesn't want us living on the surface,' he said. 'Why even hunters aren't supposed to go far from the Delve, or have anything to do with other magical folk. Because if we start getting mixed up with spriggans and who knows what else…soon we won't be piskeys any more.'

And only an hour ago he'd been telling her it didn't matter to him that she was half-faery. 'You sound like Mica,' she said accusingly. 'No, worse – you sound like Betony. Do you really believe that's what makes us piskeys? Refusing to change or learn or adapt in any way, and treating every outsider as a threat?'

'That's not what I meant!'

'We pride ourselves on our honesty and hard work,' Ivy went on fiercely, 'and how generous we are with each other. We think we're so much better than those selfish faeries and greedy spriggans. But you've seen all the armour and weapons in the Treasure Cavern, the same as I have. Our ancestors weren't kind, peace-loving folk. They attacked faery wylds and spriggan tribes and destroyed them—'

'It was a different time,' Mattock interrupted. 'A harder time, when everyone had to struggle to survive. We're not like that now.'

'Only because there's nobody left to fight,' Ivy shot back. 'Because after we'd killed off most of our enemies and stolen their women and girl-children for our own, we hid underground where no one could find us. That wasn't a triumph, Matt. It was cowardice.'

Matt was silent.

'And now the daughters and grand-daughters of those stolen women are dying. It started with my mother and Nettle because they had no knocker blood to give them resistance, but it won't end there. And if men like you don't stand up for them—'

'This isn't about the Delve!' Mattock tore off his cap and slapped it against his thigh. 'You're the one I'm worried about. I thought you might give me a chance, if I could only make you understand how I feel about you. But now I don't know any more.'

Ivy felt as though someone had punched her in the heart. 'What do you mean, how *you* feel?'

Matt sighed. 'What do you think, Ivy? For nearly a year now I've been watching you, thinking about you, wanting to be with you. I've listened to your troubles, and helped whenever I could. I've even risked my life for you once or twice, when it came to that. But you've never treated me as anything but a friend.' He turned the cap over in his hands. 'And now I know why.'

'Stop right there.' Ivy clenched her fists, struggling against the urge to cuff him. 'If you felt about me that way, why didn't you say so? Where were you at my last Lighting, when all the other girls had dance partners, and I was sitting in the corner with Cicely? Yes, you've been kind and helpful and – and all those other things. But how is that different from what Jenny or any other good friend might do? I'm no mind-reader, Matt. You should have told me.'

'I tried,' he said. 'More than once. But you always cut me off or changed the subject.'

Ivy opened her mouth to deny it, then realised with a pang of guilt that he was right. He'd been trying to talk to her back in the adit, less than two hours ago. 'I'm sorry,' she said. 'I didn't realise.'

'It doesn't matter.' He knocked his cap into shape and put it on again, looking resigned. 'Even if you had known, it wouldn't have made any difference. Would it?'

Ivy had no idea how to answer. She'd never imagined any of the young men in the Delve would want her that way, least of all someone as big and strong and good-looking as Matt. And for the past few weeks she'd been too busy trying to save her people to think about anything else.

But if they could defeat Betony and bring all the piskeys to the surface, or better yet find a way to purge the Delve from poison and make it safe again...wouldn't she want to make a life for herself among her own people, if she could?

The rain was tapering off, the storm clouds rolling away towards the west. A woman emerged from the bus shelter, shaking out her umbrella. Ivy watched three cars and a lorry rumble past, and finally said, 'I don't know. Maybe.'

Hope dawned on Matt's face. 'Then it's not too late,' he said, moving closer. 'Come back to me, Ivy. Get rid of that spriggan rubbish you're carrying, and let me bring you some good honest ore from the Delve instead.'

'Get rid of it?' Ivy clutched the straps of her pack. 'What are you talking about?'

'Throw it away, put it back where it came from, I don't care. Just don't let him own you any longer.' He touched her wet hair, let his hand fall to her cheek. 'Show me you're still the Ivy I grew up with.'

He thought that Martin *owned* her? That he'd bought her loyalty, maybe even her love, with a crock full of old jewellery? The idea made Ivy's stomach curdle, brought a choking fury to her throat. She knocked Matt's hand away.

'I'm the same person I've always been,' she said. 'I took this treasure to help my family, not myself, and I don't have time to waste making *you* feel comfortable about it.'

'Ivy, please—'

'No. That's my final answer, Matt.'

She'd meant about the treasure, not about anything else. But Mattock's bleak expression said otherwise. 'You've made your choice, then,' he said. 'I see how it is. Goodbye, Ivy.'

He moved to go, but Ivy caught his arm. 'You can't be serious,' she said. 'What about the Delve? What about Jenny? You can't just give up on them because of me!'

The look he gave her then was as cold as she'd ever seen on Mica's face, or even Betony's. Ivy faltered, and her hand dropped to her side as Mattock turned his back on her and walked away.

Ivy stood by the roadside for a long time after Mattock had gone, staring at the pavement. Then she took a deep breath, shouldered her pack, and set off to look for the train station. She'd seen signs for it when she and Matt were walking to Ralph Pendennis's shop; it couldn't be far.

But try as she might to focus on the task at hand, her thoughts kept wandering back to her quarrel with Mattock, and her worries about what it might mean. Now that Jenny could no longer come to the surface, Matt was the only remaining link between Ivy and the Delve. If he washed his hands of her, she'd be left with no way to find out what was happening to her fellow piskeys.

But then, Ivy thought with sudden bitterness, it wasn't as though she'd been doing much for them anyway. She'd already warned Jenny and Matt about the poison, and encouraged them to warn others. What more could she do without going into the Delve herself, risking her life and – if she were caught – putting Marigold and Cicely and perhaps even Molly in danger as well?

It took Ivy several minutes to work her way back to the train station, and even longer before she figured out how to get the information she needed. Her ears burned with humiliation when she had to confess to the man at the ticket window that she didn't understand any of the railway maps and timetables, and the impatient sighs and mutters of the people in the queue behind her made her feel even worse. But once she was satisfied that the trains to London ran several times a day, that the journey would take five or six hours, and that she could easily afford to buy a ticket with the money Ralph Pendennis had given her, Ivy was glad that she'd made the effort.

Still, she couldn't leave right away: she'd have to stop at home first, or her family would wonder what had become of her. How she'd explain to Marigold that she needed to be gone for a day or more, Ivy wasn't sure yet – but at least she could change into dry clothes while she was thinking about it. She slipped up the street to the doorway of an abandoned shop, and willed herself back to the cottage.

The instant she materialised in the barn, she knew something was wrong. Dodger was prancing restlessly in his box, nostrils flared and dark eyes rimmed with white. He snorted at the sight of her, and let out a fearful whinny.

'Shh,' said Ivy, shoving her pack under an old feed bucket and hurrying to soothe him. 'It's all right. No one's going to hurt you.' She blew in his nostrils and patted his shivering neck until he quieted, then unlatched the box door and glanced inside. But Cicely had done a thorough job of mucking it out that morning, and there were no rats or snakes hiding in the straw that Ivy could see.

Still, it wasn't like Dodger to be so skittish. Ivy shut the box, looking around the barn for other signs of trouble. But nothing seemed out of the ordinary, so she gave the horse a farewell pat and headed outside.

All seemed quiet as she crossed the yard, the cottage as peaceful as it had ever been. But when she passed the kitchen window a sweet, sickly smell wafted towards her, growing thicker and more cloying with every step. Had Cicely left something on to burn? Ivy broke into a run, sprinting up the path to the front door. It was locked.

'Cicely!' she shouted, fumbling for her key. 'Mum! Are you there?' She unlocked the door, shoved it open – and the stench of charred *something* billowed out towards her. It curled like a black, slimy worm around her tonsils and oozed down the back of her throat, burning as it went. Ivy clutched the doorframe and her stomach at the same time, afraid she was going to be sick.

'Mum!' she coughed, when she could speak. The blood was pounding through her ears, but beneath its pulse she could hear the gurgle of running water – or was that someone sobbing? She groped across the front room, dimly noticing the scorch-marks around the kitchen entrance, the bubbled paint and blackened tiles beyond, the smoky tang of burnt wood mingling with that hideous nightmare odour.

Then Cicely emerged like a ghost from the hallway, all white face and staring eyes. One braid was soaked, her right arm dripping to the elbow, and her clothes were streaked with ashes and blood. She opened her mouth and closed it again, then whirled and dashed back the way she'd come. Speechless with dread, Ivy chased her down the corridor to the bathroom.

Water streamed into the bath, gurgling in the half-plugged

drain. Marigold lay in the tub with her back to them, her whole body trembling. She did not move as they entered, but Ivy could hear the harsh rattle of her breath.

'Mum,' whispered Ivy, clutching the sink for support. From this angle she couldn't see how bad Marigold's injuries might be, but the clumps of burnt hair floating around her and the pinkish-grey colour of the water confirmed Ivy's worst fears. There'd been an accident while she was gone, and her mother had been horribly burned.

'I did everything she told me,' Cicely blurted, though she was shaking almost as much as Marigold. 'She said *water* and she said *bath* and she said *don't tell the humans, don't let them take me away*. And I had to smash the thing on the ceiling with a broom because it kept screaming and I didn't know how to make it stop—'

Ivy snatched her little sister into an embrace, clutching her wet head against her shoulder. 'You did right,' she told her. 'If you'd called the neighbours for help they'd have taken her to the hospital, and that's not a safe place for magical folk.' She released Cicely and wrapped a towel around her for warmth. 'What happened?'

'I don't know,' Cicely sniffed. 'I took Dodger for a ride after you left and I was gone for maybe an hour. When I got back I took off his saddle and rubbed him dry and put everything away like you showed me, but all of a sudden he started whinnying and prancing like he was scared, and it took me forever to calm him down. And when I came back to the cottage the door was open and everything smelled like smoke, and Mum was...just lying...' She buried her face in her hands.

Ivy knelt beside the bath, stroking the remnants of her mother's hair. Even on her good side it felt dry and brittle, and bits of it came away in her hands. She'd learned a little about treating burns from Yarrow, enough to know that Marigold would need to drink plenty of fluids to make up for all the moisture she'd lost, and that her wounds would have to be cleaned and packed with honey before any dressings went on. But if the burns went deep or covered a large area of her skin, then not even Ivy and Cicely's best care could save her — without magical intervention, their mother would die.

'I'm so sorry, Mum,' Ivy said brokenly. 'If I'd known something like this could happen...'

The water sloshed as Marigold rolled over. The right side of her face was livid with burns, her arm red and blistered beneath the singed remnants of her sleeve. She fumbled for Ivy's hand and groped up her arm, tugging her closer.

'What is it?' asked Ivy, leaning down to listen — and with that, Marigold's fingers brushed her temple.

— not here? Where is she, then? Tell me at once, or —

— faery witch, I'll make you regret the day you ever crossed me —

Shocked, Ivy jerked away, and Marigold's hand fell. But though their contact had lasted only an instant, the memories her mother had shown her were seared deep into her mind. She stumbled back from the tub, shaking in rage and horror, sick with the knowledge that the cottage she'd believed safe and the family she'd thought protected were no longer safe or protected at all.

Because Betony had found the house and tricked her way inside, looking for Molly. And when Ivy's mother had refused to cooperate...the Joan had burned her.

nineteen

'Ivy?' asked Cicely. 'What's wrong? Why are you angry?'

Anger was hardly the word for what Ivy was feeling. A boiling, consuming hatred filled her, a black storm of rage that went beyond anything she'd felt before. It shivered every muscle in her body; it whistled through the marrows of her bones. It made Ivy want to tear apart everything she saw, or smash it to pieces – but she couldn't let herself give in to it, not yet. She clenched her teeth, dug her fingers into her palms, and breathed until the red fog across her vision faded away.

'Cicely,' she said when she trusted herself to speak, 'I need you to be very, very strong and very, very brave. Can you do that for Mum – for me?'

Her little sister nodded and stood up straight, like a guard waiting for inspection. Ivy put her hands on her shoulders.

'I'm going to look for someone who can heal Mum with magic,' she said. 'But it might be a day or two before I get back, so you'll have to look after her all by yourself. I'll help you get her out of the bath and dress her wounds, and we'll make her as comfortable as we can – but after that, it's up to you. All right?'

Cicely nodded again. Her eyes were wide and fearful, but she didn't look away.

'Call the secretary at the dance school, and tell her Mum's been taken ill and can't come in for a few days. But don't tell her anything more than you have to. And if anyone comes to the door while I'm gone, don't let them in. Do you understand?'

A third nod.

'Good.' Ivy let her go. 'Then let's get started.'

Once she and Cicely had drained the bath, tended Marigold's wounds and carried their limp, moaning mother across the corridor to bed, the heat-storm of Ivy's fury had cooled to icy resolve. She waited long enough to make sure Marigold was sipping the water Cicely held to her lips, then returned to the sink and washed her sticky hands, scrubbing around and between her fingers until every trace of blood and honey was gone. Next she changed into dry clothes, stuffed Ralph Pendennis's money in her pocket, and put her copper bracelet back on. Her muscles burned and her feet dragged with fatigue, but Ivy had no time for weakness. She grabbed her coat off the bed and stalked outside.

She didn't care any more whether swifts were supposed to be in England at this time of the year, or how many hungry predators might be lurking in the skies above. She didn't care that piskeys weren't supposed to change shape; she didn't care if every human in the district was watching when she did. All she cared about was flying, far and fast and fearless, until she reached her goal.

Only a short time ago she'd been full of worries, self-doubt and uncertainty about the future. Now there were only two things in all the world that she wanted, and she was ready to do whatever it took to make them happen.

First she would find Martin, wherever he was, and bring him back here to heal her mother.

Then she would go to the Delve, and kill Betony.

Ivy broke into a run, footsteps crunching as she sprinted down the drive. Then she hurled herself into bird-shape, and soared away.

It felt strange to be airborne after so long on the ground, and Ivy must have been even more out of practice than she'd thought: her body felt weirdly heavy for all its swiftness, and the sharpness of her bird-vision was dizzying. The tiniest movements at ground level shouted for her attention – a woodpigeon startled into flight, a badger waddling across the road, the scurry of a mouse through the rust-coloured bracken. Even the late autumn landscape, so drab to her human eyes, had transformed into a blaze of hot-metal hues: bronze, tin, and molten gold, with the glowing blue-silver traces of animal spoor woven through it.

How could she have forgotten how extraordinary the world looked through a bird's eyes, how full of beauty and life? Under any other circumstances, Ivy would have been appalled that she'd ever taken it for granted. But she had no time to think of such things now, not with her mother's life at stake. She forced herself to focus on the long bars and featherings of cloud before her, and beat upward into clearer sky.

The city of London lay well to the north-east: Ivy remembered that much from the maps she'd seen in Redruth. Flying at top speed, she should reach its outskirts by nightfall – assuming the weather stayed favourable, and that no mishap drove her from her present course. But though gulls cursed and crows jeered as she flew by, and a cloud of starlings whirled up to spiral around her, she saw no birds large or fierce enough to pose a threat. It seemed that for the moment, luck was on Ivy's side.

Still, she was determined not to be caught off-guard, by a hobby or anything else. Beak clamped shut to silence her habitual swift-scream, Ivy rose until the cold bit into her thick feathers – until all the other birds dropped below her, and there was nothing but sky as far as her eyes could see. Then she drove onward, wings drumming the air, following the dark thread of the roadway across Bodmin Moor, then over the winding ribbon of the Tamar into Devon.

At this height the colours of the land were dulled with distance, and the earth spread itself out in a tattered brown patchwork, blotched here and there with the iron-grey stains of human cities. One of those cities looked large enough to give Ivy pause, but she'd only been flying an hour, so it couldn't possibly be London. She banked northward, correcting her course, and carried on.

Over Devon and into Somerset she flew, ever watchful of the sky around and below. Late into the second hour of her flight she heard the low thrum of an engine, and glanced around to find a helicopter following in her path. But it was miles away and beneath her, a thing of no consequence. Soon it veered southward and disappeared, and once more Ivy was alone.

Gradually the sky darkened and the sun slid behind the horizon, its dying fires glowing briefly before nightfall stamped them out. The once-ugly towns and cities became beautiful with light, and Ivy felt a strange peace come over her. She'd made it through dusk – the most dangerous time for a swift – without a single battle. She was tired and hungry, but the winds were still in her favour, and the inner compass that was her legacy as both a piskey and a bird assured her that she was flying in the right direction. Soon she would reach London, and her quest to find Martin and save her mother could begin.

Ivy tucked her wings and dived, slicing through the chill air to the warmer draughts below. She had less to fear from other birds now: the only predators she knew of that hunted in full darkness were owls, and she could easily outfly those. Confidence growing, Ivy levelled her course and pressed on.

That haze of radiance on the horizon – could it be? The scattered diamonds of light below her were clustering together, stringing themselves along the golden chains of motorways and major roads. Towers lit with blue, green, and white-gold rose up from a sea of lesser buildings that spilled out far to the north and east – so far that even Ivy's searching bird-vision could not find the end of it. She'd never imagined a city so dazzling, or so huge: it had to be London.

She angled into a glide smooth as pouring water, feeling the wind ripple over her wing-feathers as the rooftops and streets below came into sharper focus. The longest part of her journey was over. Now all she needed was a safe place to change shape and some harmless-looking humans to talk to, so she could get directions to Thom Pendennis's shop.

Several awkward conversations and two frustrating false starts later, Ivy found herself on a narrow, dimly lit street to the north of the city centre, gazing up at the dull gold letters of a sign reading T. PENDENNIS, ANTIQUITIES. Most of the humans she'd talked to had warned her that the shop would be closed by now, and it was, but Ivy refused to let that discourage her. She rattled the door and pounded on the metal-shuttered window, then changed to swift-shape and fluttered up two floors to the roof, searching for a way in.

Ivy didn't care about selling the treasure now; she hadn't even brought it with her. Still, Thom Pendennis was the only person she knew of who might be able to lead her to Martin. If she could get inside the shop and hunt around, perhaps she'd be able to find out where Thom lived – but one way or another, she had to talk to him tonight.

The hole she eventually found beneath the eaves was a snug fit, and she had to push through a clotted mess of dead grass, old newspaper and bird droppings to reach the attic behind it. But after a bit of scrabbling and a few awkward flaps along the rafters, Ivy had enough room to change back to her own shape – if only at piskey size. Quick as a mouse, her skin-glow lighting her way, she searched the inner walls until she found another hole, this one with a faint light shining through it. She stuck her head into the gap for a cautious look-round, then wriggled into it feet first and dropped.

She'd landed on the top of a tall cabinet, where a mould-spattered plastic curtain had been left to gather dust with an old scrubbing brush and a bar of soap. The streetlamp glowed dully through a curtained window beside it, revealing a small toilet that looked as though it hadn't been used in years. Taking swift-form again, Ivy fluttered down from her perch and lighted on the tiles. Then she grew to human shape, opened the door and stepped out into the hallway beyond.

This floor of the building seemed deserted: the only light she could see was her own skin-glow, and the boards at her feet were velvety with dust. Ivy looked in one door after another until she found the staircase, then hurried down past a small landing and another shut door to the ground level.

The shop was a single large room, twice as wide as it was deep, with plastered walls and wooden beams worn smooth by age. Glass cases lined the walls, displaying chipped bottles and bits of broken pottery, crudely made statues, and other objects that to Ivy looked more like rubbish than treasure. A smaller cabinet held jewellery, including a few pendants, bracelets and pairs of ear-hoops that were pretty in their way, but nothing so fine as the treasure she and Martin had found.

So where were the pieces from the Grey Man's hoard?

Ivy walked around the room, the floorboards creaking beneath her feet. There were a few items she hadn't noticed at first glance, mostly old documents and sets of coins hanging in frames upon the walls – but no, they weren't from the spriggan trove either. Perhaps all Martin's treasure had been snapped up so quickly by eager buyers that none of it was left?

Or else that door behind the till led to another room, where Thom kept his more valuable pieces. Ivy hurried over and tried it. The knob turned so reluctantly at first that she thought it must be locked, but when she twisted harder, the door clicked open.

It wasn't a showroom at all, only a small office. But behind the desk and chair stood a wooden cabinet with three drawers that looked like it might hold something important. Ivy slipped around the corner of the desk, crouched and tried the bottom drawer. It rattled, but stayed shut. She tried the next drawer up, and the next. All were locked.

Exhaustion swept over Ivy, and she sagged against the cabinet in despair. She was no faery tracker, like the Blackwings Martin had mentioned. If she couldn't find Thom's address she'd have no way of finding him, let alone Martin, until morning – and those few hours could make the difference between life and death for Marigold.

She had only one hope left, and that was the desk itself. Perhaps Thom had hidden a spare set of keys somewhere. Heedless of any noise she might be making, Ivy tugged open the top drawer and began pulling out everything she saw. She'd emptied its contents onto the desk and was picking up and shaking each item in turn when she caught sight of a thin, box-shaped protrusion on the drawer's bottom edge. She slid her fingers along it, and a key dropped out into her hand.

So luck was with her after all. Eagerly Ivy turned and fitted the key into the lock at the top of the cabinet. A twist, a click—

And a hand clapped over her mouth.

Ivy struggled, but her assailant only seized her tighter, dragging her back against his body and pinning her arms to her sides. It was like being in the hobby's talons all over again, the same blind terror of a small creature trapped in a predator's grip, and for an instant she was paralysed by it. But then she heard his voice in her ear, low and husky with surprise:

'Ivy?'

Her heart did a rolling dive into her stomach. She spun around in her captor's loosening grip – and there he stood in the half-darkness, thinner and paler than she'd last seen him, but alive, whole, and undeniably real.

'Martin,' she gasped, and flung herself into his arms.

twenty

The last time she'd hugged Martin, he'd stiffened and pushed her away. But this time his arms tightened around her, and he dropped his face against her hair.

'I'm sorry,' he murmured. 'If I'd had any idea it was you…' He drew back with obvious reluctance. 'But what are you doing here?'

Ivy's knees were still wobbly from shock and relief. She gripped his forearms, steadying herself. 'I was looking for you,' she said. 'I thought Thom might be able to tell me where you'd gone. I never thought I'd find you like *this*.'

Martin's gaze fell to the bracelet on her wrist. He touched it lightly, as though he weren't quite sure it was real. 'Looking for me,' he repeated. 'Why?'

Was that sadness in his voice, or only weariness? He looked almost as tired as Ivy felt. She wanted to ask where he'd been all this time, why he was here now – but no, all that could wait. She straightened up and let him go.

'My mother's hurt,' she said. 'She was burned fighting my aunt Betony, and if you don't come back to Cornwall with me right away…' Her voice faltered. 'She's probably going to die.'

For several seconds Martin regarded her in silence. Then he turned and walked out into the shop.

'Where are you going?' Ivy scrambled around the desk and went after him. 'Didn't you hear me?'

'I heard.' He spoke quietly, his back to her. 'But I can't help you. You'll have to find someone else.'

'There is no one else! The Delve's healer makes ointments and medicines – they help sometimes, but they can't heal like you can. And Mum's burned so badly, all down her arm and the side of her face…'

'I believe you. I wish I could help. But I can't leave this place.'

'What?' She grabbed his elbow and pulled him around to face her. 'You came back to Cornwall the last two times after selling Thom your treasure. Why is it any different now?'

'I wasn't under the *tenkyz* then.' He bit the words out, not meeting her eyes. 'I didn't know who I was, and Thom wasn't sure yet either, so there was nothing to bind me to him. But now I have no choice.'

A *tenkyz* was a magical fate or obligation, a set of conditions that had to be met or everyone bound by it would die. But that didn't make what Martin was saying any easier to understand.

'But Thom's only a human, isn't he?' Ivy asked. 'He doesn't have magic, so how can he have power over you?'

'Because,' Martin said bitterly, 'my father gave it to his father thirty years ago, in exchange for protection from the piskeys who'd killed his brother.'

Thirty years ago. Nettle had told Ivy once that it had been thirty years since anyone had seen a spriggan. *A thin, miserable bit of a thing it was too, all by its lonesome. But it fought like a demon until young Hew smashed its head in, or so he and the other lads said.*

'There were three Pendennis sons at the time,' Martin continued. 'The oldest was oath-bound to uphold their family's bargain with the piskeys, and the middle son had no interest in dealing with magical folk at all. But the youngest, Thom's father William, agreed to take my father safely away with him to London – if he bound himself and his descendants under a *tenkyz* to serve and obey him and his family for three generations.'

He gestured at the shop. 'All this is merely the respectable front for Thom's real business – finding and selling spriggan treasure. And now that Walker's too sick to work any more, I'm the new errand-boy and night watchman.' His lip curled. 'Unpaid. Of course.'

'But you said you didn't know who your parents were. What makes you think Walker is your father?'

'I don't know exactly what happened, and neither does he. My best guess is that my faery mother found out about the *tenkyz*, and decided she'd rather wipe my mind and abandon me than see me turned into a slave. But fate has a way of coming around eventually, no matter how you try to avoid it.' He sighed. 'I'm not a fool, Ivy. I know how unlikely it is that the first spriggan I met would turn out to be my father, and I certainly didn't trust Thom enough to take his word for it. But once I met Walker and heard his story…I couldn't deny it any more.'

The resignation in his voice made Ivy's stomach clench. She'd never heard Martin sound so defeated. 'But Walker has to do what Thom tells him,' she said. 'How do you know he's telling the truth?'

Instead of answering, Martin took her hand and led her through the shop to the staircase. He took her up the steps to the landing she'd passed on her way down, opened the door and motioned her through.

Beyond was a narrow hallway much like the one she'd seen upstairs, with rooms leading off it on both sides. A door to her left stood half-open, revealing a shadowy space cluttered with crates and old boxes. To her right lay another room, empty except for a battered-looking chest and a pallet of blankets in the corner. Martin guided her past both to a third door, then held a finger to his lips and ushered her in.

Like the other room it was pitifully bare, except for the curtains at the window and an old fringed carpet on the floor. Along the back wall stood a brass bed topped with a thin mattress and a few ragged blankets. And in the bed lay a gaunt-faced spriggan with silky white hair, eyes closed and mouth pinched with pain. Ivy glanced at Martin, then back at the sleeping man. The resemblance was unmistakable.

'That was the first clue,' said Martin. He drew her out into the hallway with him and shut the door again. 'And when he started talking about a faery woman he'd loved once, and how he'd always suspected he had a child she'd hidden from him, I started to wonder. But even then, I didn't say anything. Not until he mentioned the Grey Man.'

Ivy's heart skipped. 'What?'

'Well, he didn't call him that exactly. But when I asked what he could tell me about his ancestors, he said his mother used to tell him he was descended from Coleman Grey, one of the greatest spriggan chiefs of legend. A mighty warrior, who had troves all over Cornwall, and died in battle with the piskeys. Sound familiar?'

It did, but Ivy couldn't bring herself to accept it. If Martin was trapped here in Thom's shop, unable to leave of his own will, then who would help Marigold? She started to say that he might have let something slip about his past or her spriggan dreams by mistake, but Martin shook his head.

'It's no use, Ivy,' he said. 'I didn't tell Walker anything until I was sure. But I'll tell you what finally convinced me.' He folded his arms and looked past her into the shadows. 'The first few times Thom's father sent Walker back to Cornwall for more treasure, he went back to all the spriggan haunts he remembered from his childhood. Places I recognised, when he described them – like that cave by the sea you and I visited, and one or two others I'd checked out on my own. But he never found any more of our people, there or here.'

His grey eyes focused on hers, full of the same sadness she'd seen when he looked at her bracelet. 'He thought he was the last spriggan left alive, until he met me. And before I met him…I'd come to much the same conclusion. He has to be my father, Ivy. There's no one else, living or dead, who could be.'

Ivy closed her eyes, feeling hollow inside. 'And now he's dying.'

'He is,' said Martin. 'He's been getting weaker for months, not only because he's old but because he'd run out of treasure to give Thom and didn't know where to find more. He stretched out his last hoard as long as he could…but it wasn't enough.'

Now she understood why Martin had gone back to the carn in such a hurry. He'd been trying to meet the terms of the *tenkyz* on Walker's behalf, and save the old spriggan's life.

'How long does he have left?' she asked.

'He sleeps most of the time now. I don't think he'll live much longer.' Martin glanced at the closed door. 'But it makes no difference, Ivy. Thom ordered me to guard the shop for him. If I go anywhere without his permission…'

Ivy didn't need him to finish the sentence. If Martin broke the terms of the *tenkyz*, for any reason, both he and his father would die. 'And he's not going to give you permission,' she said. 'Is he?'

'No.' His voice was flat. 'Once he was sure I was Walker's son, he wouldn't even let me leave the shop long enough to find you and say goodbye.'

So he would have come back to her, if he could. He'd only broken the spell on her bracelet because he knew he'd never see her again. Ivy put her hands over her eyes, pressing back the threatening tears.

'Then there's no hope,' she whispered. 'My mother's going to die.'

Martin did not reply, and the ache inside Ivy grew as she realised he probably hadn't even heard. But before she could turn away, he seized her by both shoulders.

'No,' he said with sudden fierceness. 'You're wrong. I'm not the only male faery who can heal: I'm not even that good at it. You're the only one I've ever—' He paused and went on more carefully, 'There are others who might help. If you ask them the right way.'

'But I don't know any other faeries—'

'Yes, you do.' He turned her towards the stairwell. 'I told you about them. Rob and his rebels – the faeries who live in the Oak.'

Not *an oak* or even *that big oak*, but *the Oak*, as though it were the only one in the world. A shiver rippled through Ivy and her heart beat faster, though she could hardly tell why.

'But they don't know me,' she said. 'And when they fought the Empress, my mother was on the wrong side.'

'That won't matter, if you can offer them something they want badly enough. And you can.' His arm tightened around her shoulders. 'You can tell them where to find me.'

Ivy whirled, staring up at him. 'No,' she breathed, and then more loudly, '*never.*'

'Why not? It isn't a betrayal; I'm telling you to do it. Tell Rob and Rhosmari and the others that you'll lead them to the place where I'm hiding, if they'll send a healer to save your mother.

A life for a life – that's as fair a bargain as any faery could ask for. They won't say no.'

'Yes, and a life is what it'll cost you!' Ivy shook herself free and backed away. 'You'll die the minute they take you out of here!'

'Better that,' said Martin, 'than spending the rest of my life as a slave. I've had enough of surviving at any cost, Ivy.' He reached out, fingers hovering next to her face. 'Everything I've ever cared about is lost to me now, one way or another. And I have nothing left to give you, except this.' His thumb brushed her cheekbone. 'Please. Take it.'

There was nothing theatrical about him now, none of the evasions or sly mockery he used as a mask for his true feelings. He meant every word he said. Ivy turned her face into his palm, and brought her own hand up to cover his.

'You'll do it, then,' he said. 'Promise me.'

The idea of handing him over to his enemies made her heartsick. But what choice did she have? There was still hope for Martin as long as he was alive, but there would be none for Marigold unless she found a healer soon.

'I promise,' Ivy said hoarsely.

The tension melted out of Martin's body. 'Good,' he said. 'Now let me show you where you need to go.' And he pressed his fingers to her temple.

The memory came in a single flash, a half-second glimpse of vision: a bird's-eye view of gentle, unfamiliar countryside, where a winding road crossed an old stone bridge, and a solitary human house stood dwarfed by the largest tree Ivy had ever seen. She could *feel* where the place was, just as Martin had felt it when he first visited it in bird-shape, and with surprise she realised that it was barely a half-hour's flight away.

'The nearest town is Aynsbridge,' said Martin. 'And the house is called Oakhaven.' He stepped away from her, head up and spine straight, like a man going to his execution. 'Good luck.'

Was this the end? The next time Ivy saw him, would it only be to watch him die? She wanted to tell him how sorry she was for all he'd suffered, what his sacrifice meant to her, how much she wished she could undo the past two months for both of them and make everything right again. But her mind was blank with grief and weariness, and the words refused to come.

'Ivy.' His voice was rough. 'Go. Now.'

She went.

She'd pictured the street outside the shop and willed herself into it, thinking to save herself the trouble of climbing two flights of stairs. But as soon as Ivy materialised on the pavement a wave of exhaustion crashed over her, and she had to clutch the lamp post for support.

After the first dizzy moment, it wasn't hard to guess why. She hadn't eaten since breakfast, she'd walked to Redruth carrying a heavy pack, she'd lifted Marigold out of the bath and dressed her wounds, and then she'd flown from Cornwall to London in just under five hours. Add to that all the shape-changing and size-changing she'd done just getting into Thom Pendennis's shop, and it was no wonder she felt drained.

But she couldn't rest yet. She still had to get to the Oak. Ivy pushed herself upright, limped a few steps along the pavement, and heaved herself into bird-shape.

Fatigue dragged at her body, making her feel twice her normal weight. But her wings beat with grim persistence, forcing her onward and upward until the street with its closed shops, half-lit windows, and line of parked vehicles dropped away. She wheeled and headed south-east, towards the memory Martin had shown her.

As she winged away from the city centre, a breeze blew in from the east and the clouds thinned and stretched before it, letting the cold stars shine through. The moon emerged, gleaming like the edge of a talon hooked into the night sky. She angled between two tall buildings, startling a cluster of dozing pigeons into flight, and flapped on.

What would the faeries of the Oak do when they found Ivy at their door? Surely they wouldn't be frightened of one lone piskey-girl, not when they'd been brave enough to stand up to the Empress herself. But if they had any idea how Ivy's ancestors had treated the faeries of Cornwall, she could hardly expect a warm welcome. She could only hope, for her mother's sake, that Martin hadn't offered his life in vain.

Gradually the lights and bustle of London faded behind her, and the glimmering skein of its river vanished into the distance. Ivy flew steadily onward, one dogged mile after another, until she reached the great motorway that ringed the city.

She was only a short distance from the Oak now, and the

thought should have heartened her. But a haze was creeping over her vision, and her wings felt heavier with every stroke. If she collapsed at this height, she would plummet to her death. But she couldn't stop to rest yet, not so close to her goal.

None of the places she was flying over felt familiar. How could they, when she'd never been outside Cornwall before? And yet they were familiar to Martin, part of the memory he'd put into her mind. The village of Aynsbridge glided beneath her, its cluster of lights scattering into the intermittent flashes of the cottages and country houses beyond…and all at once she could *feel* the Oak with her bird-senses, hear the giant shape of it like a deep voice calling to her out of the night.

She was going too fast, Ivy realised dimly, and tried to slow down. But her wings were clumsy with weariness, and before she knew it she was tumbling out of control. Buffeted from one air current to another, she descended in a crazy spiral, only managing to orient herself at the last minute—

A house leaped up in front of her, its windows dazzling her with light. Ivy let out a scream of terror and tried to bank away, but her momentum was too strong. Wings splayed and talons flailing, she smashed into the glass, bounced off it in a blinding instant of agony, and crashed into the garden below.

twenty-one

It was pain that shocked Ivy back to consciousness, a sharp bone-grinding in her elbow that tore a scream from her lips and would have jolted her upright, if there hadn't been something – or someone – holding her down. But once the flare of agony died to a throb and the roaring in her ears subsided, she heard people talking all around her.

The first was a girl, distraught: 'I thought you were going to put her to sleep first!'

'She was unconscious,' said the man beside her, sounding like a younger version of Gossan. 'I didn't think I needed to.'

Where was she? Ivy tried to look, but her eyelids were too heavy and her vision refused to focus. All she knew was that she was lying in a room with creamy walls and a dark square of window – not the Oak she'd been aiming for, but a house. Maybe even the same house she'd smashed into, right before she fell…

Panic stabbed her chest, but she forced herself to breathe through it. She had to stay calm, gather her strength, so she could escape before these humans figured out that she wasn't one of them.

'Well, you've done it now, so no use arguing about it.' A woman's voice, light but firm. She let go of Ivy's shoulders and added, 'Go on, heal her.'

Heal? Did she mean with magic? But that didn't make any sense. What would a faery healer be doing in a human house?

'Do you need an anchor?' asked the girl.

'For a broken arm? I don't think so.' The young man's hand cupped her elbow, and Ivy flinched – but this time his touch was light, and in seconds the bone-deep ache in her arm eased away. 'There.'

The pain was gone. It *was* magic. 'Please,' Ivy whispered, though her mouth was so parched she could barely speak. 'I need – I need to—'

'Don't try to talk.' That was the girl again, soothing. 'Rest, and get back your strength.' The bed shifted as she sat down. 'I'm Linden. Rob is the one who healed you, and behind you is Peri. She's the one who found you in the garden.'

Rob. So she had come to the right place, after all. And the faint herbal scent that wafted from Linden, more subtle than any perfume, assured Ivy that she was a faery too. Yet the woman – Peri – smelled human, and so did the house… Ivy tried to put the pieces together, but none of them fit.

'How?' she croaked.

'I could ask you the same thing,' said Peri. 'When I heard a great *thump* at the window and saw a bird fall onto the lawn, I

247

wasn't expecting to go out and find a girl instead. I thought only male faeries could change shape.'

'So did I,' said Rob. 'Where did you come from, and what brought you here?'

'*Rob*,' Linden protested, but Ivy waved a hand feebly.

'No, don't,' she mumbled. 'Have to…need to tell.'

Linden sighed. 'So much for resting. I'll get her some water.'

Even freshly healed and lying in bed, Ivy felt weaker than she'd been in her entire life. It took all her concentration to sketch out even the most basic details of her story: her faery mother had been horribly burned that afternoon, and there were no magical healers nearby who could save her. 'But then someone…told me about the Oak,' she whispered, and took another sip of water. 'So I flew here…as fast as I could.'

Her vision was clearing now, and she could see her surroundings: a plain but spacious bedroom on the top floor of Peri's house, with a window overlooking the back garden and the shadowy bulk of the great tree beyond. No wonder the house was called Oakhaven.

'Someone in Cornwall?' asked Peri. She smelled and sounded human, but her face was a bewildering contradiction: arched brows, angled cheekbones, and eyes so dark they were almost black, framed by a cataract of silky hair even paler than Martin's. 'Who would that be?'

Queasiness twisted Ivy's stomach. She didn't want to talk about Martin, not yet. Not until she was certain there was no way to get the help she needed without betraying him. 'A faery who knew my mother,' she said. 'He told me I could call him Richard.'

Rob frowned. He was lean and long-faced, with hair the same rusty shade as Mattock's but none of his solidity; he reminded Ivy more of a coiled whip, or a rapier poised to strike. 'That's a strange common-name for a faery,' he said. 'We don't usually name ourselves after humans.'

'We don't usually call ourselves after weapons either,' Linden replied, 'but that didn't keep Peri from naming herself Knife.'

Until now Ivy had thought all the Oakenfolk would be slim and sharp-boned like Rob, or even Peri. But this round-faced girl her own age, with the rosy cheeks and brown curls tumbling over her shoulders, could easily have been mistaken for a piskey. 'Knife?' she echoed, to cover her surprise.

'It was my hunter's name,' said Peri. 'When I used to be a faery, and lived in the Oak. Even my husband still calls me Knife sometimes, when he forgets himself.' Her mouth curved, as though she were enjoying some private joke. 'But that's another story.'

She spoke lightly, as though faeries turned into humans every day. But Ivy knew better, and it shocked her. 'You *used* to be? You mean you gave up your magic? Why?'

'To be with my husband, of course.' Peri rose and walked around the end of the bed. 'And speaking of Paul, the chairlift's broken again. I'd better tell him what's going on before he explodes from curiosity.' She took Ivy's empty water glass and strode out.

'It's a wonderful story,' Linden said with a smile, when the sound of Peri galloping down the stairs had faded. 'You should hear it if you get the chance. But we've kept you awake long enough.' She hopped off the edge of the bed, brushing creases from her skirts. 'We'll see you tomorrow.'

'Tomorrow!' Dismay pierced Ivy, and she struggled to lift herself up from the pillows. But she was still weak, and even that slight effort left her winded. 'I can't…wait that long. My mother…'

'You don't have a choice,' said Rob. 'Queen Valerian will decide what to do about your mother, once she and the rest of the council hear your case. But you're in no condition to come to the Oak tonight.'

'And even if you were,' put in Linden before Ivy could speak, 'there's only one other faery here skilled enough to heal wounds like your mother's, and he can't fly in the dark any more than Rob can. So you'd have to wait for daylight anyway.'

It was a fair point. Ivy had been so desperate to get to the Oak as quickly as possible, she hadn't considered how impossible it would be to turn around and fly back to Cornwall the same night. And after all these people had done for her, it would be foolish – even rude – to argue with them.

'I…I'm grateful,' she said. 'For your help. I'm in your debt.'

'Perhaps,' said Rob, studying her with his dark, foxlike eyes. 'Perhaps we can help each other. Time will tell.'

'And you needn't worry about staying here,' Linden assured her. 'Peri and Paul will take good care of you…' She trailed off, tilting her head to one side. Then with a *tsk* of exasperation she plucked something from between the mattress and the bed-frame and held it up.

'No wonder Timothy can never find his guitar picks,' she said, handing it to Rob, who looked amused. 'He's probably stuck twenty under there and forgotten about them.'

Who was Timothy? Ivy's eyes slid to the collection of framed photographs on the wall. One showed Peri crouching next to a handsome blond man in a wheelchair – Paul, she guessed, from Peri's comment about the lift. Then came an older couple who could be Paul's parents, and finally a lanky boy bent over a guitar who bore a slight family resemblance as well. The boy's hair was dark and he looked about Ivy's age, but the light could be deceiving, or Peri might be older than she'd thought...

'Is Timothy their son?' she asked.

Linden gave a startled laugh. 'Oh no,' she said. 'He's Paul's cousin, who lives here sometimes when he's not at school.' Her face sobered to wistfulness. 'Peri...doesn't have any children.'

'They have you,' said Rob, with a gentleness that surprised Ivy. 'Come. It's getting late, and we still need to talk to Queen Valerian.' He took Linden's hand, she gave Ivy a parting smile, and the two of them vanished.

Ivy closed her eyes, telling herself to relax. Linden at least seemed warm-hearted and ready to believe her story, though Rob was more guarded, as she feared the queen and her councillors would be. Still, they hadn't refused her outright, which was promising, so perhaps it wouldn't hurt to rest for a few hours.

After all, she'd need all her wits and strength about her if she was going to plead her mother's case tomorrow…

She'd barely finished the thought before she fell asleep.

'Get down, lad!'

Helm's hand gripped his shoulder, flattening him against the ledge where the two of them lay hidden. A jutting rock poked the boy's chest and he winced, but made no protest. A warrior did not complain.

It was just after nightfall on the sixth day of their journey. For the past week they'd been travelling westward along the coast, staying small and creeping under cover of hedge and dry bracken, searching for other spriggans who might be willing to take them in. But they'd had no luck so far, not of any kind: the weather was harsh, their snares empty more often than not, and when they'd grown to human size and stopped in a town to beg, they'd been sent off without so much as a crust in hand. Now they lay on an outcropping near the seaside, watching as three piskeys sauntered boldly along the sand below.

Judging by the long poles slung over the shoulders of the first two and the dripping basket carried by the third, these young hunters had just got back from their dusk fishing. The thought of cooked fish made the boy's stomach clench with longing, but he made himself keep still. Helm was as hungry as he was: if the older spriggan could be patient, so could he.

'You have your knife?' Helm spoke low in his ear.

The boy nodded.

'Be ready, then.' He raised himself on his arms, pulling one foot up beneath him as he readied for the spring. Then, fluid as water, he

252

changed shape. His head swelled to grotesque size, his limbs thickened to muscular stumps, and his bristling beard flowed over his chest nearly to his belt. Then, with a wild howl and his club brandished high, Helm launched himself off the ridge and landed in front of the piskeys.

The youngest dropped his basket of fish and stumbled back, gibbering with terror. The older ones paled, but they flung aside their fishing poles and reached for their knives. None moved fast enough. As Helm swung his club and sent the first hunter sprawling, the boy dropped down behind the second and stabbed him in the back. Then the boy spun, seized the remaining piskey by the throat, and raised his knife for the final blow.

Helm had told him not to hesitate. But seeing the other boy's terrified face, the tears brimming in his wide brown eyes, he couldn't do it. He'd never been so close to a piskey before – never realised how much like spriggans they were. And this one was even younger than he was, untrained and weaponless. Killing him would be wrong. He gave the piskey a shake and pushed him away.

With a sob the young hunter fled back towards the boat, staggering and slipping on the sand. The spriggan-boy sheathed his knife and began picking up the fish that had fallen from the basket. Three, four, five—

'That was ill done,' growled Helm, shifting back to his own shape. 'Didn't I tell you, no survivors? He'll bring the knockers down on us.'

The boy had no answer. He picked up the last fish and put it in the basket, then followed Helm up the ridge, leaving the two fallen piskeys behind.

They moved swiftly along the cliffs, keeping to the rockiest ground so as to leave no footprints. Fishy water dripped through the basket, soaking the boy's ragged trousers, and he was tempted to pull one out of the basket and eat it raw. But it wasn't safe to stop, even for a moment. They had to get away from the beach, and the piskey village that surely lay nearby.

It was two hours before Helm called a halt to their march, clambering down the rocks to a cave that was little more than a crack in the cliffside. The boy's legs felt like jelly and his stomach was cramped with hunger, but that was no more than he deserved for his cowardice. He should have killed that last piskey, unarmed or not…

Yet deep down he was glad he hadn't. He'd seen enough death already. At Helm's curt order he emptied the basket and began breaking up the drier parts for fuel, while the older spriggan sharpened a stake to cook the fish on.

'Why do they hate us?' the boy asked. 'The piskeys?'

Helm's knife paused mid-stroke, as though the question surprised him. But then he went back to his whittling.

'It's an old story,' he said. 'Old enough that no one living can swear to it. But they say that once, long ago, the piskeys, the knockers and the spriggans lived together in peace as one tribe.'

The boy found that hard to believe, but he loved stories. He settled back against the wall of the cave, wrapping his grimy cloak around him, and listened as Helm went on.

'The piskeys were a merry folk, with a gift for herb-lore and talking to animals. The knockers were stout, hard-working lads skilled at mining and metalwork. And we spriggans, shape-changers descended

254

from the giants of old, were the proudest warriors and bravest soldiers who ever were. For it was our duty to protect all the others, and keep the humans from stealing our treasure.'

He laid his knife aside, took flint in hand and crouched over their pile of kindling. With a deft strike and a few puffs he set the tinder aglow, then fed it with sticks until the flames began to crackle. 'For many years all was well,' he continued, 'until Joan the Wad, the queen of the tribe, grew old and died. The new Joan was a piskey-maid, fresh and lovely as dew on a spring morning, and all the young men set to wooing her, for the one she chose would rule with her as the Jack O'Lantern. But there were two boys she favoured above all others, one a knocker and the other a spriggan, and she loved them both so well she could not choose between them.

'For weeks the two lads courted the Joan with all their might, each striving to best the other and prove himself worthy of her hand. They had once been friends, but now they became jealous rivals, and the whole tribe was divided by their squabbling. At last a wise woman, a seer, came to the young queen and warned that if she did not choose before tomorrow's sunrise, she would lose her power and her throne. So with tears and sighs the young Joan summoned her knocker and spriggan suitors to her private chamber, that she might tell which one of them she had chosen.

'At dawn all the people gathered before the house, expecting the queen to come out and present their new Jack. But as the minutes passed, they grew restless. They called to the Joan, but she did not appear. So at last they broke the door down and rushed inside – and what a sight! The lovely young maiden lay dead upon the floor, while

her two rivals struggled in mortal battle, each shouting that the other had murdered her.

'Now all the knockers swore that their lad must have been the Joan's choice, for he was true-hearted and honest, while the spriggan-boy was a lying shape-changer who could not bear to see her marry another. And the spriggans claimed that she had chosen their brother and that the knocker-lad was false, for he had slain the Joan with his left hand and shouted, "This hand did not slay her," while holding up his right. Their quarrelling grew fierce and soon came to blows, and a battle broke out in which many knockers and spriggans were killed.

'At first the piskeys were undecided, for some believed the spriggan lad and others the knocker. But alas, they were soon swayed to the knockers' side. For all agreed that the giants had been greedy and violent and cruel, and their children could be no better. They disowned us and cast us out, calling us liars and murderers, and swearing that never again would any of them willingly give his daughter to a spriggan. And our people have been wandering ever since...'

When Ivy came back to herself, she was huddled in a cocoon of blankets, with a pillow over her head. She surfaced from the tangle, still disoriented from her unexpected dream...and found the bedroom suffused in golden light.

'Oh no.' Ivy snatched up the clock on the nightstand, but it only confirmed her fears. 'No!' She scrambled out from under the bedclothes and jumped to the floor, looking frantically in all directions. It was unthinkable that she'd slept so long, unbearable that Peri and the others had simply let it happen. They'd taken her jacket, her mud-streaked jeans, her socks and shoes – what had they done with them? She had to get dressed and over to the Oak at *once*—

'Oh good, you're awake,' said a cheerful voice, and a red-haired faery woman even shorter than herself appeared in the doorway.

'There's no need to worry,' she said, handing Ivy a pile of neatly folded clothing. 'Everything's quite all right. I'm Wink, Queen Valerian's attendant; she sent me over to get you ready. And you're feeling much better after that rest, aren't you?'

Physically, Ivy did feel better: her strength had returned, and she could think clearly again. But when she thought of the hours she'd wasted lying in this bed when she could have been pleading her mother's case and convincing the faeries of the Oak to help her, she wanted to vomit.

'I need to talk to the queen straight away,' she said, snatching her jeans from the pile and pulling them on. 'There's no time to waste. Please, could you tell her—'

She was arrested by Wink's hand on her arm, small but firm. 'I *said* everything was all right. Rob and Linden told us all about you last night, and Queen Valerian came over to bring you some of her special tea – she's a healer herself, you see, only with herbs instead of magic. But you were already asleep, and after she'd had a good look at you, she said you had the worst case of spell-fatigue she'd ever seen. So she asked Rob to make sure you slept for at least twelve hours, and she told *me* to make sure you didn't leave this room until you'd had a proper breakfast.' She whisked a cloth off the bedside table, and thrust a steaming tray at Ivy. 'There it is. Now eat.'

Ivy sank down on the edge of the bed, clutching the tray. There was a bowl of porridge drizzled with honey and sprinkled with dried berries, a heap of scrambled eggs on a slab of grainy toast, several chunks of apple, and a mug of hot chicory. Before now she'd been too distraught to even think of food, but now she realised she was starving. She picked up a spoon and began to eat.

'Peri had to go out this morning,' said Wink, patting her skirts and looking distractedly about the room. 'But she gave me something for you, if only I can remember where I put it…'

Ivy barely heard her; she was too busy trying to make up for lost time. But when she put down the bowl of porridge and reached for the plate, she found something tucked in beside it. Wondering, she drew it out. It was a dark grey feather longer than her hand, striped with bands of cream.

'I don't understand,' she said, turning the feather in her fingers. 'Why would Peri give me this?'

'She said it was lying on the lawn, right where she found you last night. She wasn't sure how your shape-changing worked, so she thought you might need it.' Wink's eyes were bright with curiosity. 'Do you?'

Incredulous joy welled up in Ivy. She set the tray aside, stood up, and flung herself into bird-shape.

Wink let out a squeak and threw her arms over her head as Ivy flapped past her, circled the room and landed atop the bedpost, strong talons gripping the wood. She turned her head and caught a flash of her reflection in the window, all curved beak and hooded eyes.

No wonder her vision had seemed so much sharper than before, and the weight of her body unfamiliar. No wonder she'd travelled all the way from Cornwall to London without meeting a single predator; no wonder the pigeons of the city had scattered in alarm when she flew past them on her way to the Oak...

She was a peregrine.

Ivy dropped off the bedpost and changed back to her own form, smiling. Now she knew the secret of taking falcon-shape; she'd thrown herself into flight without hesitation, without even caring what she became. Just as she had last night when she'd raced away from Molly's cottage, so consumed with worry for her mother that she'd had no fear left for herself.

All along, she'd believed she had to think about how falcons looked and moved in order to become one. But she'd thought the same about becoming a swift at first, and it hadn't worked then either. It was Cicely's scream that had startled Ivy into flight the first time, just as it was Marigold's need that had made her not only fast, but fearless.

All this time, she'd been obsessed with what *she* wanted. But she hadn't gained the wings she longed for until she stopped thinking about how much they meant to her, and started thinking about how much they could mean to somebody else.

Wink straightened up, flushed and indignant. 'What was that about?' she asked.

'I'm sorry I frightened you,' Ivy said. 'I just needed to check something.' She picked up the tray from the bed and sat down again. 'I'm grateful Peri thought to return the feather, but I don't need it. She can keep it, if she likes.'

twenty-two

Most trees looked thin and fragile in late autumn, but not the Oak: it was even more formidable with the full stretch of its mighty limbs exposed, every twig jutting sharp and black against the sky. It dominated the whole bottom of the garden, with branches high as the top of the Delve's engine house and a trunk nearly as wide – no wonder Rob and his fellow rebels had chosen this tree for their stronghold. Following Wink down the path from the house, Ivy found herself hanging back and treading carefully, as though the Oak were a sleeping giant she feared to wake.

Yet Wink had assured Ivy there was nothing to fear. 'There are wards around the garden,' the Queen's attendant had told Ivy as they came down the stairs from the bedroom, 'so no humans except Paul and Peri – and Timothy, when he's here – can see us going in and out of the Oak. The wards keep out uninvited faeries too, so it's a good thing you crashed into Peri's window; you wouldn't have got much further without her help anyway.'

Ivy found it hard to believe that knocking herself unconscious and breaking her arm was a good thing, but once she'd thought about it some more, she had to agree. For one thing, her weakness had made her an object of the faeries' pity, instead of a potential threat. And if she hadn't lost that wing-feather in Peri's front garden, she still wouldn't know that she could become a peregrine.

There was only one problem with what Wink had said: Ivy wasn't a faery, uninvited or not. But if she confessed to being a piskey before she'd had a chance to tell the queen her story, they might turn her away. So she'd held her peace, and followed Wink out into the garden.

And now at last Ivy stood at the foot of the great tree, gazing up through its lattice of branches at the grey mid-morning sky. 'This way,' said Wink behind her, but when Ivy turned to look, she was gone...

No, not gone. She'd merely shrunk herself to a tenth of her former size, and darted between the roots of the Oak. Ivy had guessed the Oakenfolk must be smaller than the average piskey, but she hadn't known they were *that* small.

Still, she'd have to follow Wink's example to get inside the Oak. Ivy concentrated, and the world swelled to monstrous size around her. At this size the hole beneath the roots gaped like the entrance to a mineshaft, but the sight of Wink's face peering up at her assured Ivy it wasn't that deep. She climbed over the edge and dropped to the bottom.

Facing them was an arch-topped wooden door, almost broader than it was tall. Wink hauled it open, puffing with the effort, and led Ivy up a set of stone steps to ground level. Turning right, they emerged from an archway—

And the heart of the Oak opened up before them.

It was like the inverse of the Great Shaft: stretching up and away from the earth rather than down into it, and growing lighter and airier as it rose. Galleries ringed its walls, with archways and corridors leading off them, and the whole place was swarming with faeries. Winged females flitted from one circular landing to another, while males flashed into bird-shape to cross the open space between them. They walked in and out of doors, leaned over the balconies, talked in pairs and small groups. There had to be at least as many faeries here as there were piskeys in the Delve, perhaps more.

But that wasn't the only surprising thing about the Oakenfolk. Most of them were dressed in modern human clothing, like Ivy herself. But there were also a number of women in old-fashioned dresses like Linden's and Wink's, and a scattering of men in finely tailored clothes that looked neither old nor new. The faeries of the Oak seemed to be made up of at least two if not three distinct groups, each with its own culture and history – much like the piskeys, knockers and spriggans had been in the story Helm had told last night.

'We'll have to fly up to Queen Valerian's apartments,' Wink told Ivy, leading her across the packed-earth floor. 'There used to be a staircase, but it got smashed when the Empress attacked the Oak, and nobody had the heart to rebuild it. Follow me.'

She stepped forward, her translucent wings blurring into

motion. In seconds she was gliding upward, passing one door-ringed gallery after another to land on the ninth and topmost floor of the Oak. Ivy paused, judging the distance, then took swift-shape and darted after her.

'I didn't know you had *two* bird-shapes,' exclaimed Wink, as Ivy landed and changed back. 'That's wonderful! You must tell me some time how you do it. Just wait a minute.' Picking up her skirts, she hurried to an archway draped in velvety curtains, and slipped through it into the corridor beyond.

That must be the entrance to the queen's apartments. Ivy closed her eyes, willing herself calm. But she only had a moment to compose herself before Wink reappeared again.

'Queen Valerian's ready for us,' she said. 'I'll take you in.'

Queen Valerian's audience chamber was more plainly furnished than Betony's stateroom in the Delve, with a carved wooden throne instead of the granite desk the Joan favoured. It had three tall windows to let in the sunlight, rather than a fireplace and hanging lamps. But as she walked up the carpet to stand before the faery queen and her council, Ivy felt just as small and self-conscious as she ever had approaching her aunt.

Not that the queen looked anything like Betony. Valerian was tall and slender, with a face so calm it was almost plain and straight brown hair falling past her shoulders; there was nothing haughty or imposing in her appearance, only a quiet dignity that somehow made Ivy all the more certain of her power. She'd never felt tempted to kneel before Betony, but it felt wrong not to bow to this woman, even though no one had asked her to do so. So when Ivy stopped at the foot of the throne she made a little curtsey, and bent her head respectfully.

'Welcome to the Oak, Ivy of Cornwall,' said Queen Valerian. 'Rob and Linden have told us your story, but my councillors wish to ask you some questions before we decide whether to grant your request.'

It was hard to stand there with so many strange faeries staring at her, their expressions wary or at best unreadable. The only one she recognised was Rob, but Wink had whispered some hasty introductions in Ivy's ear as they entered, so she knew who his seatmates were: the dour piskey-like woman to Rob's left was called Thorn, and the blond on his right was Campion, the Oak's librarian.

On Valerian's other side was a sharp-faced man with untidy hair and a neat beard – she hadn't quite caught his name, but it had sounded like *rock*. Then came Rhosmari, a young woman with a mane of spiral curls and the most beautiful deep brown skin Ivy had ever seen. It was a relief when Ivy caught sight of Wink scurrying up to the empty seat at the far end: at least there was one person on the council who didn't intimidate her.

'I know your need is pressing,' the queen continued, 'but if your mother has lived through the night, there is good reason to believe she will survive a little longer. Be patient with us, if you can.' She looked to her right. 'Rob?'

Rob unfolded himself and rose. 'You told us last night that you had flown here from Cornwall,' he said. 'Yet to our knowledge there have been no faery wylds in Cornwall for over a hundred years. And when the Empress rose to power, she captured every wandering faery she found and forced them into her service. So where did you and your mother come from?'

Was he implying she was a liar? Ivy resisted the urge to glare at him. 'My mother was born underground and raised among the piskeys of Cornwall,' she said. 'She didn't even know she was a faery until five years ago, when the Empress captured her.'

'So she did serve the Empress, then.'

So did you, Ivy wanted to say, but she held her tongue. She wasn't sure she liked Rob, especially knowing he was Martin's enemy, but he'd healed her last night and she owed him a debt. 'Yes,' she said. 'But not willingly.'

'Few faeries did. What is your mother's name?'

'Marigold.'

She saw the change in Rob's face at once. His jaw tightened, and his eyes became cold. 'I know her,' he said. 'She joined the rebellion after our first victory against the Empress, but instead of staying to fight with us, she ran away. When the Empress came to attack the Oak, she fought on the enemy side and killed one of my best men. And after that—'

'She was trying to get back to her family!' Ivy burst out. 'She ran away to find us as soon as she could, but when the Empress captured her again, she lost hope. She didn't want to fight, but she didn't have any choice.' She was about to explain that Marigold had been desperate to save Ivy and her siblings from the poison in the Delve, but Rob cut her off.

'Your mother had a choice,' he said. 'She made the wrong one. And if she cared so little for her fellow faeries, why should we put our own lives at risk by going into enemy territory to save her?'

The stocky woman beside him – Thorn – made a scoffing noise. 'Enemy territory? That's a bit dramatic, don't you think? From all I've heard, Cornwall's just a great empty nothing these days, as far as we faeries are concerned.'

'But there's a reason it's empty,' said Rhosmari, turning to reveal a pair of jewel-blue butterfly wings that made Ivy bite her lips with envy. 'I've seen loreseeds of the ancient battles between the piskeys and the faeries of Kernow, and they were terrible. In the end, most of the faeries were dead or taken captive, and the survivors fled into England and Wales, too frightened to return.' She looked at Ivy. 'Isn't that true?'

This was going every bit as badly as Ivy had feared. No wonder Martin had urged her to betray him: what hope did she have of convincing these people to trust her otherwise?

'Yes,' she said. 'But you don't understand. We're not—'

'I understand,' said Queen Valerian. 'Like your mother, you have no interest in faery concerns. Your only thought is for your family.'

No, Ivy wanted to say, *it's not like that*. But maybe it was. Yes, she'd been shocked to learn about the violence of her piskey ancestors, and finding out that her own mother was a faery had forced her to reconsider the prejudices she'd been raised with. But she still thought of faeries as a foreign people, not like the piskey friends and neighbours she'd been trying so hard to save.

She couldn't say she *cared* about the Oakenfolk: how could she, when she barely knew them?

'Yet I have three hundred faeries under my protection,' the queen continued, 'and I will not be another Empress, sending them into peril against their will. I have no doubt that your mother's need is great. But healers skilled enough to treat injuries like hers are rare, and the cost of such healing is greater than you know.'

Her gaze locked onto Ivy's, and Ivy had the unnerving feeling that Valerian was looking *through* her, to a vision of something greater and deeper beyond. 'So if you want our help, you must give us better reason to do what you are asking. What can you offer us?'

Ivy's stomach tightened. Everything in her cried out against doing this, but she'd given Martin her promise, and she could see no other way. Still, she'd have to choose her words carefully, or the Oakenfolk might suspect her true feelings and think she was leading them into a trap.

'If my mother has wronged you,' she said, 'then she can answer for that herself, if she lives. But I do know one thing. If she hadn't made the mistake of trusting someone who betrayed her to the Empress, she would never have had to fight in any of those battles you talk about at all.' She drew a deep breath. 'The faery who deceived her was called Martin. He's a liar and a murderer, and I know you've been looking for him. And if you help me…I'll tell you where he is.'

Rob went rigid. Rhosmari's hands flew to her mouth. Ivy went on, 'The piskeys of Kernow are no threat to you. They live underground, and they haven't fought any battles in years…'

She trailed off, because none of the council seemed to be listening. Rob had sunk back onto the bench, staring into space. Thorn and Campion were conversing in heated whispers, and the bearded man was heading over to join them. Rhosmari sat with head bowed, while Wink put a consoling arm around her. Only Queen Valerian kept her eyes on Ivy, her expression grave.

'We will consider your offer,' she said. 'Allow us to discuss it a little while in private, and I will call for you when we are ready.'

When Ivy left the audience chamber, she nearly bumped into Linden, who'd been standing just outside the curtain. With no sign of embarrassment, the faery girl beckoned Ivy down the corridor into another room – Wink's chamber, by the cheerful look of the place – and shut the door behind them.

'I wasn't eavesdropping,' she said quickly. 'Queen Valerian asked me to wait outside in case she needed me to fetch something – I do that for her sometimes, when Wink's busy in council. But is it really true? You know where Martin is?'

'Yes,' said Ivy.

Linden let out her breath. 'I can't believe it. We've been searching for over a year. Rob thought we'd never find him.'

So Martin had been right. Despite all the evil the Empress had done, Rob was still determined to see her murderer brought to justice. And judging by the way the rest of the council had reacted, he wasn't the only one.

'That girl who was sitting next to Wink,' said Ivy. 'Rhosmari. What did Martin do to her?'

The words had scarcely left her mouth before she remembered: Marigold had told her the story, right after Martin disappeared two months ago. But Linden was already talking, and it would have been rude to interrupt.

'The same thing that he did to your mother,' she said. 'Tricked her into trusting him, and betrayed her to the Empress. And for Rhosmari it was especially awful, because her people – the Children of Rhys – had been safe from the Empress until then, and her getting captured put all of them in danger too. It turned out all right in the end, but Rhosmari was so hurt…I don't think she's ever quite got over it.'

Ivy could understand why. If Martin had done anything to threaten or endanger the Delve, she wouldn't find it easy to forgive him either.

'And it wasn't just the Empress that he killed,' Linden went on, prodding the coals in Wink's brazier to life and setting the kettle on to boil. 'He murdered a good friend of Rob's too – a human friend, just a harmless old man. I mean, it was the Empress's fault really, it was on her orders, but Rob never knew who did the actual killing. When he found out that it was Martin…I've never seen Rob so upset. He said he'd seen Martin that same night, before and after, and he'd never let on it was him or shown any guilt about doing it.'

Ivy sank onto the brightly cushioned sofa, feeling numb. None of this should surprise her, not after what she knew of Martin's past. But he'd never done Ivy harm, or deceived her in any significant way; he hadn't killed or even injured anyone, in all the months she'd known him. And last night in the shop he'd touched her so tenderly, and given his very life into her hands. It was hard to reconcile that Martin with the cunning, remorseless killer Linden described.

But at least now it made sense that Rob would want to see Martin punished. It was hard to imagine anyone mourning the Empress, but an innocent man...

'And there've been problems with the other faeries as well,' said Linden, spooning tea leaves into the pot. 'The ones outside the Oak, I mean. They're glad to be free of the Empress, but they're also frightened that nobody's in control any more, and they know we haven't caught Martin yet. Some of them think he killed the Empress so he could rule in her place, and since then he's just been biding his time, plotting to come back and take over.'

The idea of Martin wanting to be Emperor was so absurd, Ivy had to choke back a laugh. Being responsible for thousands of faeries, having to listen to their grievances and settle their disputes, was the last thing he would want. 'You think they'd follow him if he did?' she asked.

'I don't know.' Linden looked troubled. 'Maybe. They don't know what to make of Queen Valerian – they don't understand why she hasn't just seized power and set herself up as the new Empress. They think that means she's weak, because they're so

271

used to having someone thinking and giving orders for them, instead of encouraging them to choose their own leaders and think for themselves.'

She swirled the teapot, poured two cups and handed one to Ivy. 'The Empress had got rid of all the other queens when she came to power, you see. And after that she was forever sending faeries from one place to another, so they could never get attached to any one wyld or even have proper families any more, let alone work out how to govern themselves. Now she's gone they have all these choices to make, and it's making them terribly anxious. I think they'd almost be glad if Martin did come back.'

And if the Oakenfolk saw Martin as a political threat, it made even more sense that they'd want to capture him. It would show the other faeries that Queen Valerian wasn't weak after all, and quash any rumours of Martin becoming the new Emperor. Ivy laced her hands around the earthenware cup, its warmth radiating into her palms. 'Are you sure you should be telling me all this?' she asked.

Linden blinked. 'Why shouldn't I?'

'Well,' said Ivy, 'if I were an enemy, I could use that information against you.'

'But you're not.'

All Ivy's life she'd been warned not to deal with faeries, that they were cruel and calculating and made deceitful bargains. She'd never imagined that any of them could be as innocent as Linden.

'I'm a piskey,' she explained. 'You heard what Rhosmari said

272

back there: my people did terrible things to yours. There's no reason you should trust me with your secrets.'

'Oh, it's no secret,' said Linden. 'You could easily find out all that yourself, just by visiting another wyld or two. And we faeries did some pretty terrible things to each other in the past as well, so I don't think we can go about judging people because of their ancestors. All we can do is try to be better now…'

A tinkling bell-chime interrupted her, and Linden quickly set her tea cup down. 'That's the Queen,' she said. 'We should go.'

'The council has agreed,' Queen Valerian told Ivy. 'We will accept your bargain.'

After what Linden had told her, Ivy wasn't surprised. But the relief she felt was mingled with an aching sense of loss. Even if Martin preferred to break the *tenkyz* and die rather than face a lifetime of imprisonment, even if it was no more than he deserved for his crimes, Ivy would always be haunted by the knowledge that she'd been the one to betray him.

'I'm grateful,' she said, but the words came roughly, and she could not meet Valerian's searching gaze.

'Broch has been training as a healer these past months,' the queen said, gesturing to the sharp-featured man. 'He is willing to journey back to Cornwall with you, and use his skills to help your mother. And Thorn will accompany him, as my representative.'

Linden started at this news, and Wink looked shocked. But Thorn gave a curt nod, as though this was no more than she'd expected.

'If your mother lives,' Valerian continued, 'and you are satisfied that she is fully healed, then Thorn and Broch will escort you back to the Oak, so that you can lead us to Martin.'

Ivy hated to say it – hated even to think it – but the possibility had to be faced. 'And if my mother dies?' she asked.

'Then you are released from your obligation,' said Valerian. 'And you may choose whether you still wish to help us or not. But whatever happens, it is my hope that you will consider the Oakenfolk your friends and allies, as we have sought to be yours.'

Meaning that even if Broch failed to save Marigold, the queen hoped Ivy would keep her half of the bargain anyway. But much as she had come to appreciate the faeries' hospitality and goodwill, Ivy had no intention of selling Martin's life so cheaply. There might still be some way of freeing him from the *tenkyz*, if only she had time to find it. 'I appreciate your kindness,' she said, and made a little bow.

'Then go with my blessing,' Queen Valerian told her gently. 'And may the Great Gardener give you safety on your way.'

twenty-three

'But Thorn,' pleaded Wink, hurrying after the other faery as she and Ivy came out onto the landing, 'you've never gone so far from the Oak before. You've never been *anywhere*, except for that time we all went to Wales to fight the Empress. Why now?'

'Why not?' asked Thorn irritably. 'I don't see any point in sitting here like a mushroom, when I can make myself useful.'

'Yes, but you can't fly on your own wings, not all that distance. Broch'll have to carry you, and you're going to be terribly sick…'

Thorn dismissed this with a snort. 'We'll meet you on the lawn in ten minutes,' she said to Ivy, then turned back to Wink. 'And you, stop that hand-wringing or I'll thump you. I'll be perfectly fine.' She marched off the edge of the landing, wings buzzing to life behind her, and zoomed away.

Wink watched her go, her forehead lined with distress. Ivy had to wonder why the little redhead would be so protective of a woman who clearly had no interest in being coddled – but that was none of her business. Besides, Rob was striding towards her now, with Rhosmari close behind him, and the last thing Ivy wanted was to be questioned about Martin. Hurriedly taking her leave of Wink, she changed to swift-shape and flashed away.

Once she landed on ground level and made her way outside, it wasn't long before her new companions came to join her. Broch's bird-form was a rook – a slow flier compared to Ivy's peregrine, but large enough to carry Thorn and their combined baggage with ease. As they launched themselves into the noonday sky, Ivy heard Thorn muttering curses; the faery woman lay flat with her arms flung around Broch's neck, and her legs gripped his sides so hard they trembled. But the rook's wingbeats stayed smooth and even, and eventually Thorn began to relax, sitting up a little and even opening her eyes a crack before squeezing them shut again.

But as they flew on, angling south-west to avoid the roar and stench of an airport and riding the winds over a long, rambling stretch of downland, it soon became clear that the faery woman was more than just uneasy; she was unwell. Her face had turned ashen, dark circles ringed her eyes, and she kept making faces as though trying not to be sick. It seemed Wink's concerns about her had been justified.

Yet Valerian was a healer as well as a queen, and surely she knew Thorn's weaknesses even better than Wink did. So why would she choose her to make this journey – indeed, why send an emissary to Cornwall at all? Ivy's mother wasn't a queen or any kind of leader; she was just an ordinary faery woman, with no particular power or influence. So this was hardly a diplomatic mission.

On the other hand, the queen had said that skilled healers like

Broch were rare, so perhaps she'd sent Thorn along to protect him. Certainly Thorn's stocky build and fierce expression made her look like a soldier, even if she didn't appear to have much fight in her at the moment...

Then Broch swooped downward, his long glide carrying him down to a little valley where a stream ran cold and clear. He came to a flapping halt on the rocky bank, and Thorn slid off him and dropped to her knees. With a falcon's scream of frustration at the delay, Ivy wheeled to join them.

'It's not wasted time,' said Broch, shifting out of bird-shape to talk to Ivy as Thorn, bent double, retched into the grass. 'If we can Leap back instead of flying, we'll save hours on the return journey.'

'It's wasted if my mother dies before we can get to her,' Ivy said. 'You're a healer – isn't there something you can do to fix this?' She gestured at Thorn. 'Surely you could put her to sleep, if nothing else.'

'And I'll just hang onto him in my sleep too, I suppose?' Thorn snapped, straightening up with difficulty and wiping her mouth on the back of her hand. 'Anyway, he can't just go flinging healing spells about like so much thistledown – he's got to save all his power to help your mother. Have some sense.'

'You see the problem,' Broch said drily to Ivy. 'But don't worry. We'll get to Cornwall as quickly as we can.'

Broch was true to his word, and Ivy could tell that Thorn too was doing her best to endure the long flight without complaint. But they still had to land several more times before the countryside started to look familiar to Ivy. As they crossed into Cornwall she took the lead, flying faster than before and determined not to stop again. They'd reach Marigold in an hour, if the others would only keep up. She flapped westward, the sun blazing in her hooded eyes.

The sky was dusky and darkening to nightfall when they reached the cottage. As Ivy glided down to land in the cobbled yard she glanced about for any sign of danger, but all seemed quiet. Broch and Thorn followed her, both of them transforming as she did to human shape and size, and the three of them hurried up the path to the house.

But the door was locked – and Ivy had left her house key inside. 'Cicely!' she shouted, rapping the knocker. 'I've brought help! Let me in!'

She pressed her ear to the wood, listening for an answer, but all she could hear was the pounding of her own heart. Had her little sister fallen asleep? She knocked again, harder. 'Cicely! Open the door!'

Still no answer. Thorn and Broch exchanged looks, and then Thorn cleared her throat and spoke. 'It smells like humans have been here,' she said. 'And not too long ago, either.'

Fear twisted inside Ivy. She'd been gone almost twenty-four hours – anything could have happened while she was away. What if one of their human neighbours had seen the smoke drifting from the kitchen, and come over to investigate? What if they'd found out Marigold was injured, and insisted on calling an ambulance? Her mother could be trapped in hospital right now, with Cicely helplessly watching as the doctors did all the wrong things, and by the time she found them it could be too late…

'The curtain moved,' said Broch in a low voice. 'There's someone inside.'

'Blight,' muttered Thorn. 'What if it's a trap?'

But before any of them could move the lock clicked open, the latch rattled, and the door opened wide. Ivy stepped forward – and froze, her stomach lurching with dismay.

It wasn't Cicely who had answered the door. It was David Menadue.

'What are you doing here?' Ivy demanded. 'Where's Cicely? Where's my mother?'

Molly's father ran a hand over his face and up into his hair. 'Sleeping,' he said thickly. 'Both of them. Your sister was exhausted after being up all night, and Marigold…'

That was all Ivy needed to hear. Her mother was still here, and alive. She pushed past David and raced down the corridor to the bedroom.

The first thing that hit her was the sweet-sour stench, even worse than she remembered. Behind her Thorn made a gagging noise, but Broch followed Ivy into the room without breaking stride. Only his flared nostrils and the curl of his upper lip betrayed that he could smell it too.

Marigold lay on her back, the limp hanks of her remaining hair snaked out across the pillow. Her eyes were closed, her body stiff, and when Ivy peeled the dampened sheet away from her body she didn't even flinch. If not for the faint rasp of her breathing, she might have been dead already.

Carefully Broch removed the honey-soaked dressings from Marigold's arm and face, eyes narrowing as he examined the burns beneath. 'These are the worst injuries I have seen,' he said at last. 'It will take a great deal of power to heal them, and the shock may be more than your mother's body can endure.' He gave Ivy a penetrating look. 'Are you certain you want me to do this? Or I should say, are you certain it's what she would want?'

Ivy stared at him. 'Of course it is. Why would you even ask?'

'Because,' said Broch with a hint of impatience, 'you have a choice to make. I can try for a complete healing, if you are prepared to take the risk that she may not survive it. Or I can give her a milder infusion of power to strengthen her body and ease her pain, and then leave her to heal on her own. The scars will be permanent, and she may never get back the full range of movement in that arm...but she will live.'

Ivy shut her eyes, unable to look at her mother's white, pain-lined face. The thought of Marigold spending the rest of her life disfigured and crippled, forever reminded of what Betony had done to her, was unbearable. Yet what would be the use of Broch making her whole if she died while he was doing it?

'I don't know,' she whispered. 'I don't know what she'd say.'

'I do,' said David Menadue, walking to join them. His hair was rumpled and his eyes bleary, as though he'd just woken up from a too-short and not very comfortable sleep – which, Ivy realised as she caught sight of his jacket hanging over the bedside chair, he probably had. What was he doing here? Why didn't he seem surprised about anything that was going on?

'Your mother talked to me a little,' he went on before Ivy could ask, 'when I arrived this morning. I think she must have been delirious or she wouldn't have said some of the things she…well.' He cleared his throat. 'Anyway, she made it very clear that she'd rather die than go on living like this.'

Broch met the human man's gaze and held it, as though trying to judge whether he was telling the truth. Then he said, 'Very well.' He tossed the stained and sticky dressings into the bin, and turned to Thorn. 'Are you ready?'

'Of course,' said the faery woman crossly, shoving past David to join him. She still had one hand pressed to her stomach, but the colour was coming back into her face. 'Where do you want me?'

'Here.' He pointed to the chair, and Thorn sat down. 'And now Ivy.' He gestured to his other side. 'Stand here, if you will.'

David Menadue shifted uneasily. 'Is there…anything I can do?'

'You can close the door behind you,' replied Broch, not looking up. 'And don't bother us until we're done.'

For a few seconds Molly's father hesitated, his eyes on Marigold. Then he bowed out and shut the door.

'Why do you need me?' Ivy asked. 'I'm no healer.'

'Neither is Thorn,' Broch replied. 'But for a healing this deep, I'll need you both.' He went down on one knee beside the bed. 'Though I won't draw magic from either one of you, unless I have to. I'm just using you as anchors.'

Linden had said something to Rob about an anchor too. 'What does that mean?' asked Ivy.

'Small or superficial wounds are easily healed,' Broch said, in the crisp tones of a scholar. 'But when a patient is severely injured, the healer has to put intense concentration and a considerable amount of their own power into healing them, and that can cause…difficulties.'

'Such as?'

'It depends,' began Broch, but Ivy persisted, 'On what?'

'On how close the two of you were to start with, of course,' snapped Thorn. 'It's all very well making someone better, but if you don't know what you're doing and your magic ends up all muddled with theirs…'

'It can be awkward.' Broch's mouth twitched, halfway between a grimace and a smile. 'That's why many healers don't do deep work on anyone but close friends and relatives if they can help it. Or else they make sure they've got at least one anchor with them: someone who knows either the healer or the patient well, and can remind them where one ends and the other begins.'

And with Ivy and Thorn beside him, Broch would have two such anchors. Clearly he was taking no risks – and it also showed how demanding he thought this spell would be. No wonder Queen Valerian had said that the cost of such healing was more than Ivy knew.

Had Martin known the risk of not having an anchor when he'd poured his magic into saving Ivy's life? Or had he been as unaware as she was of how that impulsive healing would connect them? She touched the copper bracelet on her wrist, wondering if she would ever have the chance to talk to him again and find out.

'Now,' said Broch, interrupting her thoughts, 'we begin.' He stretched out his hands with deliberate slowness, laying one on Marigold's head and the other on her heart. Then he closed his eyes, and his fingers began, very softly, to glow.

This was nothing like Ivy remembered from her own near-death healing, which had been brief and violent – a concentrated burst of power that had jolted her whole body and shocked her back to life at once. Broch worked with painstaking caution, magic curling from his hands in rosy wisps and slow golden spirals to spread, inch by inch, across Marigold's burned side.

'Thorn,' he said between his teeth, and the faery woman put a hand on his shoulder.

'Broch,' she replied, her voice gruff but strangely gentle. Broch bent lower, a shudder running through him, and the livid burns on Marigold's cheek and arm began to change.

First the raw wounds smoothed over, healthy pink flesh rising in their place. The stench that had permeated the room faded away. Then the magic swirled faster, spiralling down Marigold's arm and arcing across her chest, and her mother's harsh breaths became even. Even the scorched parts of her hair were growing back now, golden-brown waves unfurling where before there had been only frizz and stubble. The colour returned to her cheeks, and the tension in her face eased away. She looked like a healthy, beautiful woman resting peacefully in bed, and soon there was no sign that she had ever been injured at all.

'Mum?' whispered Ivy, and Marigold's eyes fluttered open. She focused on Ivy, and her lips curved in a smile. She reached up to touch her cheek, and Ivy's eyes welled up as she smiled back.

'Broch!' barked Thorn, jumping up to catch the faery man as he crumpled. She dragged him back into the corner, where he slumped with head lolling, spent.

Ivy watched them until she was sure Broch would be all right, then turned back to her mother. 'Mum,' she said softly, 'I have so much to—'

Marigold's breath hitched, then stopped. Her smile faded, the light went out of her eyes, and her arm fell limp to the bed.

'Mum?' Ivy grabbed her mother and shook her. 'Mum!'

Thorn thrust Ivy aside, bending to listen to Marigold's chest and check her pulse. When she straightened up, her expression was grimmer than ever.

'No good,' she said. 'Her heart's stopped.'

'No.' Ivy stumbled back, eyes locked on her mother's still body. 'Not now, not after all this—' A sob broke from her, and she flung the bedroom door open and ran out.

She collided with David Menadue in the hallway; he caught her and said sharply, 'What is it?' while at the same moment, Cicely's door flew open and Ivy saw her pale, frightened face. But Ivy had no words to give either of them. She wrestled free of David's grip, staggered through the sitting room and burst outside into the cold evening light, blinded with tears.

She'd flown so far and sacrificed so much to save her mother: she'd pushed herself harder and taken greater risks than ever before. But it had all been for nothing, because Marigold was dead.

And it was Betony's fault.

Ivy braced her hands on her knees and drew a long, shuddering breath. Then she rubbed her sleeve across her wet face and walked back into the cottage. From Marigold's bedroom she could hear Thorn and David Menadue arguing while Cicely wept, but Ivy paid no heed to any of them. She stooped under the wardrobe for the sword she'd taken from the Grey Man's trove, pulled it free of the scabbard and tested its edge with her thumb. Then she sheathed it again, buckled it around her waist, and willed herself to the Delve.

'Ivy? Surely it can't be – yes it is! *Ivy!*'

Fern wasn't the first neighbour Ivy had heard calling after her, but she didn't break stride. She'd got this far into the Delve by moving fast and not stopping for anyone, though she'd left Jenny's brother Quartz goggling when she pushed past him in the Narrows, and she'd been swarmed by excited children when she passed the Upper Rise. But she'd turned the sword at her side invisible before plunging into the hillside, so while her fellow piskeys might be surprised to see her marching through the tunnels, they had no reason to suspect she was there for anything more than a visit. The Joan had never publicly condemned Ivy as a traitor or admitted to banishing her, after all.

Still, she was coming into Long Way now, and the door of her old home cavern was only a few paces ahead. If Mica had heard

Fern's shout, he'd come bursting out into the tunnel any minute. Was she really prepared to fight her own brother to get to Betony? And would she have any chance of beating him, if she did?

Ivy's hand dropped to the hilt of her sword, gripping it hard. *Stay inside, Mica*, she thought. *Don't make me do this.* She stepped to the far side of the tunnel, watching the door as it cracked open—

But no, it wasn't moving at all, it must have been a trick of the light. Ivy relaxed and quickened her pace, galloping down the stairs to the next level. The work day had ended over an hour ago, so by now most of the men would be home with their boots off and their feet up, and the piskey-wives would be calling their children for dinner. If she kept away from the common caverns, she had a good chance of getting to Betony without anyone noticing...

'Ivy?'

His voice was soft, as always. But after the things he'd said to her in Redruth, Ivy knew better than to think he was on her side. She spun and whipped out her sword.

'I don't have time to argue with you, Matt,' she said. 'So walk away now, and forget that you ever saw me.'

Mattock moved cautiously out of the side tunnel. 'What are you doing here? Mum told me she'd seen you, but I couldn't believe...' His brows creased. 'Why are you holding your hand like that?' He stepped forward – and the point of the sword bumped his chest. His eyes widened.

'I told you,' Ivy said, 'walk away.'

Mattock raised his hands in a gesture of surrender and began walking backward, his miner's boots scuffing loudly on the granite floor. 'Just tell me what this is about,' he urged, but Ivy set her jaw.

'It's none of your business,' she said. 'This is between Betony and me.'

'Not any more it isn't,' said her brother curtly from behind her, and his powerful hands seized her arms, wrenching them behind her back. The sword clattered to the floor at her feet, and Ivy struggled to reach it, but Mica was as strong as any knocker in the Delve, and he held her fast.

'I'm sorry, Ivy.' Matt sounded shaken, but he didn't move to help her. 'We can't let you do this.'

So he'd known her brother was there all along. 'Traitor!' Ivy spat at him, twisting and wrenching against Mica's hold. 'Coward!'

'Stop it, you little fool! You're only making it worse.' Mica gripped her wrists tight, lashing them together. 'Ivy, daughter of Flint, I arrest you in the name of the Joan.'

Ivy kicked back against his shin as hard as she could, but her rubber soles were no match for his boots. 'She killed our mother, Mica!' she shouted. 'She threw a fireball at her and *burned* her! How can you take her side after—'

Mattock pushed his wadded-up handkerchief into her mouth. She was still trying to spit it out as Mica flung her over his shoulder and carried her away.

twenty-four

Ivy huddled at the back of her tiny cell, sick with despair. Mica had freed her hands and Mattock had pulled the gag out of her mouth before they left, but that was little comfort – not after they'd carried her deep into the diggings and stuffed her into a hole in the tunnel wall, then heaved a great slab across the entrance to trap her in. She couldn't will herself out, because travel-magic didn't work underground; she could take any shape or size she wished, but she'd never get past that block of unyielding granite. There was no enemy here for her to fight, no tools she could use to break free. She had no food, no water, no hope of rescue – and she was all alone.

Her only consolation, if it could be called that, was that she wouldn't have to face the Joan's wrath right away. As she'd heard Mica and Matt discussing on the way down, Betony was busy preparing for a great banquet in the Market Cavern tonight, where she would give a speech to honour Nettle's memory and confirm Jenny as her new attendant. So it wouldn't be until much later, perhaps even tomorrow, before she could spare the time to deal with Ivy.

Still, a few hours more or less wouldn't change the inevitable outcome. There would be no trial for Ivy, no chance to defend herself or call on her allies for help. Betony would simply burn Ivy to ashes where she stood, because no one – not Mattock, not Jenny, not even her own brother – had the courage to stop her. Then she'd go back to ruling the Delve as she saw fit, while the rest of Ivy's people sickened and died one by one. Cicely would be left without a family, and Molly without protection. Martin would spend the rest of his life as a slave to Thom Pendennis...

And Ivy would never see him, or any of the other people she loved, again.

The first tear fell, threading hot down Ivy's cheek. Then the tightness in her chest shattered into jagged shards of grief and she was sobbing, rocking, pressing her face against her knees. She'd been so unhappy and restless in her exile, so obsessed with saving her people and proving Betony wrong, she'd taken the most precious things in her life for granted – like the family she still had in Marigold and Cicely, and her growing feelings for the young man who'd saved her life and shown her how to fly. No matter how false Martin might have been in the past, he'd been nothing but true to Ivy, and she loved him, spriggan or not. But she hadn't fully realised that until this moment, and now it was too late.

Ivy wept until she had no tears left, only a hollow ache inside her. Then she wiped her wet cheeks with both hands and slumped against the wall, exhausted by the force of her emotions. She hated crying: it never made anything better. But at least she'd got it out of the way before Betony came. She sat there in weary silence, until her eyes closed and she drifted into a shallow, fitful sleep.

'Faster, lad! They're catching up!'

In the stark moonlight shadows spilled black across the ground, and every rock gleamed like a whetted knife. The boy sprinted after Helm, small legs pumping furiously to keep up with the old warrior's loping strides. He didn't dare look back, but he could hear the shouts of the knockers chasing after them, and it sent a ripple of gooseflesh over his skin.

He'd thought they'd be safe in that seaside cave, if only for the night. But once the piskeys found the bodies of their fallen comrades, they'd wasted no time hunting the spriggans down. Helm had whistled up a wind to blind their enemies, and he and the boy had changed to human size as they fled. But what they'd made up in speed they'd lost in endurance, and as their strength flagged the piskeys kept up their relentless pursuit. Soon they'd be in range of their enemies' slings and arrows, and if that happened, the two of them wouldn't live to see tomorrow's sunrise...

Unless one of them gave himself up, so the other would have a chance to get away. And if it came to such a sacrifice, the choice was obvious. Helm was the seasoned warrior, the one most likely to survive – why should he die because of a stripling boy? He gulped, blood pounding through his ears, and began to slow his pace. But he must have dropped behind too quickly, because the older spriggan rounded on him.

'Hoy there, what d'you think you're doing?'

'Drawing them off,' muttered the boy, and turned to run.

Helm grabbed his arm. 'None of that nonsense,' he growled. 'The Grey Man didn't give his life just so you could throw yours away.' He wrestled the boy back on course and gave him a shove, pushing him to the front of the trail. 'You owe it to him, d'you hear me? Whatever happens to me or you or both of us, whatever it costs you, you stay alive – and keep running.'

When Ivy woke she was gasping for breath, as though she'd been running with Helm and the boy. Poisoned air was seeping into her cell, making her lungs burn and her throat ache. Mica's knocker blood gave him some immunity, so he probably hadn't thought twice about the poison when he put her down here. But Ivy took after their mother, and if she stayed in this cell much longer, Betony might not need to execute her.

She scrambled to her feet, willing her skin-glow brighter as she scanned the rugged walls. It was no use trying to plug up that crack at the top of the door, not when the poison was already in here with her. And the gap was far too narrow for her to squeeze through, even at her tiniest size. In desperation Ivy threw her weight against the slab that trapped her, then splayed both hands against the stone and tried to shift it sideways. But it stayed just as firmly planted as before. Ivy backed up to the wall, ready to leap and kick out with both feet – not that she hadn't tried all those things at the beginning, but she couldn't bear to just lie down and wait for the end to come.

She was gathering her strength for the jump when she heard it – a grinding rasp of stone on stone, shockingly loud in the silence of the diggings. The door of her cell had moved.

So Betony had found time to deal with her after all. Ivy fought back her rising terror and dropped to a crouch, readying herself to spring. If her aunt wanted to kill her, she'd have to fight off a furious peregrine first…

'Ivy?' The whisper came urgently through the gap in the door. 'It's me. I've come to rescue you.'

Her fists unclenched. 'Matt?'

'I know it looked bad, before.' He heaved the slab again, and now she could see his face, earnest and anxious in the light of their shared skin-glow. 'But Mica had already seen both of us, so I didn't have any choice but to play along… There. Can you get out?'

It was a narrow gap, but wide enough for Ivy. Ignoring the hand Matt offered her, she slipped through and stepped quickly out of his reach. She wanted to believe him, but what if this was a trap?

'Betony knows you arrested me,' she said. 'She's never going to believe I escaped on my own.'

'She doesn't know anything,' said Mattock. 'I let Mica think I was going to tell her we'd caught you, right after we put you in here. But I never did.'

'But he wasn't the only one who saw me. What about the others?'

'I thought of that too. So I made sure to tell my mum and Quartz that you'd come to have a private word with Betony, and it wouldn't be right for any of us to go gossiping about it.'

And to think she'd worried that travelling with Martin was making *her* deceptive. 'Oh,' said Ivy faintly.

'I would have come sooner, but it took a while before I could get away without anyone noticing. And I took a couple of wrong turns coming to find you – Mica knows the diggings a lot better than I do. But I think I've got it now.' He glanced both ways down the rough-hewn tunnel, then took Ivy's arm and set off. 'Right now everyone's feasting in the Market Cavern, and the Joan's about to make her speech. There should be enough time to get you out of here and up to the Great Shaft, if we're lucky.'

Ivy hurried to keep up with him, resisting the urge to pull away. She knew her own mind now, if she hadn't before; whatever future might lie in store for her, she wouldn't be spending it with Mattock. But this was no time to get into an argument about it. 'Do you know what happened to my sword?' she asked.

'Mica took it,' Matt replied. 'I don't know what he did with it, but does it matter? You don't need it now, do you?'

Ivy hesitated, not sure how to answer. Wearing the sword to the Delve had been more an expression of her own rage and grief than anything else, a symbol of her resolve to get to Betony and confront her at any cost. But now that she'd had time to think about it, she realised how futile a gesture that had been. Even if she'd been skilled in swordcraft, how could anyone fight off fire?

Still, she hated to lose the weapon when she'd brought it all this way, just as she hated to go sneaking out of the Delve with nothing but her own life to show for it. If only there was something she could do to help her fellow piskeys, before she left them forever…

She pulled back, forcing Matt to a stop. 'Wait,' she said. 'That feast in the Market Cavern.'

'What about it?'

'The Joan's about to stand up in front of the whole Delve, and make a speech. Everyone will be watching her, won't they?'

'Yes, of course, but…' He broke off, his face turning pale. 'Ivy, no.'

'Why not? It's the perfect time. If I confront her now, she won't be able to hide.'

'But she'll kill you!'

'Maybe.' *Probably.* 'But I saved the Delve from Gillian not that long ago, so to a few piskeys at least, I'm a hero. If Betony executes me, they'll want to know why – and maybe that's all it will take. Maybe…' She stood taller, her conviction growing. 'Maybe my death is exactly what our people need, to make them stop believing in Betony.'

Matt caught her face between his hands. 'No,' he whispered. 'Don't do this. You have too much to live for. If not for me, then think of your sister. Think—' He swallowed. 'Think even of *him*, if you have to. Just…please, Ivy. Don't throw your life away.'

So he did love her, after all. He might even follow her, if she agreed to leave the Delve in peace. After all, Mica wouldn't stay ignorant forever, and Ivy knew from bitter experience how her brother reacted when someone he trusted deceived him. After disowning Ivy and refusing to acknowledge his own mother, he'd hardly make an exception for his best friend.

But Mattock must have known that too, when he came here. He'd made his choice. And so had she.

'Show me the way out of here,' Ivy said. 'You can go wherever you want after that, and do whatever you think is best. But I'm going to the Market Cavern.'

Matt slumped and let his hands fall, defeated. Without another word, he turned and led Ivy down the narrow passage. They turned left, right, and left again, the tunnel growing steadily wider as they walked, until at last it opened onto a broad gallery with a ladder at the far end. There it was: the exit to the Silverlode. And once they climbed out of the diggings, the Market Cavern would be less than twenty paces away.

But she and Mattock had only taken a few steps when something glinted in the shadows at the edge of the tunnel, and a dark figure stepped out into the circle of their shared glow. As his own skin lit up, the light reflected off a gleaming strip of metal in his hand – a sword. *Her* sword, newly polished and sharpened, and pointed deliberately towards them.

'You slurry-brained fool, Mattock,' said Mica. 'I knew I'd find you here.'

twenty-five

Mattock stepped in front of Ivy, spreading his arms wide to shield her. 'Put the sword down, Mica,' he said. 'You're not going to touch her unless you kill me first.'

'Really?' said Mica. 'I knew you fancied her, but I never guessed you were quite that serious about it. Still, you can't really think she's going to let you court her, especially not after you gagged her and stuffed her in a cell. I may not know my sister as well as I used to, but I do know that much.'

'And you think I'm going to let you put me back in that cell again?' snapped Ivy, ducking around Mattock. 'I'll spit myself on that sword before I do.'

Mica looked exasperated. 'Why would I do that? I didn't even enjoy stuffing you in there the first time around.' He thrust the sword back into its sheath. 'There. Does that make you feel better?'

'I don't know,' said Ivy warily. 'Should it?'

'Oh, for pity's sake.' He unbuckled the weapon and tossed it to the floor. 'Of course I had to arrest you, especially with Matt right there and me with no way to know whose side he was on. Once I realised you were planning to march up to Aunt Betony and point that sword at her, it was the only way I could think of to keep you from getting yourself killed.'

Ivy stared at him. Next to her, Mattock's arms wilted to his sides.

'You pair of useless pebble-wits,' said Mica. 'You deserve to get married and have children as stupid as you are.' He shoved Matt out of the way, marched forward and pulled Ivy into a rough embrace. She stood stiffly a moment, unable to believe she could have misread him so completely, then gave a little, hysterical laugh and hugged him back.

'I thought you hated me,' she said. 'I thought – when Betony banished me from the Delve, I thought you were on her side.'

'Well, I had to make *her* believe that, didn't I? Otherwise she'd have exiled me too, and there'd have been nobody who knew about the poison in the Delve. The best way I knew to help was to stay here, and try to finish what you and Dad had started.'

'So that's why you were spending so much time in the diggings,' exclaimed Mattock, and Ivy said at the same time, 'You mean… by poisoning yourself?'

'That's dross,' said Mica scornfully. 'Dad wasn't trying to poison himself either – he was trying to find the source of the poison so he could get rid of it. Why do you think he went haring after Gillian's smoke-spell? He thought the poison was her doing, and this was his chance to destroy the curse and save us all.' His face sobered, and now Ivy could see the shadow of grief in his eyes. 'I only wish it was that easy.'

'So you don't think there's any way to get rid of it?' she asked.

Mica shook his head. 'I don't think it's magical, either. It's something in the rock itself, not just in one place but all over, and the more and deeper we dig the worse it's going to get.' He grimaced. 'We're never going to find some glowing green lump we can pull out and show to Aunt Betony, if that's what you were hoping.'

'So all this time, we've been on the same side?' said Matt in disbelief. 'Why didn't you tell me?'

'Why didn't *you*, you great hillock?' Mica gave him a clout on the arm. 'When you started sneaking off at all hours without me, I was fairly sure it had something to do with Ivy. But I figured you'd tell me if anything came of it. How was I to know you were conspiring with her and Jenny to turn the whole Delve inside-out?'

Ivy started. 'Who told you that?'

'Jenny, of course,' said Mica. 'When I thought Matt was going to tell the Joan we'd arrested you, I dashed down to see her, hoping she'd catch Matt before he got there and convince him to give her the message instead. I knew she'd been up to the surface at least once, so I was ready to twist her arm if I had to – but I was pretty sure she'd want to help anyway.' He looked rueful. 'I just never guessed, until she told me, how much she'd been helping you already.'

'Oh, Mica.' Ivy put a hand to her forehead. 'I had no idea. If I'd known…we could have been working together all along.'

'Well, maybe that's not such a bad thing. Betony's been keeping a close eye on me ever since you left, and if she'd had any reason to suspect I'd been talking to you we'd all have been down the shaft.' He gave an embarrassed shrug. 'Anyway, it's not like I gave you much reason to believe I was on your side.'

Which was as close to an apology as he'd ever given her. Ivy stepped forward and hugged him again, saying quietly, 'I wish you could have seen Mum, before she died. I know you weren't happy to find out she was a faery, but…she never stopped loving you, Mica.'

Her brother's jaw clenched, and he looked away without answering. Once Ivy would have taken that as rejection, or at least denial – but now she knew better: he was grieving, and struggling to hide it.

'I have to go now,' she said, stepping back. 'Betony will be starting her speech any minute. Get out of here while you can and find Cicely, she's going to need you when I'm…'

Dead. She couldn't say the word, couldn't even make her mouth shape it: if she thought too much about what she was doing, she'd never have the courage to go on. But Mica didn't wait for her to finish.

'Not a chance,' he said. 'If you're worried about her, send Matt. But I'm not letting you go up against Aunt Betony alone.' He kicked the sword towards her. 'Here, I sharpened it for you. I'm taking this.'

He stooped into the shadows by the edge of the tunnel, and

pulled out their father's thunder-axe. A spark of magic glinted off the blade as he hefted it to his shoulder.

'I'm not leaving either,' said Mattock, and put his hand on his hunter's knife. 'Whatever happens, I'm with you to the end.'

Ivy looked from him to Mica and back again, her heart too full to speak. At last she buckled the scabbard around her waist and hooked her arms through theirs.

'All right then, let's do this,' she said. 'Together.'

'...a faithful servant, wise counsellor, and an upstanding citizen of the Delve. Nettle's presence among us will be greatly missed...'

Betony's crisp voice echoed through the Market Cavern, audible even in the passage beyond. Breathing slowly to spare her sore lungs, Ivy crouched by the entrance and studied the festive gathering inside. The granite walls were draped with banners, the ceiling hung with copper chains and dangling shards of crystal that sparkled in the light, and everyone had dressed in their finest clothes to honour the occasion. But still the great cave seemed dark and gloomy, its edges blurred with a shadow that not even the hanging lamps could banish.

All her fellow piskeys – over two hundred of them – stood dutifully facing the dais at the far end, their only movement a slight shuffling of the feet. A baby wailed, and was hushed by its mother; an old woman wheezed into her cupped hands, trying to suppress a cough. Near the back of the crowd two of the younger piskey-boys began to squirm, and one of them cast a longing glance towards the door. Hastily Ivy ducked out of sight.

'We'll never get through that lot without being noticed,' said Mica in her ear. 'They're packed to the walls in there.'

Her brother was right: even though the long tables and benches had been cleared away and there should have been plenty of space for everyone, they'd all squeezed close to the platform to get a better view of the ceremony. She'd hoped to slip invisibly along the edge of the crowd, and not reveal herself until she leaped up onto the platform with Betony. But there was no chance of that now.

Yet if Ivy waited until the Joan's speech was over and the crowd began to break up, it would be too late. If she were to have any hope of making it out of this alive – or at least making her death count for something – the whole Delve needed to hear what she had to say.

'…my pleasure to present to you,' Betony went on, 'Nettle's chosen successor, and my new attendant.' She held up a glittering, square-linked chain with a golden medallion hanging from it. 'Jenny, step forward.'

'We've got to do something,' Mattock said as Jenny climbed up onto the platform, delicately lifting her long skirts to keep from tripping. 'The ceremony's nearly over.'

'We could go up Elders' Way and break through the wall,' said Mica, reaching for his thunder-axe. But Ivy stopped him.

'No,' she said. 'We won't win anyone over by smashing up the Delve.'

And now that she thought about it, sneaking through the crowd unseen and popping up like a will-o'-the-wisp wouldn't impress them either. Most of her people loved a good prank, but this was no laughing matter. If Ivy wanted them to listen to her, she needed to prove to them that she was a true piskey at heart – honest, forthright, and brave. She rose, and laid her hand on her sword-hilt.

'Matt,' she said, 'I need you to stay back here by the door, and not move unless I call for you. If anything happens to me and Mica, you'll be the only one left who can help the Delve.'

'What are you doing?' hissed Mica, as she stepped forward. 'You can't just march in there and expect them to let you through!'

'If that's true,' Ivy replied, 'I'm doomed anyway.' Then she straightened her spine, raised her head, and walked straight into the Market Cavern.

'Let me through, please,' she said to the piskeys standing at the back of the room. 'I've come to speak to the Joan.'

At first Ivy got only scowls from the hunters and knockers, and one or two piskey-wives turned to shush her. But as soon as they recognised her, their faces cleared and they moved aside for her at once. Whispers buzzed around her as row by row, Ivy picked her way through the centre of the crowd towards the dais.

Up on the platform, Betony was draping the medallion around Jenny's neck. 'To be chosen as the Joan's attendant is a great honour,' she began, then frowned as the growing murmur reached her ears. She turned, cold gaze sweeping the crowd – and her eyes fixed on Ivy.

The colour drained out of her face, as though she had seen a ghost. But she was not the Joan of the Delve for nothing. She pointed at Ivy and snapped out, 'Gossan! Arrest this intruder!'

Fear struck into Ivy, and she almost drew her sword. But she fought the impulse, and kept her hands at her sides. 'Why?' she called back, before the Jack could move. 'What have I done wrong?'

Dead silence followed, while the piskeys looked at each other in confusion. One young hunter took a tentative step towards her, but when he saw that none of the others were doing likewise, he drew back again.

'You are impertinent and disruptive,' said Betony. 'You dishonour this ceremony. If you have something to say to me—'

'I do,' said Ivy in the loudest voice she could muster. 'I say that you murdered my mother.'

Shocked exclamations burst all around her. 'Here, lass,' said Hew, shouldering through the crowd, 'you're not yourself, you know that can't be true!'

He took her arm, not unkindly, but Ivy pulled away. 'You have no idea what's true,' she said. 'All you know is what the Joan chooses to tell you.' She pushed to the front of the crowd, holding Betony's glare with her own accusing gaze. 'But yesterday she tricked her way into the cottage where my mother was living, and burned her so badly that she died.'

'You are out of your wits, girl,' said Betony. 'Why would I trouble myself with your mother? She left the Delve six years ago to return to her own people – her *faery* people. She is no concern of mine.'

Faery. The shock of it rippled through the whole cavern, and the piskeys closest to Ivy began to back away. Out of the corner of her eye she saw Gossan motioning to the hunters and knockers under his command – they'd be on her in seconds, if she didn't move fast. With a desperate burst of energy, Ivy plunged forward and leaped up onto the platform.

'Yes!' she shouted, turning to face the crowd. 'My mother was a faery, with no piskey blood in her at all. But so was Nettle, the woman you came here tonight to honour. And if my faery blood makes me untrustworthy, then what of yours? Most of your grandmothers and great-grandmothers were faeries too!'

As soon as she finished, she knew she'd made a mistake. Her people's mistrust of faeries went as deep as their fear of spriggans, and they'd be mortally offended to hear her say such things about their ancestors. And Betony knew it too, because the smouldering anger in her eyes flared into triumph.

'Even if that were so,' she said, 'it would be ancient history. My people are all true piskeys, and so was Nettle, whatever you may believe. But' – her tone became biting – 'perhaps your faith in the goodness of faeries explains why you were so easily manipulated by Gillian, when she used you and your sister to prepare her attack on the Delve.'

The crowd became agitated, turning to one another in dismay. Betony gave a grim smile. 'I have said nothing about your treachery until now, for the sake of my brother's memory and what remains of your family's honour. But—'

'Honour!' Mica shouted from the back of the cavern. 'There's no honour in twisting the truth as you do!'

Ivy winced. She hadn't wanted her brother to give himself away so soon. But there was no stopping Mica when he was in a temper, and already he'd hefted Flint's thunder-axe and raised it high for all to see.

'You know who our father was,' he announced to the piskeys around him. 'You know he gave his life to save the Delve. And you know what Ivy did too. She fought Gillian and cast her down the Great Shaft, she led our people to safety, and then she came back to free all the piskeys who'd been trapped in the Claybane – including the Joan herself. No traitor would do that!'

'You think not?' retorted Betony, her voice cutting through the rising clamour. 'Well, she is your sister, after all. But the rest of us are not so blind. Time after time, Ivy has broken the Delve's laws and despised our sacred traditions. She freed the spriggan that you, her own brother, had captured; she went up to the surface by daylight, alone; she allowed your sister, an innocent child, to fall into Gillian's clutches. And when she saw the damage that *her* folly had caused us, she violated our secrecy and endangered our safety once again, by bringing Gillian's half-human daughter inside the Delve.'

She rounded on Ivy. 'Can you deny that everything I have said is true? Do you dare even to try?'

A hush fell over the cavern, and all eyes turned to Ivy. Inwardly she raged at how her aunt had trapped her, and she almost wished she could lie. Perhaps she could, if she tried hard enough...

But Mica and Matt knew the truth, and lying would only lose her the few allies she had. Besides, it wasn't the piskey way.

'No,' Ivy said. 'But there's more to the story than—'

Betony swept her aside and strode forward. 'By her own admission, she is guilty! And now she returns to the Delve to accuse *me* of wrongdoing, and try to turn my own people against me. What more proof do you need of her treachery?'

By the look of the cavern now, the piskeys needed none. A row of Gossan's hunters had surrounded the platform, their hands on their knife-hilts, while the knockers closed in on Mica and wrenched the thunder-axe from his hands. The old aunties shook their heads at Ivy, and the uncles called hoarsely to her to come down. Some of the younger piskey-wives cast nervous glances about the chamber, and began herding their children towards the exit.

'Wait!' shouted Ivy, darting in front of Betony again. 'If you won't hear anything else I have to say, listen to this! It isn't safe to stay in the Delve any more. There's poison in the—'

Her jaw froze in mid-sentence, all her muscles locking up at once. Off-balance, she teetered forward and fell off the edge of the platform, hopelessly trapped in her aunt's binding spell. As Gossan's hunters seized Ivy and wrenched her to her feet, Betony gave her a contemptuous look. 'We have heard enough of your *faery tales*,' she said, and turned away.

twenty-six

Ivy stood rigid and helpless in the hunters' grasp, unable even to speak. They hadn't disarmed her yet, but they didn't need to: Betony's spell bound her fast, and she couldn't have drawn her sword if she'd tried. All she could do was roll her eyes towards the platform where Betony stood with folded arms and a little smile of malice on her lips, waiting for Gossan and the others to drag her away...

'Wait!'

Jenny was trembling, but her expression was resolute. She walked forward, holding out her newly awarded chain of office. 'I don't want this,' she said. 'Not any more.' Then she dropped it at Betony's feet.

'What?' The Joan stared at her. 'What madness is this?'

In her shock, Betony had lost hold of the binding spell. At once Ivy shrank to Oakenfolk size, too small for the hunters to hold her, then darted between their legs as they turned about in confusion. Racing along the foot of the platform, she vanished into the shadows behind it, blessing Jenny for the chance to escape.

But the older girl was still talking. 'Ivy's right,' she said as she turned to face the crowd, her hands clenched in her feast-day skirts. 'There *is* poison in the Delve. Nettle died of it, and we're all suffering because of it, and it's not going to get better, no matter what the Joan says.'

'How dare you,' said Betony in a low, venomous tone. Jenny swallowed, but she didn't back down.

'I've helped Yarrow care for the sick and dying. I've seen her records.' She cast a pleading look at Yarrow, but the healer refused to meet her gaze. 'There are more people sick now than there were two months ago. The Joan's spells aren't making any difference.'

Betony seized her arm. 'You ignorant, *foolish* girl. This is how you repay my trust? Get out of my sight!'

She tried to drag her off the platform, but Jenny wrenched free and spoke to the crowd again, louder and more urgent with every word. 'The only way for us to get better is to go up to the surface, like Ivy did! And if Betony's too proud to accept that her spells aren't enough to save us – if she'd rather watch us all die than admit she was wrong – then she doesn't deserve my loyalty. Or yours!'

The crowd of piskeys were shifting restlessly now, glancing at each other. Even the hunters had begun to look uneasy. 'Enough!' snapped Betony. 'Be quiet!'

Oh, Jenny, thought Ivy, crouching in the shadows. *And you believed she would never fear you.* The piskeys of the Delve might doubt Ivy's word, might even be willing to let Betony execute her as a traitor, but they'd never believe anything but good of their own faithful, good-hearted Jenny.

'But that's not the only wrong she's done,' Jenny called out, her voice cracking with the effort. 'Before Nettle died, she told me everything. She told me the Joan banished Ivy's mother for trying to warn her about the poison, and let her own children think she'd been taken by the spriggans. And she told me that Betony's been trying to kill her niece – Molly, the girl who helped save us from the Claybane!'

Gasps rose from the crowd. Every family in the Delve had been touched by the Claybane in some way; many of the piskeys still remembered all too well how it felt to be trapped in that dark curse. They knew the blood-debt they owed to Molly, Gillian's daughter or not, and now they knew she was Nettle's niece as well…

'But that's not right, the Joan doing that,' said Hew, his heavy brow creased with distress. 'That's none of it right.' Murmurs of agreement and disapproval broke out all over the cavern, and a shrill voice cried out, 'Hear Jenny! Down with the Joan!'

Betony turned white as salt. Then she let out a snarl, and lunged at Jenny.

'Jenny!' shouted Mica. 'Look out!'

But the warning came too late. Betony's hands exploded into flame, and the fireball engulfed Jenny in an instant. Her wings shrivelled to ashes, her fair hair went up like a torch, and she dropped to the dais in a heap.

'JENNY!' screamed Ivy, leaping onto the platform and throwing herself down beside her. But the girl she'd grown up with was little more than a pile of blackened rags now, far beyond help or healing. 'Jenny, no – oh, Jenny, Jenny…'

Mica sank to his knees, Flint's thunder-axe sliding from his grip. Gossan and his hunters stood rigid, staring at the platform in horror. Then Jenny's mother burst into hysterical sobs, and her neighbours rushed to comfort her.

Rage kindled inside Ivy, and she dragged herself to her feet. She fumbled for her sword, pulled it from the sheath, and stumbled across the dais to Betony. 'Kill me too, then,' she rasped, levelling the blade. 'Just like you killed her. And my mother.'

The Joan's lips twitched, then twisted. Her body shuddered, and a faint sizzling rose from her fingers as she lifted her clawed hand high. Ivy shut her eyes, bracing herself for the searing agony to come—

'No,' Betony breathed, and then in sudden frenzy, 'No! No! *No!*'

Ivy's eyes flew open. Her aunt had stumbled back, clenching and unclenching her hands. She looked like a madwoman, her hair and robes dishevelled, the pallor of her face a stark contrast with the dark shadows beneath her eyes.

'No!' she shrieked again, gripping her right wrist and shaking it wildly. 'I am the Joan! Joan the Wad!' But no spark appeared at her fingertips, or even the tiniest wisp of smoke.

Was it possible? Had she lost the ability to make fire?

A shiver rippled up Ivy's spine, followed by a rush of feverish elation. Betony was defenceless: with one thrust of her sword she could free the Delve from her aunt's unyielding rule. Marigold would be avenged, and the power of the Joan would pass to another – perhaps even to Ivy herself. And maybe then, Jenny's sacrifice would not have been in vain…

Betony whirled on Ivy, her dark eyes afire with hate. 'This is your fault,' she snarled. 'Wingless, half-faery filth!'

Ivy's hand clenched around the sword-hilt. She drew back the blade to strike – and a look of savage triumph flashed over Betony's face.

She wants this, thought Ivy, astonished. *She wants me to kill her. Why?*

'Do it!' Mica shouted over the crowd. Hardly anyone was paying attention to Ivy and Betony now; they were too busy arguing, wailing, clutching at one another. 'Do it now!'

Of course she had to kill Betony: it was the only way to make sure she would never hurt anyone again. Even if she'd lost her powers for the time being, they might come back, and then the Delve would be at her mercy. After all, a ruler who'd lost the confidence of her people could always control them by force.

Yet Ivy hesitated, wracked by indecision. If Betony wanted her to do this, she must have a reason. Had she lost all desire to live, as soon as she realised her fire-making powers were gone? Would she rather die than see another woman ruling the Delve in her place? Or was this her last attempt to win back her people's sympathies by making herself a victim, and Ivy the murderer?

But surely the other piskeys wouldn't see it that way, not after what Betony had done to Jenny. Surely they'd consider her death justice, or at least something that had to be done. Surely they'd listen to Ivy and heed her warnings about the poison, once the Joan was out of the way...

Yet even as the thought flashed through her mind, she remembered Linden's words: *They don't understand why she hasn't just seized power...they're so used to having someone thinking and giving orders for them.* And Valerian's quiet affirmation, *I will not be another Empress.*

The people of the Delve were used to being powerless too. Did she want to be another Betony?

'Well?' demanded her aunt, flinging her arms wide. 'You heard your brother. Isn't this what you've wanted all along – to destroy me, and take my place? Strike me down, then! Show the Delve how strong you are!'

Ivy looked into the Joan's blazing eyes, her anger fading to a deep, strangely peaceful conviction. Perhaps Betony was manipulating her even now; perhaps one day she'd regret not killing her when she had the chance. But she would not murder her aunt, no matter how much she'd done to deserve it. If the piskeys of the Delve couldn't see that Betony was not a leader worth following, if they weren't ready to choose life for themselves instead of waiting for her to choose it for them, then killing her would make no difference. Ivy exhaled, and began to lower her sword.

Betony saw it. Her lips parted, letting out a hiss of thwarted rage. Then with the speed of a striking adder she darted forward, and thrust herself onto the blade.

Screams echoed through the cavern. Ivy staggered, shoving at her aunt in a desperate attempt to pull the sword free. But it was already buried to the hilt, and the other woman's falling weight twisted it from her grasp. Betony crumpled to her knees, gasping, then toppled to the floor.

'She's murdered the Joan!' shouted one of the hunters, and the Market Cavern erupted into chaos. Gossan vaulted onto the platform and caught Betony in his arms, shouting for the healer. Children wailed and fled in all directions, while their mothers rushed after them. With a furious effort Mica wrestled free of the knockers holding him, and snatched up his thunder-axe again.

'Get out of here, Ivy!' he shouted, swinging it wide as piskeys scattered before him. 'Fly!'

Betony's eyes sought Ivy's, pain-dulled but glittering with malice. 'They'll never follow you now,' she whispered.

No, they wouldn't – especially once they'd seen what Ivy was about to do. But the hunters of the Delve were swarming up onto the Dais, and there was no other way to escape. With a scream of anguished fury, Ivy transformed to peregrine-shape and hurled herself into the air.

All the piskeys ducked, shielding their faces in terror. But Ivy soared high over them, diving at the last instant to shoot through the open door. She veered up the staircase that led to the upper levels of the Delve, flapping onward until the tunnels grew too dark for even a falcon's night-vision to see. Then she dropped back to piskey-shape and broke into a run.

'Stop!' she heard Matt shouting behind her. 'Everyone calm down!'

He was holding the others back, buying her time. But what would that cost him? And what would happen to Mica? He'd called out for Betony's death, loud enough for the whole cavern to hear – and even with a thunder-axe, he couldn't fight off all the knockers in the Delve by himself. Any minute now, Gossan would rise in anger from his wife's side, and order the hunters to arrest him…

A sob tore at Ivy's throat, and her chest knotted with grief for the brother she feared she would never see again. But she put her head down, and kept running.

One blind, reckless flight up the Great Shaft later, Ivy crawled between the bars and collapsed onto the muddy ground. Then she mustered the last of her strength, and willed herself back to Molly's cottage.

She was stumbling up the path to the house when Cicely came pelting out to meet her. 'Ivy! Ivy, you won't believe—' She stopped, her brown eyes widening. 'Where have you been? Is that *blood*?'

'It's not mine,' Ivy said. 'It's…it's nothing you need to worry about. What won't I believe?'

'Mum!' Cicely's face transfigured with delight. 'She's alive! David saved her! Come and see!'

A *human* had brought her mother back to life? Numb with

astonishment, Ivy allowed Cicely to drag her inside and down the corridor to the master bedroom. There sat Marigold propped up against the pillows, with Molly's father seated by her side.

'But how did it happen?' Ivy asked, once she and her mother had finished hugging and laughing and crying enough to speak. 'Thorn told me you were dead!'

'She *was* dead,' said Thorn from the doorway. 'I may not be a healer, but I do know that much. That's what I kept trying to tell *him*' – she jabbed a finger at David Menadue – 'when he started pushing on her chest and puffing into her mouth like a lunatic.'

'CPR,' said Molly's father, a little sheepishly. 'I thought if I could keep her alive long enough to get her to hospital…'

'Or in this case, until Broch woke up enough to help,' said Thorn. 'But by then it didn't take much magic to set her right. She'll be weak for a few days, that's all.' She frowned at Ivy. 'What happened to you?'

'I don't want to talk about it right now,' said Ivy, and turned to David Menadue. 'But who told you about…well, everything? What made you come here in the first place?'

'He rang to talk to Mum, the night you flew off to London,' Cicely piped up, before Molly's father could answer. 'He wanted to know why she couldn't come to the phone, and I tried to put him off, but he could tell I was upset and he kept asking questions and I – I couldn't lie.'

'Molly had told me a few things, after her mother died,' added David. 'So I wasn't as unprepared as I might have been.' He looked wryly at Marigold. 'Though I admit, finding out that I'd married one faery and fallen in love with another still came as quite the shock.'

Fallen in love? The words thumped into Ivy's heart like stones. How could that be? They'd only met a couple of times...

Yet David had rung the cottage at least twice since then that Ivy knew of, and possibly any number of other times that she didn't. And for the past few weeks Marigold had been away from the cottage much more than usual, and stayed out late on more than one occasion – could she have been going to meet Molly's father then?

Of course she could. She was a faery: she could travel by magic, and there were few places between Cornwall and London that she hadn't already been. Even the phone call that had so upset Cicely could have meant something quite different than they'd thought – not Marigold pleading with David for more time to pay the rent, but asking him to be patient while she sorted out her feelings...

'David,' said Marigold gently, 'perhaps we should talk about this later. Ivy's tired.'

She didn't say *and filthy*, but she didn't have to. Reluctantly, Ivy let go of her mother's hand and left the room, Thorn following after her.

'Broch's sleeping,' the faery woman told Ivy in her crisp, no-nonsense tone. 'And I'm about ready to turn in myself. But tomorrow, we're going back to the Oak – and now that everything's settled here, you should come with us.'

Settled? Ivy had never felt so far from it. The joy of finding

Marigold alive had distracted her for a while, but no happiness could erase the sorrow she'd carried back from the Delve. And if losing Jenny and her brother – and possibly Matt as well – wasn't bad enough, Thorn had just reminded her that she'd promised to hand Martin over in exchange for her mother's life.

But she couldn't explain any of that to Thorn. So Ivy said, 'All right,' and went into the bathroom and shut the door. She turned on the shower as high as it would go, and stepped into it with all her clothes on. She stood with head bowed, watching all the dirt and ash and blood that caked her body spiral away – and then at last, silently, she wept.

'Come on, lad! Almost there now!'

The boy struggled after Helm as they raced across the moor, crunching through dry heather and dodging bristling thickets of gorse, scrambling over stone hedges into pastures cropped short by sheep and cows. When they'd veered away from the cliffs and headed inland, he'd known the older spriggan had a plan – but they'd been running for over an hour, and the piskeys behind them were getting closer all the time. Where could they be going?

Soon he had his answer, as they crested a low hill and staggered down the slope beyond. Below them a ring of tall stones stood like grey-robed sentinels in the moonlight, and Helm clutched the boy's arm, bringing him to a halt.

'Can't go…much further,' he panted. 'Make our stand here.' He limped towards the stone circle, and the boy followed.

As they drew closer, three more stones emerged from the shadows at the centre of the ring – two stubby, smooth-worn pillars no taller than waymarks, and between them a round boulder with a hole in the middle. Helm hurried around the outside of the circle, touching each of the tall stones in turn, then took the boy's arm and led him inside.

Never had he stepped into a place that felt more ancient, or more powerful. He could sense the tingling of magic all around him, like a web of power laced between the stones, and he stood in the heart of it, silent with awe.

Yet he could hear the piskeys shout as they came over the top of the hill and spotted them, see them running down the slope with bows and thunder-axes in hand. What was the use of this place, if it couldn't shield them from their enemies? Where in this open circle of stones, this empty stretch of withered ground, were they supposed to hide? Distressed, he turned to Helm – and to his surprise, the old warrior gripped his shoulders and kissed him roughly on both cheeks.

'It's a hard road I'll be sending you on, lad,' he said. 'And I can't say where it'll lead you. But I'll tell you this. My old mam was a wise woman, gifted with the Sight, and she was in the birthing cave with your mother when you were born. And when she came out she said to your father and me, "If that one lives to be a man, he'll be the saving of our people."'

The boy drew back, shaken. 'Me? But…how?'

'Aye, well, that's for you to find out.' Helm looked out through the circle, his weathered face lined with anxiety. The knockers were fanning out to surround them, moving with the confidence of hunters sure of their prey. 'That's why the Grey Man chose to keep you unawares as long as he could, for fear that if you knew too much the

prophecy might not come true. But now we've come to this place' – he wrapped his arms around one of the stubby pillars, muscles straining as he lifted it from the ground – 'I know – we've been – on the right course – all along.'

The boy watched, bewildered, as Helm staggered across the grass with the stone and dropped it into a new position, no longer in front of the holed stone but close beside it. Then he heaved up the other post and moved it to the opposite side.

'The piskeys use this place for healing,' he said, wiping his hands on his jerkin. 'But we spriggans remember it has other uses too. Look through that hole, lad, and tell me what you see.'

Cautiously the boy approached the hoop of stone, then crouched to peer through it. At first he saw only the taller pillars on the far side of the circle, dark against the glittering stars. But then Helm stepped up behind him, laying a hand on each of the two posts. The net of magic around them shivered—

And everything changed.

The boy's mouth dropped open. The ring of standing stones had vanished, the stars were drowned in a sea of cloud, and the post Helm had moved was back in its former position. But it looked older and more battered now, with a thick crust of lichen upon it, as though it had stood there for hundreds of years...

Something whizzed through the air and Helm grunted, head snapping to one side. The piskeys were using their slings, and a flying stone had grazed his brow. Blood trickled down his face, but still he clutched the stones on both sides of the portal, unwilling or unable to let go.

319

'Get on with you, then!' he said. 'Go through it!'

The boy hesitated, but only for an instant. There was nowhere else to go now, and even an unknown future was better than certain death. He ducked and scrambled through the hole.

The world blurred, inverted, and righted itself again. Mist swirled before his eyes as he tripped and fell full-length onto the gravel. From the far side of the portal he heard the hiss of an arrow, and Helm's huff of breath as it struck.

'No!' screamed the boy, and flung himself at the portal, reaching out to seize Helm and drag him through. But as soon as the old spriggan's hands fell away from the stones, the hole turned black and a soundless explosion knocked the boy flying. His head struck something hard, white fire exploded behind his eyes, and he knew no more.

twenty-seven

Ivy flailed awake and fell out of bed, landing with a thump on the floor. Her heart drummed wildly in her chest, and her mind reeled with disbelief at how the dream had ended. Could it be? Was this the answer she'd almost given up seeking, the reason she'd been having these strange dreams all along?

Cicely stirred and rolled towards her, half-wakened by the commotion. 'It's all right,' whispered Ivy, climbing in beside her. 'Go back to sleep.'

Her little sister sighed and burrowed under the covers, her eyes drifting closed again. Ivy tried to calm herself and follow her example, but her thoughts were racing with excitement and a new, unexpected hope. She'd thought her dreams had to be about Martin's great- or great-great-grandfather, because the story had happened so long ago. But if Helm had sent the boy hundreds of years into the future…

Then the Grey Man's son could be Martin himself.

If it was true, it could change everything. Yet she had to be certain. These memories could be the key to Martin's freedom, but if Ivy were wrong, it would cost him his life.

Ivy groped for the night-stand, found her copper bracelet, and put it on. It had no power in itself, not any more: the finding spell was long broken. But Martin had given it to her as proof of his trust and friendship, and it seemed only right to wear it now. Folding her hands over her breast, Ivy lay back and closed her eyes.

She'd struggled so long to keep Martin at a safe distance, part of her was still afraid of opening her mind to him. She was a piskey and he was a spriggan, after all. But she had a Joan's blood on her hands now, and her people had rejected her. What did she have left to lose?

Nothing but her pride, and Ivy had little enough left of that. If she wanted to have any hope of saving Martin, she had to do this. She willed herself to relax every muscle, put her own fears and sorrows aside, and focus her thoughts on him.

The first memories came in flashes, fragments of disconnected thought that felt at once intimate and remote. She stumbled blindly along an unfamiliar road, her head full of fog and emptiness where her memories used to be. A shrill blare cut the night behind her and she scrambled for the hedge in terror, only to be knocked spinning into the dark. And when she woke again, she was in a room full of gleaming metal objects and noises that made no sense, with strange faces peering in at her from every side…

He was riding away from the *hospital*-place in a thing called a *car*, with a grim-faced woman beside him. He was climbing out a window in the dead of night, restless with hunger and the gnawing, irresistible need to escape. He was kneeling on the floor in a drab little West End flat, weeping over the body of a human he'd never wanted to kill. He was peering through the stage curtains of a tiny theatre, watching Lyn and Toby argue about whether to cast him in their production of *Othello*…

The visions came faster and faster, whirling dizzily through Ivy's mind. She saw, she felt – and more than that, she understood. When Martin had poured his magic into her to save her life, he'd inadvertently given her all his memories as well, including some that he himself had long forgotten. But Ivy hadn't been ready to use that gift, let alone appreciate it, until now.

Yes, Martin had made some bad choices in his life, done things that even he couldn't excuse or forgive. He'd deceived and betrayed people who'd done him no harm, and he'd turned his back on mercy when it was offered him. But he'd also been the boy who'd taken pity on a lonely woman weeping in the darkness, and who'd spared the life of a frightened piskey-child at the risk of his own.

The memories slowed to a trickle, then died away, leaving her with one last image – Martin kneeling beside a battered, unconscious girl lying among the rocks, touching each of her cuts and bruises and healing them one by one. He stooped and kissed her brow, then lifted her in his arms and carried her away.

And when Ivy opened her eyes, it was morning.

*

'You're leaving?' Cicely dropped the plate she'd been scrubbing into the dishwater and grabbed a dishtowel to dry her hands. 'Right now?'

'I'm afraid so,' Ivy told her. 'I have a promise to keep.' She glanced at Thorn and Broch, waiting in the kitchen doorway. 'Fly on ahead. I'll catch up with you in a minute.'

'You mean…you're going away with them?' Cicely looked stricken. 'But what about Mum and me?'

Ivy took her by the shoulders. 'It's only for a little while,' she said. 'But you don't really need me to look after you, not any more. Look how brave you were when Mum was hurt. She wouldn't be alive right now, if not for you.'

'But I wasn't brave at all.' Cicely's lip trembled. 'I was terrified the whole time, and when Molly's dad called I started crying and told him practically *everything*, and now…'

Ivy put an arm around her. 'Come with me,' she said, and led her down the corridor to their bedroom.

'And now what?' she asked, shutting the door behind them. 'He saved her life, Cicely. And he loves her. If she loves him too, isn't that a good thing? Dad's gone now, and Mum being lonely isn't going to bring him back.'

Her sister sniffed, but she nodded. Ivy slipped a hand under her chin and tilted it up. 'And you were brave, in every way that matters,' she said softly. 'No matter how scared you were, you didn't give up or run away, and you made sure Mum was looked after. I'm proud of you.'

Cicely's eyes brimmed, and she gave a wavering smile. Ivy

kissed her cheek. 'I have to catch up with Thorn and Broch,' she said. 'But when I get back, I'll teach you how to travel by magic, if you like.'

'Really?' Her face brightened. 'Can you teach me how to turn into one of those big, beautiful birds like you do, too?'

So Cicely had seen Ivy fly away, when she'd left to find help for their mother. And now she knew for certain what she'd only suspected before: that she'd made that desperate flight to London not as a swift, but as a falcon.

'I don't know,' she said, giving her sister a farewell hug. 'But we can certainly try.'

With no great need for urgency, and with Thorn's sickness and Broch's fatigue to slow them down, Ivy expected their journey would take most of the day. But once her falcon had caught up with Broch's slow-flapping rook, they only had to fly a short distance before the three of them could land and start travelling by magic instead. Following the faeries' lead, Ivy willed herself from one landmark to another, revisiting all the places they'd stopped along the way. By midday, they were back at the Oak.

The outside of the great tree looked much less forbidding now that Ivy had met the faeries who lived there – and especially now that she had the hope of saving Martin to sustain her. She followed Broch and Thorn up to the queen's apartments and would have accompanied them into the audience chamber as well, but Wink plucked her elbow and drew her aside.

'Queen Valerian wants to talk to Thorn in private,' she

whispered. 'Why don't you come and have tea with me, until the rest of the council arrives?'

So Ivy had to wait, and it seemed like hours before Linden poked her head through the doorway and said, 'They're ready.' But once she walked into the chamber and saw the whole council seated on the dais – especially the queen, with those searching grey eyes that seemed to look right through her – she wished it had taken longer.

Ivy had promised to show the Oakenfolk where Martin was hiding, and she was prepared to keep her word to the letter. But she was also determined to help him escape before Rob and the others could catch him. And once these faeries realised what she had done, Ivy feared they would never trust her or look on her as a friend again.

'Broch tells me that he has healed your mother,' said Queen Valerian. 'Are you ready to fulfill your part of the bargain?'

'Yes,' Ivy said. 'He's in London. I can show you where.'

'Good.' Valerian turned to the council. 'Rob, you are in command. Go with Ivy, and take as many of our people with you as you think best. Is there anyone else who wishes to go?'

'I do,' said Rhosmari. She cast an uncertain look at Ivy, who gave her a faint smile in return. She'd feared this girl before, thinking she must hate Martin as much as Rob did. But now she'd seen Martin's memories, she knew better.

Martin had manipulated Rhosmari cruelly, earning her trust only to betray her to the Empress. But instead of taking revenge on him, she'd forgiven him and let him go free. He'd scoffed at her mercy then, but he'd never forgotten it – and in the end he'd repaid her by saving the life of Timothy, the human boy she had come to love. If anyone but Ivy could believe that Martin was capable of repentance, it would be Rhosmari.

'There may be a fight,' Rob warned her. 'And knowing Martin, it'll be ugly. Do you really want to see that?'

'Yes,' said Rhosmari, with a lift of her chin that reminded Ivy painfully of Jenny. 'I am the ambassador from the Green Isles, remember, and it is our prison that Martin escaped.'

Except that Martin had escaped *before* he could be sent to prison, not afterward, so it was hard to imagine why the faeries of the Green Isles should care whether he were captured or not. But if Rhosmari wanted to believe that her reasons for going were political as well as personal, Ivy wasn't about to argue with her.

'We should wait for nightfall,' she spoke up. 'There will be fewer humans about to interfere.' And Thom would have closed up the shop and gone home by then, so she could talk to Martin alone.

'That was my thought as well,' said Rob. 'But we'll need at least one human to help us. I suggest Timothy.'

Ivy didn't have to ask why. Timothy had fought Martin before and beaten him, and unlike the faeries he could wield cold iron, which would stop Martin from using magic to escape. She could only hope it wouldn't come to that.

'I agree,' said Valerian. 'Peri can contact him for us.' She nodded at Linden, standing by the door, and the brown-haired girl slipped out. 'Ivy, I would like to speak to you in private, if you are willing. The rest of you may go.'

After Rob and most of the others had gone, the queen rose and led Ivy to her own modestly furnished but far more comfortable chambers. For some time she questioned Ivy about what Cornwall was like, while Wink served them a simple meal of soup and bread and Thorn sat in the corner, listening to every word. And though Ivy took care not to give away anything that might endanger the Delve or hint at her friendship with Martin, she somehow ended up telling Valerian most of her story.

'It seems to me,' said the queen when Ivy had finished, 'that there is much our people could learn from yours – and you from us, as well. If only your fellow piskeys could put aside their fears and prejudices, as you have…but from what you say, it sounds as though that will not happen easily. Still, the hardest heads are not always the hardest hearts,' and she smiled at Thorn, who reddened, scowled, and looked away.

Ivy had no idea what that was about, but she did feel better having talked to Valerian, even if she couldn't bring herself to speak of the troubles that haunted her most. And she was impressed once again by the faery queen's willingness to be patient with her subjects and earn their confidence and loyalty, rather than intimidating them and bending them to her will. She could only hope the next Joan of the Delve would be more like Valerian than Betony.

And later, as the sky darkened towards evening, four birds

left the Oak and winged their way towards London – Rob in his robin-shape, a faery called Llinos in the form of a small songbird, another named Tylluan who flew as a brown owl and carried Rhosmari on his back, and Ivy as a peregrine falcon, leading them all.

'The shop is on the other side of these buildings,' she whispered to Rob, when all of them had landed in a shadowed alley and transformed to human shape. The major roads of London still swarmed with traffic, but the side-streets were growing quieter as the shops, cafes and galleries closed up for the night. 'Where's Timothy?'

'I'll find him,' said Rob. 'Llinos, Tylluan, scout the area and secure it. Rhosmari, wait here with Ivy.' He pulled the hood of his jacket over his dark red hair, and set off towards the main road. The others vanished likewise, and Rhosmari and Ivy were left alone.

A misty rain began to fall, speckling Ivy's coat and the dark spirals of Rhosmari's hair with silver. The two girls stood quietly, gazing out at the darkened street. Until now, Ivy had been wondering how she could get away and talk to Martin without rousing the other faeries' suspicions. But if she had only Rhosmari left to contend with, it might not be as difficult as she'd thought…

Yet Rob and Timothy might return at any moment, so she had to act quickly. Did she dare to tell the other girl what she had in mind? Or would that be stretching Rhosmari's sympathies too far?

'So,' said Rhosmari, shivering and rubbing her arms. 'How did you know we were looking for Martin? And how did you know he was hiding here?'

Ivy had been dreading that question. 'I heard some things,' she said, careful to sound offhand. 'I tracked him down.'

Rhosmari was quiet. Then she said, 'You must hate him very much.'

'Do you?' asked Ivy.

'No.' Her dark eyes slid to Ivy. 'And you didn't answer my question.'

Maybe she should have been afraid of this girl after all. 'I didn't have any choice,' Ivy admitted. 'It was the only way to save my mother.'

Rhosmari nodded slowly, as though this made sense. 'Are you sure Martin's still here, though? He couldn't have escaped, or moved on?'

'I could find out,' Ivy said, trying not to sound too eager. This was it, the excuse she'd been looking for. 'I could fly up to the roof of the shop, and sneak in through the attic. That's how I spotted him the first time.'

'Oh, but—'

'Don't worry, I'll be careful,' Ivy said. 'Tell the others to wait for my signal. I won't be long.' Then, not daring to wait for Rhosmari's answer, she changed to swift-form and darted away.

twenty-eight

'Martin…? Martin! Are you there?'

Ivy crouched on the first-floor landing, tapping on the door. But no answer came, so she turned the knob and went in.

She was halfway down the corridor when it struck her that Martin might not be here after all, that Thom might have decided to take him off guard duty and send him on another treasure-gathering expedition. But even as she formed the thought, the flutter in her stomach and the sudden squeeze of her heart told her otherwise. She knew Martin was nearby. She could feel it.

'Martin?' she whispered again, afraid to speak louder. She'd seen a faint light at the back of the shop as she flew past, and Thom Pendennis might still be working in his office.

'I can't, Ivy.'

His voice drifted back to her from the bedroom at the end of the corridor, rough with weariness. She pushed the door open and there sat Martin with his back against the wall, one leg drawn up and the other stretched out in front of him, as though he'd been there for a long time.

'I thought I'd be ready, by the time you came.' Martin unfolded himself and got up to meet her. 'But it's too soon. My father's not dead yet, and I...can't leave him like this.'

He gestured to Walker, lying in the bed. Ivy watched the two spriggans a moment, struggling between anger and pity. Then she took Martin's hand and led him out into the corridor, shutting the door behind them.

'Martin,' she said, 'that man is not your father.'

He stared at her. 'What?'

'I don't know whether he lied to you,' Ivy said, 'or just tricked you into lying to yourself. But your real father died a long time ago.' She stepped closer to Martin, her heartbeat quickening. 'Please, there isn't much time. Let me show you.' Then she brushed the hair back from his face, and pressed her fingers to his temple.

She'd never tried this before, and at first she wasn't sure it would work. But as she closed her eyes and let Martin's lost memories flow through her mind, his sharp intake of breath and the tremor that shook his body told her that he was seeing it exactly as she did. She showed him everything she'd witnessed in her dreams, and when they came to the final, moonlit night when Helm had sent him through the portal, Martin's hands closed hard on her arms and she felt a streak of wetness run down the side of his face.

But Ivy wasn't ready to break the connection yet. She had too much to tell Martin and not enough time, so she shared her own memories with him as well, from the time they'd parted two days ago until this very moment. He felt her grief and rage as she marched into the Delve, her hopeless misery in the dark of her prison cell, the horror of Jenny's death and the shock of stabbing Betony, and all the turbulent emotions that had followed – things she had never told Valerian, or anyone else. And by the time it was over they were clinging to each other, Martin's hands buried in her hair and Ivy's cheek pressed damply to his collarbone, and there were no more questions to be asked, or answered.

'Don't let Rob and the others take you,' Ivy whispered. 'You don't owe Thom Pendennis anything, you can leave whenever you want…'

Martin released her, and walked back into the room where the old spriggan lay. He crouched by the bedside and said with surprising mildness, 'You crafty old beggar, Walker. You really had me fooled.'

The spriggan's eyes fluttered open. 'Aye, well,' he rasped, 'you can't blame me for trying.'

'I can,' said Ivy hotly, but Martin held up a hand.

'No,' he said. 'I don't blame him. He was desperate, and frightened, and he had to do what Thom said. I'd have done the same thing, in his place.' He rose, gazing down at Walker. 'He guessed I was half-faery by my looks, and he told me a story that would make it plausible he might be my father, if I was looking for one. The only thing I don't understand is how he knew to tell me about Coleman Grey.'

'That?' Walker gave a croaking laugh. 'That was a bit of spriggan luck, boy. My mother did use to say that, about him being our ancestor. I thought it might make you more proud to claim me if you knew it, but I never guessed it'd work so well.'

Perhaps it was even true, thought Ivy. The Grey Man could have had another child that Martin never knew about, or perhaps Coleman Grey had been Martin's grandfather and Walker was a distant cousin. It would explain the family resemblance...

Martin put a hand on the old spriggan's shoulder. 'It's over now,' he said. 'You're dying anyway, and keeping me here won't help you. Let it go.'

Walker's body sagged, as though he'd been freed from some great burden. Then, little by little, his face began to change. His eyes moved closer together, the irises turning hazel; the sharp cheekbones receded, and his jawline grew square and coarse. His gossamer hair thickened to iron-grey, and when the transformation was complete he looked nothing like Martin at all.

'Thank you,' he whispered. Then his gaze became fixed, and he let out a slow, rattling exhalation. He did not move again.

Martin closed Walker's eyes, then backed away. He turned out the light with a gesture, took Ivy's hand, and they walked out to the corridor together. Then without a word he led her to the stairwell, and began heading downstairs to the shop.

'Wait,' she said. 'Thom's still down there.' She could hear the man moving about the floor below, whistling tunelessly to himself. There was a sound of ripping cardboard and rustling paper, as though he were opening boxes.

'Oh, I know he is,' said Martin. 'I'm counting on it. But feel free to wait here, if you like.'

Apprehensive, Ivy followed him down the stairs and into the darkened shop, whose shuttered windows let in only faint gleams of light from the street outside. She paused to look through one of the cracks, but all seemed quiet – perhaps a little too much so.

How long would Rob and the others wait for Ivy's signal, before they came after her? And what would Martin do when they did?

'Thom Pendennis!'

She'd never heard Martin speak in that tone before, every syllable snapping like a whip. It didn't merely demand attention: it commanded obedience. It was the voice of the Grey Man's son.

The office door creaked open, and a man stepped out. He was short and heavyset, with thinning hair and a broad, doughy face, and he carried a packing knife loosely in one hand. 'What do you want?' he asked. 'I'm busy.'

'What I want,' said Martin, 'is for you to return to me all the treasure I brought you, when I still believed that wretched slave you kept upstairs was my father. I know you still have most of it. You can pay me for the rest.'

Thom's hand clenched around the knife. 'What are you talking about?'

'You know very well, Thom. You guessed I was a spriggan the first time I walked into your shop, and you and Walker hatched this little scheme to trap me if I ever came back again. He had no son to carry on the *tenkyz*, so the two of you threw out all the bait

335

you could and waited to see if I'd bite. And you did it well, I'll grant you that. I might never have guessed I'd been played, if not for my piskey friend here.'

He draped an arm around Ivy, then went on, 'Come to think of it, I've changed my mind. I'll take the full value of the treasure in cash, right now, from the safe you keep in your office. And you can give it to her.'

Ivy started in protest, but Martin put a finger to her lips. *Now is not the time.*

In the half-light, Thom's small eyes were wary. 'You think I tricked you? I wouldn't be so sure. You step out that door without my permission, you'll find out who you really belong to.' His gaze flicked to Ivy. 'And I'm not giving either one of you anything.'

'That's very unfortunate,' said Martin. He dropped his arm to Ivy's waist, pulling her against his side. Then he spread his fingers, and the air began to move.

It was a light breeze at first, almost playful. It ruffled the pad of paper beside the till, and sent a pen rolling onto the floor. But soon it picked up speed, spinning off in whirling tendrils that lashed the walls and licked at the edge of the carpet. Pictures shook and rattled, and the door of one tall cabinet whipped open, glass cracking and tinkling in shards onto the floor.

'What are you doing?' shouted Thom, lunging forward with the packing knife in hand. But Martin flicked a finger, and a gust of wind hurled him through the office door. Ivy heard him grunt as he hit the desk, and then he clawed his way back to the doorframe again, the breeze making a wild halo of his scanty hair. 'Stop it! You're wrecking my shop!'

He was right. By now Ivy and Martin were standing in the eye of a whirlwind, while framed coins and documents dropped from the walls, books flapped about the room like frightened pigeons, and murderous-looking fragments of glass and splintered wood spun all around them. Inside one of the shuddering cabinets, a clay statue toppled and broke in half, and Thom groaned.

'I wouldn't come out here, if I were you,' Martin called above the roar. 'That is, not without a great deal of money.'

Thom cursed bitterly, and slammed the office door. It blew open again at once, but it wasn't much longer before he reappeared, a fistful of flapping bills clutched in one hand. 'Take your money!' he yelled. 'Take it and get out!'

Martin closed his hand, and immediately the wind died away. 'That was fun,' he remarked, and stepped forward to pluck the money from Thom's grip. He leafed through it, then handed it to Ivy.

'You may go,' he said to Thom. 'I imagine you'll want to ring the police and tell them about the hooligans who came in at closing time and smashed up your shop. It's a lucky thing you were able to get away.'

Thom snatched up his coat and wrestled himself into it. He edged his way around the shop, slipping and stumbling on the debris, then unlocked the door with shaking hands and fled into the night.

Ivy slammed it shut after him and whirled back to Martin.

'They'll see him,' she said. 'They'll come for you. You have to get away.'

'That wasn't in the bargain,' said Martin. 'You can't break your word now.'

'I'm not! I told them I'd lead them to where you were hiding, and I did. Fly out through the attic, and I'll distract them while you escape.' She tugged him towards the stairs, but he didn't move. 'Martin, please!'

'No, Ivy.' His tone was gentle, but adamant. 'All my life I've been a nomad, or a fugitive, or both. It's time to stop hiding, and face up to what I've done.' He took her hands in his. 'You taught me that.'

'But they don't understand. They think you're still a threat. They'll send you to prison, and—'

She couldn't say the words, but they ached inside her. *I'll never see you again.*

Martin drew her close, pressing his forehead to hers. 'You have a home and a family,' he said, so low she could barely hear it. 'Your people still need help, and the goodwill of the Oakenfolk and their allies could make all the difference. Don't throw it away for my sake.'

'But what about your people?' she whispered. 'The seer – Helm's mother – said you'd save them. How can you do that if you're locked up on the Green Isles somewhere?'

Martin sighed. 'I don't believe in prophecies, Ivy. But if I did, I wouldn't worry about how to fulfil them. If something's meant to be, it's going to happen anyway. And if it's not…well.' He stepped back, still holding her gaze, and raised her hand briefly to his lips. Then, with a last wry smile that wrenched at her heart, he opened the door and walked out.

It did not take long. Ivy stood alone in the wreckage of the shop, listening numbly to the flutter of wings and pounding footsteps, a hoarse shout followed by a scuffle and a sizzling crack – the unmistakable sound of iron touching faery skin. Then Martin made a choking noise, and Ivy couldn't bear it any longer. She flung the door wide and rushed into the street.

Rob, Tylluan and Llinos had formed a circle around the shop's exit, a shimmering web of magic between them. In the centre of the ring, Martin sagged in the grip of a slim, dark-haired boy with iron rings on every finger, who looked surprised to have caught him so easily. Rhosmari was hurrying up the street towards them.

'Let go of him,' Ivy said to Timothy. 'He can't hurt you now.'

Timothy gave her a dubious look. 'No offence,' he said as he bound Martin's wrists, 'but I've fought him before. I prefer not to take any chances.'

'He isn't going to fight,' Ivy said angrily. 'He gave himself up, can't you see?'

Martin opened his mouth to protest, but Rob glared at him and he shut it again. Desperate, Ivy turned to Rhosmari.

'You know why he killed the Empress,' she said. 'It had nothing to do with politics, or ambition, or – or anything like that. It was because of what she did to his friends. Tell them!'

'Friends?' said Rob, before Rhosmari could answer. 'Martin

doesn't have friends.' He nodded to Llinos and Tylluan, who moved to flank Martin as Timothy stepped back. They each took one of his arms, and when Rob said, 'The Queen's Gate,' Ivy realised the faeries were about to transport Martin back to the Oak.

There was no time to debate with herself, or with them. She had to act. 'Wait!' Ivy cried. Then she darted around Rob, caught Martin's face between her hands, and kissed him.

Time stopped. She was dimly aware of exclamations all around her, of hands reaching to pull the two of them apart, but she clung to Martin until his shock faded and his cold mouth warmed to life, returning her kiss. He had wanted this, she knew, even longer than she had. But he'd valued her friendship too much, and his own too little, to say so.

'Tell them,' she repeated breathlessly to Rhosmari, when she broke away. 'He's not who they think he is.'

'Given my history,' murmured Martin, 'that's not exactly an endorsement.'

'He's deceived you,' Rob said, but Rhosmari interrupted him.

'No, she's right. There is more to the story, and you should hear it. But not now.' She turned to Ivy, her dark eyes warm with sympathy and relief. 'Don't worry, I'll speak up for him. I can't promise anything, but I'll make sure he gets a fair trial.'

Ivy wanted to protest, and offer to testify on Martin's behalf instead. But she had no proof other than the memories he'd given her, and if Rob was so convinced that Martin had tricked Ivy, that would mean nothing to him anyway. He'd be far more likely to listen to Rhosmari, who had met Martin's dear friends Lyn and Toby and witnessed what had been done to them first-hand. The Empress hadn't murdered them, not exactly. But after she'd sent Veronica to steal away both humans' creativity, destroy their life's work in the theatre and erase most of their memories, she might as well have.

Still, Ivy had to try one last time. 'Just talk to him,' she said to Rob. 'Give him a chance to explain himself. Please.'

A muscle in Rob's cheek twitched, but his face remained stern. 'I'm not the one who will judge him,' he said, and motioned to the other faeries. Martin raised his head, and his grey eyes sought Ivy's and held them. Then the four of them disappeared.

A siren blared in the near distance, and Timothy glanced up the street. 'We'd better get out of here,' he said, pulling the iron rings off his fingers and stuffing them into his pocket. He put his arm around Rhosmari, who was shivering again, and started to lead her away. Then he paused, and looked back at Ivy.

'I'm going to Oakhaven for the weekend,' he said. 'And Rhosmari's taking the train with me. You could come with us, if you like.'

Ivy touched the copper bracelet on her wrist. The money Thom Pendennis had given her – Martin's last gift – sat heavy in her coat pocket. *You have a family*, he'd said to her, and it was true. She'd done all she could here. It was time she went back to them.

'No, that's all right,' she said. 'I'm going home.'

epilogue

'And here's my dad,' announced Molly, using her spoon as an imaginary microphone, 'with an announcement that will surprise absolutely no one—'

David Menadue, who had just pushed his chair back from the table and half-risen to his feet, gave her a long-suffering look. Molly giggled. 'Sorry, Dad. But as soon as you asked if I'd like to come down here for the weekend, it was pretty obvious.'

Her father sighed and sat down again. 'All right, yes. Marigold and I have been seeing each other for a few weeks now, and after…well, everything that's happened, we've decided we'd like to be married.' He squeezed Marigold's hand, then gave Molly an apprehensive look. 'If that's all right with you?'

Molly rested her chin on her hand, pretending to be deep in thought. 'I don't know,' she said. 'Having Ivy and Cicely for step-sisters? You know how dull and ordinary they are, and how hard we all find it to get along…'

David wadded up his cloth napkin and threw it at her. 'Cheeky monkey.'

But he sounded relieved, and privately Ivy was too. When Molly had arrived that afternoon she'd looked tired and more than a little unhappy after her long train journey, and Ivy wasn't sure how she'd take the news. It had been less than four months since her mother's funeral, after all. But Molly's parents had been estranged for years – David's work had kept him away for weeks at a time, and even when he was home Gillian had treated him with indifference. So Molly wasn't surprised that her father had fallen in love with Marigold, especially once Ivy told her how close her mother had come to dying and how David had saved her life.

Ivy hadn't told Molly about Martin, though. What had happened between them was too powerful and private, and she didn't like to say anything until she knew what the outcome of his trial before Queen Valerian and her council would be. Rhosmari had assured Ivy that the Oakenfolk wouldn't keep Martin captive for long: they didn't even have a proper dungeon in the Oak, she said, so they'd want to deal with him as soon as possible. But from the troubled look on the faery girl's face as she and Timothy walked away, Ivy feared that might not be as much of a mercy as it sounded…

She was gazing into her teacup, still lost in thought, when someone rapped at the cottage door. 'I'll get it,' said Cicely, and jumped up.

'Who could that be, at this hour?' David asked, but neither

Marigold nor Ivy had an answer. They could only listen to Cicely's padding footsteps, the rattle-and-creak as the door opened, and then...

'*Mica!*' shrieked Cicely, and burst into tears.

Ivy leaped to her feet, her chair crashing onto the floor. As she raced through the sitting room she imagined Mica's dead body laid out on the doorstep, in Betony's last act of vengeance. But no, he was on his feet, alive, with Cicely in his arms. And standing behind him, cap in hand, was Mattock.

'Sorry it took us so long to find you,' he said to Ivy. 'Are you all right?'

Ivy nodded, too overcome to speak. She waited until Cicely let go of Mica, then she stepped forward to hug her brother as well. But at the same time Mattock moved aside, and she saw the other piskeys standing behind him.

Jenny's mother and grandfather, and her little brother Quartz. Matt's widowed mother, Fern. The hunters Gem and Feldspar, with their wives and three young children. Hew and Teasel, Pick and Elvar, and several other families besides – there had to be at least thirty of them.

'What happened?' asked Ivy, hushed with disbelief, and Mica answered, 'You did.'

Even with Cicely and Marigold's help it took Ivy some time to settle all the piskeys in the barn and see that they had everything they needed for the night, and she couldn't help wondering what they were going to do in the long term. Because, as Mica explained, none of them could go back to the Delve.

'Betony's still alive,' he told her, as the two of them walked back to the house. 'She was badly wounded, but Yarrow thinks she'll recover. After you left there was a huge uproar with everyone arguing about what had really happened and who was to blame for it, and for a while I thought Matt and I were pickled for sure. But a good many agreed they'd seen Betony throw herself on your sword, and they were all upset over what she'd done to Jenny.' His voice grew hoarse, and Ivy looked away so as not to embarrass him. She knew Mica hated anyone to see him cry.

'So anyway,' he went on, clearing his throat, 'when all was said and done, we ended up with a decent number on our side. But that didn't stop Gossan from calling us down to the Market Cavern and banishing the lot of us. He gave us enough time to pack a few things, and that was the end of it.' He paused, looking up at the moonlit clouds. 'Though I think others will come, if we keep our eyes open. They just need a bit more time to think it over.'

'But why come to me?' asked Ivy. 'I mean, I know why you and Matt came, and I'm glad you did. But the others... I understand why they'd turn against Betony, but I can't see why they'd want anything to do with me.' Especially now that they knew she was half-faery, and they'd all seen her change shape.

'Well,' said Mica, scratching at the back of his neck, 'there's a rumour going around that you're the next Joan.'

'*What?*'

'I know. But it's not as strange as you might think. The Jack's been trying to keep it quiet, but pretty much everybody knows Betony's lost her power to make fire. I'm thinking that's why she tried to kill herself.'

'But...I can't wield fire either. Why would anyone think I'm the Joan?'

'Maybe because we need one,' said Mica. 'And you're the closest thing to a real leader we have. How do you know you can't? Go on, give it a try.'

Ivy held out her hand, palm up, and concentrated. But she saw no flicker and felt no warmth, and after a moment she let her hand drop to her side. 'Nothing,' she said.

Mica looked disappointed. Then he shrugged. 'It's probably for the best,' he said. 'You're already the first shape-changer to come out of the Delve in who knows how many years. If you ended up being able to make fire as well, there'd be no living with you.'

Ivy punched her brother in the side. He grinned, slung his arm around her shoulders, and they went into the house together.

Two days later, Molly had gone back to school and David to his office in London, Mica's cautious scouting of the area around the Delve had turned up five more refugees wanting to join them, and Ivy was beginning to realise her brother had been right about the other piskeys looking to her as a leader. She'd grown up with these people and most of them were older than she was, so it seemed absurd that they should be in awe of her. But from the way the men touched their caps when she came into the barn and the women lowered their eyes and curtseyed, there could be little doubt that they were.

At least they seemed to have settled into their new lodgings, even if some of them were still shy of being above ground and unwilling to venture any further than the barn door. Like true piskeys they were keeping themselves busy, cleaning and polishing everything in sight – including Dodger, who had never been so popular or well-groomed in his life. Ivy suspected it wouldn't be long before the younger piskeys started sneaking him out for rides after the others had gone to bed, but as long as they were discreet about it and put him back in his box when they were done, she saw no reason to stop them.

Still, Ivy thought that evening as she walked across the yard, she wished she could find her people a better home, a place where neither curious humans nor Betony and her followers could threaten them. There were plenty of other abandoned mines around, but she feared having them settle into one only to find it poisoned like the Delve...

A rook flapped past, and she stopped to watch it fly. Then someone coughed behind her, and when she looked around there was Thorn, with her hand on one hip and a bulging pack over her shoulder.

'What are you doing here?' Ivy asked, startled.

'Well, that's a fine polite welcome,' said Thorn, dropping her rucksack on the cobbles. 'Are you saying you've no use for an ambassador from the Oakenfolk? Because I'd been looking forward to the change of scenery, myself. And Broch figured a healer might be welcome around here too.'

Welcome? That was an understatement. Broch's skills would be invaluable, and someone like Thorn – practical, tough and skilled, and enough like a piskey in appearance that Ivy's people would find it hard to dismiss her – was exactly the sort of helper Ivy could use right now. 'But how did you know?' she asked.

'Me?' asked Thorn. 'I didn't *know* anything. All I can say is that if your queen has the Sight and she tells you to go somewhere, you go.' But she shifted uncomfortably as she spoke, and Ivy sensed that she had her own reasons for wanting to leave the Oak. It made her wonder what those reasons might be, but that could wait.

'Well,' Ivy said as Broch flew down to land beside Thorn and changed back to his own shape, 'I'm glad to see you both. But what happened at the—'

She broke off in mid-sentence, riveted by the barn owl ghosting through the air towards them. Its heart-shaped face was expressionless, but as it approached her it gave a soft, twittering cry that she heard with her mind as well as her ears: *Ivy*.

'Oh, right,' said Thorn. 'I almost forgot. Queen Valerian decided to pardon that weasel-faced spriggan of yours, so he came too.'

acknowledgements

Special thanks for their help with this book go to my lovely and insightful editor, Jessica Clarke; my brilliant art director Thy Bui and illustrator Rory Kurtz; and my faithful first-round critiquers, Pete Anderson and Deva Fagan. I am also indebted to Jackie Garlick-Pynaert, who sat down with me for a marathon brainstorming session in the early stages of this book; to Andy, Michelle, Connor and Hollie Minniss for their hospitality and friendship during my research trip to Cornwall; to Megan Larkin, Rebecca Frazer and the rest of the Orchard Books team for making me so welcome in London; to Charlotte Mattey for the beautiful fan-art that encouraged me just when I needed it most; and all the readers who took the time to write and tell me how much my faery books have meant to them and how much they were looking forward to this one. I hope you find it worth the wait.

If you liked Nomad, you'll love

Lily

Pbk 978 1 40831 640 5   eBook 978 1 40831 349 7   £5.99

Pbk 978 1 40831 350 3   eBook 978 1 40831 641 2   £5.99

Pbk 978 1 40831 351 0   eBook 978 1 40831 642 9   £5.99

Pbk 978 140831 352 7   eBook 978 1 40831 643 6   £5.99

When evil rises, good magic must fight back...

The stunning series from Holly Webb,
bestselling author of Rose

WWW.ORCHARDBOOKS.CO.UK

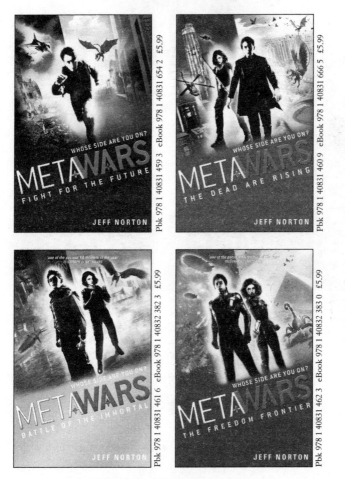

Don't miss R J Anderson's incredible
series for older readers

Pbk 978 1 40831 275 9
eBook 978 1 40831 371 8
£6.99

Pbk 978 1 40831 628 3
eBook 978 1 40831 629 0
£6.99

ONCE UPON A TIME THERE WAS A GIRL
WHO WAS SPECIAL.

THIS IS NOT HER STORY.

UNLESS YOU COUNT THE PART WHERE
I KILLED HER.